The Enchanted Journal

Adventure on the Oregon Trail

The Enchanted Journal

Adventure on the Oregon Trail

A Novel

by

Sandlin

First Edition

This is a work of fiction. Names, characters, places, and incidents either are the product of the authors' imaginations or are used fictitiously. Any resemblance to actual events or locales or persons, living or dead, is entirely coincidental.

Cover design and illustrations by Simona Molino through Fiverr.com.

Copyright © 2022 Gordon Sandlin Buck Jr.
All rights reserved.
ISBN: 9798833155448

Contents

Contents i
Dedication iii
Preface v
Acknowledgements vii

Part 1 Finding the Journal 1

Chapter 1: The Journal – April 8, 1859, Friday 3
Chapter 2: Steamboating 11
Chapter 3: Independence, April 1, 1859, Friday 15
Chapter 4: April 3, 1859, Sunday 19
Chapter 5: April 4, 1859: Monday 31

Part 2 Life on the Trail 43

Chapter 6: April 7 – The Routine 45
Chapter 7: April 15–Kansas River 65
Chapter 8: April 20–Alcove Spring 73
Chapter 9: April 28–Platte River 81
Chapter 10: April 30–Fort Kearny 85
Chapter 11: May 17–Windlass Hill 95
Chapter 12: May 17 - Ash Hollow 101
Chapter 13: May 21 – Courthouse and Jail Rocks 107
Chapter 14: May 23 – Scotts Bluff 113
Chapter 15: May 27 – Fort Laramie 121
Chapter 16: May 29 – Register Cliff 127
Chapter 17: June 4 – Cholera Strikes 137
Chapter 18: June 8 – Independence Rock 147
Chapter 19: June 17 – Pacific Springs 159
Chapter 20: June 19 – Parting of the Ways 173
Chapter 21: June 25 – Green River 183
Chapter 22: June 30 - Proposal 197

i

Part 3   A New Father 201

    Chapter 23: July 1 – Smith's Trading Post 203
    Chapter 24: July 13 – Fort Hall..217
    Chapter 25: July 25 – Upper Salmon Falls 225
    Chapter 26: Fort Boise 233
    Chapter 27: Aug 20 – Grande Ronde Valley 237
    Chapter 28: Fort Walla Walla 247

Part 4   Around the Mountain 251

    Chapter 29: Sept 4 – Camp Dalles 253

Part 5   Oregon City 263

    Chapter 30: September 22 - Oregon City............................265
    Chapter 31: Finding Milli 267

References 283

About Sandlin 285

Dedication

This book is dedicated to

Wesleigh Jean Buck Smith.

May you find your adventure!

Sandlin

Preface

AS AN AVID READER, I always wanted to write novels, and made various unsuccessful attempts over the years. Oh, I wrote books—engineering technical books, operating manuals, computer books, technical papers, and countless memos. I blamed that style of writing for preventing my writing novels.

Time travel has always fascinated me. One day, I stumbled upon Diana Gabaldon's *Outlander* series and was immediately hooked. I read the entire series and watched the videos—more than once. Diana described her writing style as unplanned, irregular, non-chronological, bits and pieces of scenes and conversations. She would put her characters into a scene or situation to see what they would do and how they would grow from the experience. I tried this approach and liked it.

James Warren Hale (1886—1966), my maternal grandfather, was primarily a laborer for the railroads; however, he was also an aspiring and prolific writer. Beginning in 1942, and likely earlier, he wrote 28 short stories, novels, and plays—about 4400 pages—in 35 journals. Although I knew he was writing "stories" during his retirement, I had no idea that he had written so many. We recently found his stories, and I've been sorting, grouping, skimming, and reading them to learn more about my grandfather. Frankly, his stories are not the best—but he still wrote them.

J. W. Hale's wife, my grandmother, Annie Lena Bennett (1890—1940), died on December 25, 1940. He finished his first story in 1942, when his children were in military service. Did he write to occupy his time after his wife's death? Was this a hobby, or did he hope to publish his work? No one knows.

This story, my own time travel adventure, may not be the best story either, but I must admit that writing it was fun. Perhaps that is what my grandfather discovered as well.

Sandlin

Acknowledgements

MY PERSONAL THANKS and appreciation to those who helped me by reading early drafts or listening to me ramble on about my novel, especially Marlo Hymel, Laura Buck Smith, Wesleigh Smith, and Lindsay Redhead. Mark Spencer provided instruction and guidance in the art of writing a novel. Susan Shackelford proof read my draft and offered suggestions which I've incorporated into this first edition.

The cover and illustrations are by Simona Molina through Fiverr.com.

Sandlin

Part 1

Finding the Journal

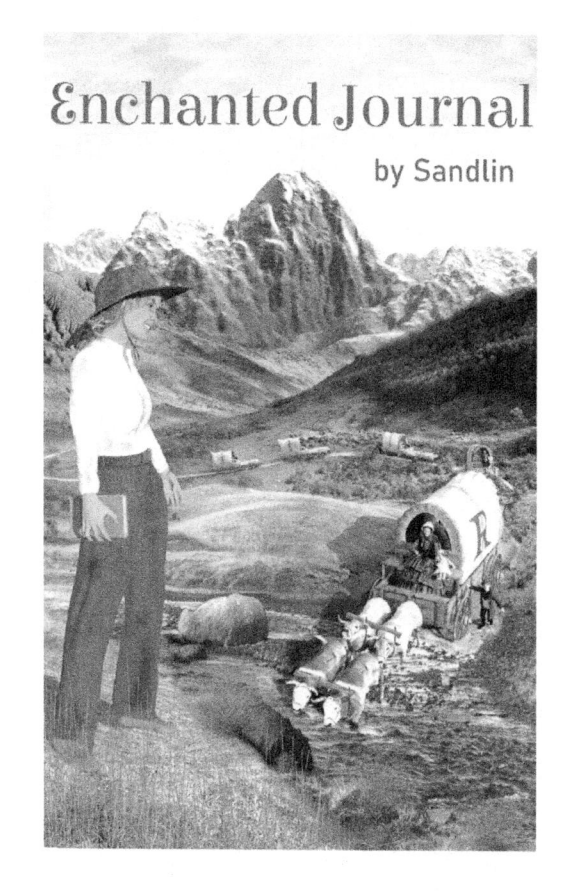

Enchanted Journal
by Sandlin

The Enchanted Journal

Chapter 1: The Journal – April 8, 1859, Friday

ABIGAIL ROBERTS WAS PICKING BERRIES—or rather looking for them on the Oregon Trail. After a week on the trail, Abigail already wished for her home in Tennessee. She could always find berries back home; here, she had to keep their covered wagon in sight and berries were scarce. Still, she was not about to wander any farther, especially after Jeff Cromwell stared hungrily at her as she left camp. Her hand dropped for the comfort of the sharp patch knife hidden in her trousers. *I've got to tell Papa that Jeff scares me.*

Yielding to a strange urge, Abigail stepped to her left and checked behind a scanty bush. A thin brown book on the dirt invited her and waited for her to pick it up. "Read me," it seemed to say. "I can help you."

Why would anyone throw a book away? Although some emigrants were already lightening their wagons by discarding heavy items, no one would toss a book at this stage of the trail. Books carried weight in entertainment and in silver.

Calling for closer examination, the brown leather journal—long forgotten but in good condition—was irresistible. Abigail picked it up between her thumb and forefinger, gingerly placed it in her open palm, and thumbed through the still pliable pages. The first few pages contained writing, but the rest of the journal was blank.

16 yrs. earlier

Sandlin

March 25, 1843

This is my personal diary and stories from my adventure on the Oregon Trail beginning today.

It has begun! We left our home in Tennessee today and are on our way to Independence, Missouri to join a wagon train on the Oregon Trail. This may well be the adventure of my life!

We sold everything—even our slaves—and packed our wagon full of supplies and equipment. We will use our farm wagon and mules to begin our journey, but Papa says we will trade for oxen in Independence. First, we must get to Memphis to catch a steamboat. I have never even seen a steamboat, but soon I will be on one!

Of course, Mama is worried. Truth be known, she would rather stay in Tennessee near family and friends. Papa is restless and excited to move to Oregon. He talks about our "Manifest Destiny" to make all North America part of the United States.

From Memphis, we go up the Mississippi River to St. Louis, Missouri, and then take the Missouri River to Independence. We will get more supplies in Independence for the long trail.

I can scarcely wait to be on the Oregon Trail! What will I do? Who will I meet?

*****

After a few pages, the writing ceased. Abigail studied her surroundings. Abigail's family was in the same location as Milli Madison's family had stopped years ago. *Poor thing, I bet she was sad to lose her journal. Looks like she only wrote in it for a few days. But I'll take good care of it. I'll read it tonight. It will become my journal.*

On her way back to their encampment with half a handful of berries, Abigail considered her own situation. Almost exactly seventeen years after Milli Madison, she, too, left Tennessee on a similar mission and route, their prairie schooner loaded with the same equipment. However, whereas Milli was excited about her journey, Abigail was not. She wished they had not left Tennessee, but what else could she do? Like her brother and sister, and even her mother, she had to follow her father's wishes.

Fifteen years old, Abigail Roberts was the oldest child of Michael and Alice Roberts. More than a tomboy, she was tall and slim, but strong and hardened by farm work. Abigail helped her mother in the kitchen, but also cooked entire meals on her own. Her mother and father taught her to manage the farm, farmhouse, and family. Abigail would make an excellent farm wife; however, none of the boys or young men in their small community attracted her.

With Milli's journal in her hand, Abigail recalled the gleam in her father's eyes when he bought Randolph Marcy's book "Prairie Traveler: A Handbook for Overland Expeditions." More than read, Michael studied the handbook late that night, his calloused hands turning pages forward and backward. All the next day, he talked about the wisdom of the handbook as they worked in the fields. After her father finished the handbook, he insisted Abigail read it. Then he read it again. At that point, Abigail knew they would head west, and she dreaded it.

Abigail sighed as she remembered her father's decision and their preparations for the Oregon Trail.

*****

WEEKS PRIOR TO JOINING THE TRAIL, as they sat around the fireplace after supper, Abigail's mother had asked, "Michael, are you sure you want to go to Oregon?"

Abigail peeked up from her sewing. As usual, Marcy's handbook absorbed all her father's attention and he had a faraway look in his eyes.

Having heard the word 'Oregon', Mike came in from the porch with his knife and whittling stick in hand. Twelve years old, he had skimmed through the camping and hunting parts of Marcy's handbook. "I want to kill a buffalo."

"Do not whittle in the house," Alice ordered. Mike returned to the porch.

"No whit," repeated Sue, three years old and playing with her rag doll on the floor.

"I'm certain," said Abigail's father. "We can make a fresh start, a new life, while I'm young enough to do it. Truth is, I'm tired of this place." He waved his bronzed arms around the log cabin. "It's worn out and wearing me out. Every year, our crops are smaller."

"But we have friends and relatives here," said Alice. "I don't want to leave."

"That's another thing. I like our family, but what about Abigail? I'm related to half the people around us and you're related to the other half. Poor Abigail! She'll end up marrying a cousin and working a poor farm. I want something better for her.

"Papa! I'm too young to marry!" insisted Abigail.

"Well, your friend Linda was too, but now she's married, pregnant, and living with her husband's parents. You can do better than that. You must marry well."

"Papa, you're always telling me I must marry well. I'm not interested in any of the boys around here."

"I know. All the more reason to leave."

"Michael," scolded Alice. "I'm not your cousin. I don't consider myself a poor farm wife, and I like our community. I married well." Alice smiled. "Abigail will, too."

"Well said." Michael pushed his chair back, ambled to Alice, and bussed her cheek. "Thank you, Alice, but I've lived all my life on this farm. Thirty-six years old and what have I accomplished?"

Alice pointed towards Sue, Mike, and Abigail. "This is not about Abigail or a new farm in Oregon. You just want the adventure. I love you and I'll go with you on your adventure, but I'm not looking forward to it."

*****

THE ROBERTS PREPARED for the Oregon Trail from their home in Tennessee. The first project was to modify their farm wagon into a prairie schooner. Abigail was well familiar with the wagon and drove it regularly, but she was dubious about living in it for six months.

"We need to raise the side boards and caulk the wagon bed so it can float if necessary," said her father. "Hold your end of this board while I nail mine." Michael pounded in his nails. "Now nail yours."

Abigail hammered nails on her end of the board with powerful and accurate strikes.

"You're a good worker, Abigail."

"Thank you, Papa. I try."

Michael Roberts had wanted his first born child to be a son and he treated Abigail as a son. Alice had named her after her grandmother and insisted that she be called Abigail and not Abby or Abe.

Their wagon measured about ten feet long by four feet wide. The rear wheels were five feet in diameter and the front wheels measured three and a half feet.

"Now to add the hooped frames and stretch canvas over them."

As they stretched the canvas, Michael marveled. "Just think, Abigail, we'll get 640 acres of prime land for free! That's four times as much as we have here. Plus, the Oregon land will be new—not worn out like this." Michael scooped up a handful of soil and scattered it away. "I do my best to keep things repaired, but I can't repair the land."

Alice emerged from the cabin to admire their results. "It's really pretty. The off white canvas goes well with the light blue wagon. Could you paint the wheels red? And paint a big 'R' on the canvas to make it easy to find among all the others."

*****

BESIDES THEIR NORMAL WORKLOAD, Abigail and her mother were busy sewing clothes for the trail. For themselves, Alice and Abigail would take three long dresses each and one long dress for church and special occasions. Although still considered long, the dresses would not drag on the ground. One dress was grey linen, another light plain woven linsey woolsey, another dark gingham. All were simple designs and quickly slipped on. They made new linen petticoats and heavy wool overcoats. Alice and Abigail knitted wool socks, mittens, and caps. They made sunbonnets and slipped them over light wood frames.

To Abigail's stack of clothes, Alice begrudgingly added trousers, a loose shirt, and work boots. Abigail much preferred her work clothes to dresses.

Alice hesitated, but added her corset to her own stack of clothes. She laughed and added a corset to Abigail's stack as well. Abigail hated corsets.

Clothes were easy to make for three-year-old Sue. Alice made three simple, straight, loose linen dresses called a wannis.

For Michael, Alice made three new loose-fitting shirts of linen and three pairs of loose trousers from heavy homespun material. He would wear his favorite felted wool hat. Alice added Michael's suspenders, heavy boots, socks, and heavy coat to his stack of clothes.

Alice had read parts of Marcy's handbook and convinced Michael to buy everyone leather walking boots. Mike and Sue usually were barefoot on their grassy farm, but the trail would be rough and rocky.

*****

WITH EVERY MODIFICATION, every purchase, every page read in Marcy's Handbook, their journey became more inevitable but Abigail silently hoped her father's plans would fall through. Then he found a buyer for their farm.

The Enchanted Journal

Abigail responded to her father's announcement by saying, "Mama, I want to cut my hair short."

"Abigail, come with me for a minute."

Her mother led Abigail into her bedroom. She held up a large hand mirror. Abigail examined the face in the mirror and saw, as she always did, her father.

"Abigail, you may look like your father and act like him, but you're not a boy. You're a girl and a pretty one at that. You can't disguise yourself as a boy for our journey."

"I know, Mama, and thank you. But the trail will be dangerous with lots of hard work. There won't be much time for prettiness. I might as well dress for comfort and not have to deal with long hair."

Alice sighed. Perhaps Abigail was correct. "All right. I'll cut it to your shoulders like your Papa's." She found her scissors and began cutting Abigail's wavy light brown locks. After all, it would grow back.

*****

THE ROBERTS COVERED WAGON PULLED UP to their church, and Lydia Bush screamed "Your hair!".

"I'm getting ready for the Oregon Trail," explained Abigail. "We leave next week."

"I know, but you should have waited and cut it on your last day here."

"Why? I'm not trying to impress anyone."

"What about Nathan?"

"Nathan is my cousin."

"A third cousin is a kissing cousin."

Abigail made a face. "To you, it is."

Lydia giggled. "I'll miss you, Abigail. You're so practical and outspoken. Who will I turn to for advice?" She wiped away a tear.

"I'll really miss your laugh, Lydia."

"Remember to write to me and tell me about your adventure. I'll bet you meet a sweetheart, maybe more than one. Be sure to tell me about them."

9

"I'm not looking for a sweetheart, and certainly not on the trail. I just want to get to Oregon and get it over with."

"Don't be in such a rush, Abigail. You're on a grand adventure; have fun. I'm jealous."

"Please write to me, Lydia," Abigail asked. "We'll be near Oregon City. We'll get there long before your letters do, but please write and tell me about life here."

"A city? I'm impressed. You'll marry some city guy and I'll be stuck on the farm. Name a daughter for me."

"First daughter or first curly haired daughter?"

Lydia compared Abigail's light brown hair to her own curly black hair. "Better not wait for the black hair. I'll name a daughter after you, too. No matter her hair."

"Don't call her Abby."

"Promise."

"Pinky Promise!" Abigail and Lydia linked their little fingers and giggled.

Their pastor stuck his head out the church door and announced the worship service.

Chapter 2: Steamboating

MEMPHIS WAS THE LARGEST TOWN Abigail had ever visited, and it thrilled her. So many people! So many sights! Perhaps her father's decision to leave the farm was a good one after all.

More than thrilling, the steamboat ride from Memphis to St. Louis would be exciting and a little dangerous. Not all steamboats arrived at their destination.

Their wooden steamboat had a rear-mounted paddle and a flat bottom for carrying heavy loads on smooth and shallow rivers. Its steam engine was coal fired and billowed black smoke. Other steamboats crowded the dock beside it.

Excited and curious, Abigail and Alice explored their steamboat. Their covered wagon was parked with the others on the deck. The emigrants slept in and under their wagons—after all, the prairie schooner would be their home for the next several months. Might as well get used to it.

Abigail peered through a window. "Oh, Mama! Look!"

A large room with a high ceiling opened below them. The room contained small tables. A stage was at one end of the room. The room was a brilliant white and trimmed with gilt.

"Honey, I'm afraid that is not for us. They probably won't even let us go inside."

"Purdy, ain't it?"

Startled, Abigail spun around to face a red-haired man a little taller than she.

The white suited man examined Abigail and her trousers curiously. "Sam Clemens, at your service, ma'am."

"Are you our captain?"

"If you're a passenger on this steamboat, I am indeed your captain. Would you ladies like a tour of our ballroom?"

"Thank you, Captain Clemens. We'd love a tour."

"Just follow me." Captain Clemens led them to a double door. "Where're you ladies from?"

"We're from Tennessee," volunteered Alice. "On our way to Independence, Missouri, to follow the Oregon Trail."

"I'm a Missouri boy, myself." Captain Clemens led them into the ballroom. "In here, we serve meals to the First-Class Passengers. At night we have music, theatre, and, of course, gambling. Where're you ladies staying?"

"We're on deck in our wagon," blushed Abigail.

"Glad to have you onboard. I've slept on many a deck in my day."

A messenger boy rushed to the captain but slowed to smile at Abigail. "Captain, sir, you're needed in the pilothouse."

"Excuse me, ladies. Duty calls." He whispered to the messenger as they left.

Alice and Abigail gazed in awe around the ballroom for a few minutes but feeling unwelcome, departed, and returned to their wagon.

"Someday," vowed Abigail, "I'll travel First Class and celebrate in the ballroom."

Alice admired Abigail's resolve. "But first, Abigail, we have a trail to follow and a wagon to ride in."

"I know, but someday…."

Abigail and Alice later tried to describe the luxuries they had seen to Michael, but he seemed skeptical.

The messenger boy reappeared. "Excuse me, ma'am," he said to Alice. "Captain Clemens sent you this basket." He smiled at Abigail and left.

The basket contained fried chicken, a cabbage slaw with vinegar seasoning, fresh bread, and an apple pie.

"Well, Alice," admitted Michael, "looks like you've made a new friend. You too, Abigail," he chuckled.

"Papa!"

"Pass the chicken, please."

As the steamboat pulled away from the dock, Captain Clemens shouted, "Mark Twain!" In a few days, they would be in St. Louis.

*****

ST. LOUIS WAS EVEN LARGER THAN MEMPHIS. After asking around, Michael located the Hawken Rifle Company.

"Abigail," Michael said, "Come with me. I want to get a plains rifle. Something that can kill a buffalo." They sauntered together, stride for stride, like father and son. Together, they entered the store section of the Hawken Company.

Rifles and shotguns lined the walls along with gunpowder, shot, percussion caps and a few pistols. "I'm joining a wagon train and want to buy a plains rifle," Michael said to the clerk. "I was told Hawkens were the best. What do you have?"

The clerk stepped to a rack and selected one of the shorter rifles with a half stock and octagonal barrel. "This is what you want," he said. "A new .54 caliber Hawken in a 32 inch barrel that uses percussion caps. We made them here." He handed the rifle to Michael, who hefted it and handed it to Abigail.

"Think you could shoot this, Abigail?" Michael asked.

Surprised, the clerk studied Abigail as she placed the 52-inch long rifle on her shoulder and sighted down the barrel.

"I think so," Abigail replied. "About the same as your shotgun."

"It will kick like the shotgun as well."

"OK, I can handle it. Why two triggers?"

"The rear trigger is a set trigger for the front trigger," replied the clerk. "Setting makes the front trigger sensitive to a light pull, so be careful. You can use the front trigger without the rear trigger, but it takes a harder pull."

"I'll take the rifle. Plus, bullets, a bullet mold, lead, and power."

The clerk nodded. "This Hawken is just right for the buffalo, deer, and elk you'll see. But if I were you, I'd also get a six-shot revolver for protection against two-legged varmints."

"What do you recommend?"

"This Colt 1851 Navy," the clerk handed a six shot revolver to Michael. "We've just overhauled it. The Navy is a .36 caliber cap and ball revolver using percussion caps. You'll need a different bullet mold, an extra cylinder, and a belt holster."

"Show us how to load them and it's a deal. Oh, and add a patch knife for my daughter."

As they stepped out, Michael said, "Abigail, always keep that patch knife hidden on you."

"Yes, sir. I understand."

Several days later, they arrived at Independence.

Chapter 3: Independence, April 1, 1859, Friday

THE POPULATION OF INDEPENDENCE, MISSOURI in 1859 was around three thousand permanent residents plus hundreds of families preparing to leave via the Oregon Trail. Independence was known for its stately courthouse in a large grassy square surrounded by a split-rail fence. Dry goods stores, butcher shops, inns, taverns, wagon shops, and blacksmith shops surrounded the square and served the emigrants.

Independence had been founded in 1827 to support the fur traders. By 1840, the fur trade was diminishing, but the emigrant wagon train era had begun and Independence was flourishing.

"Captain Bridgewater is highly recommended," said Michael to Alice. "I hope we can find him and join his wagon train."

Captain Bridgewater was well known, and they found him at Independence Court House Square, signing up emigrants for his caravan. Captain was a rugged-looking man and appeared slightly older than Michael. His loose fitting, light colored, coarse linen homespun shirt was tucked into darker homespun trousers held up by leather suspenders. A dark linen vest covered the suspenders and a high-crowned, wide-brimmed, soft felt hat covered Captain's graying head. He wore dark brown, heavy leather boots. A brown leather holster holding a pistol completed his outfit. Captain Bridgewater was ready for the trail and inspired confidence in those gathering around him.

Captain Bridgewater glanced at his Waltham Model 57 pocket watch, and returned it to his vest. He cleared his throat and explained his mission and organization.

"First, I am the captain, and if you join my train, you must obey me. I have been on the Oregon Trail many times and know what I am doing. This is my last trip. I plan to settle down in Oregon at the end of the journey.

"There are many variations to the trail, so don't be surprised if our route is not according to your guidebook or what others have told you. I'll lead you on the route I know unless we come across unexpected problems. Years ago, this journey would have taken about six months, but we should get there in about five months.

"I recommend you begin with enough food and supplies for four months to minimize the load. Buy good quality and beware of the shoddyocracy. We will benefit from the trail being well marked and established, plus having several places to resupply. We'll have to cross many creeks and rivers, but some crossings now have ferries and bridges. You'll have to pay to use the ferries—probably a dollar or so—but it is much safer and will prevent losing your wagon and supplies.

"From here, we go to Fort Kearny, a distance of some 330 miles. It should take us about 30 days. You'll be able to purchase some supplies, and mail letters at Fort Kearny."

"Are supplies more expensive there?" asked Michael.

"No, about the same as here. Fort Kearny was set up for resupplying the Oregon Trail, but other places may be more expensive. You can buy flour, salt pork, beans, and lard at Fort Kearny. You'll consume about 30 days of food while getting to Fort Kearny so it must be replenished. However, there may be hundreds of travelers at Fort Kearny so be sure to start the trail with at least four months of food."

At Fort Kearny, we'll cross the river by ferry, then travel to Fort Laramie. It is another 330 miles so will take us about 30 days.

When d'we leave?" probed a stern big man. "I'm ready. Let's git goin'."

The Enchanted Journal

"Well, I'm not ready, George," answered Captain. "I need a driver and cook for my wagon. If you're in a hurry, join another train."

George Cromwell did not like being dressed down in front of everyone, but he remained silent and took another drag on his pipe. "C'mon, Jeff," Cromwell said to the large young man beside him. "Let's git us a drink before we see what yer Ma fixed fer us."

As he trudged away with his father, Jeff cast a quizzical glance at Abigail in her loose trousers and shirt.

*****

THE ROBERTS FOUND THE LIVERY and stores recommended by Captain Bridgewater. For their family of five, they purchased:

- 500 pounds of flour in canvas sacks
- 120 pounds of hardtack
- 250 pounds of salt pork, packed in bran
- 60 pounds of ground corn
- 50 pounds of ground oats
- 2 bushels of cornmeal with eggs packed inside
- 80 pounds of rice
- 10 pounds of saleratus
- 50 pounds of salt
- 100 pounds of sugar

17

- 50 pounds of green coffee beans
- 5 pounds of tea
- 3 bushels of dried apples
- 2 bushels of dried peaches
- 10 bushels of various dried beans
- 10 pounds of butter preserved in tin canisters
- 200 pounds of lard
- Vinegar, salt, pepper, spices, lemon extract
- 5 gallons of whiskey

"Isn't that quite a lot of whiskey?" said Alice.

Michael grinned. "They tell me whiskey will be worth its weight in gold farther down the trail."

The recommended weight limit for their wagon was 2500 pounds, and their food alone weighed 1700 pounds.

Besides their food, they carried a plow and other farm implements plus carpentry tools. There was little room for anything else. Everyone had several changes of homemade clothes, two blankets, and a comforter. A Bible and three other books made up their library.

Their dairy cow, Daisy, two other cows, and two goats would follow as long as possible. Four hens were in a portable chicken coup at the rear of the wagon. The Roberts had left Tennessee with their wagon pulled by mules, but sold all the mules in Memphis except for Jake, the best. They bought six shod oxen in Independence.

On their way out of the dry goods store, The Roberts family encountered Captain Bridgewater and another man. Captain Bridgewater greeted them, "Mr. and Mrs. Roberts, meet Frank Allen. Frank will drive my wagon and cook. Well, he says he can cook; I'll find out tonight. If he can cook, we'll cross the Missouri after church service Sunday."

Frank laughed. "I can cook. Pleased to meet you, sir, ma'am. I 'spect we'll be getting to know each other right well."

"Now that I've hired Frank," said Captain, "we can load our supplies. Please excuse us."

Chapter 4: April 3, 1859, Sunday

ABIGAIL WORE HER BEST DRESS and bonnet to the Sunday worship service. Her mother had copied a dress with puffed sleeves and hand-crocheted collar from Godey's Lady's Book. After the worship service, Abigail changed to more comfortable trousers, shirt, and felted hat as soon as possible and vowed to not wear the dress again.

The Roberts left Independence and crossed the Missouri by ferry to join the Bridgewater wagon train. The captain had organized his thirty-five wagons in a semicircle on the flat open prairie with their long wagon tongues pointing outward. Oxen harnesses were on the ground beside the wagons and ready for hitching.

Hundreds of wagons were in the general area and preparing to get on the trail. Although somewhat intimidated by the hustle and bustle surrounding them, Abigail helped her mother organize their cooking area and prepare their noon day meal.

Michael and Mike pitched the family tent. They unrolled India rubber mats on the ground and placed bedrolls of heavy Mackinaw blankets over the mats. It would be cozy but everyone could stretch out.

Satisfied with the campsite and the tent, Michael went to a meeting of the men with Captain Bridgewater.

For their first camp meal, Alice prepared salt pork, potatoes, and cornbread. While these were cooking, Alice soaked beans and prepared soda biscuits for the evening meal. She made a pie using dried apples and brown sugar that Abigail had crushed in the mortar. They would eat this meal again that evening and add a few eggs to finish it in the morning for breakfast.

Absorbed in cooking, Alice was startled by a visitor's approach.

"You certainly look well organized! Hello, I'm Mary Wells."

"Thank you, Mary. I'm Alice Roberts. This is my daughter, Abigail."

"And this is my son, Henry."

Abigail peered up from grinding the roasted coffee beans. Henry was short, probably about thirteen years old and scrawny. He pushed thick eyeglasses higher on his nose and smiled at Abigail.

"Nice to meet you, ma'am," Henry squeaked. "And Abigail," his voice breaking into a lower pitch.

"Pleased to meet you, Mrs. Wells and Henry," Abigail greeted politely.

"My husband, Michael, is at the men's meeting with Captain Bridgewater," said Alice.

"That's where my Fred is."

"And my James. Hello, I'm Gladys Jones." A small, middle aged woman joined the group.

"Abigail, would you make us some coffee?"

"Yes, ma'am." Abigail rose, filled the coffee pot with water, and placed it on the fire.

"Reckon what the men folk're talkin' 'bout?" said Gladys.

"Their grand adventure," said Mary. "They're loving it."

"Was a time they'd be talkin' 'bout us," said Gladys. "Or other women, but that was long ago."

Alice laughed. Gladys was clearly the oldest of the three women. "Oh, I'm not so sure of that, Gladys. From time to time, I catch Michael glancing at a good looking woman. He can't help it, and I'm glad he still has a streak of youth."

"You can bet Captain Bridgewater looks around. He's a handsome man—single, too," said Gladys.

Alice changed the subject and waved her arm over her cooking area. "This takes a lot of effort but I suppose I'll get better at it."

The Enchanted Journal

"At least your nearly grown daughter helps you," said Mary. "My fifteen-year-old son helps if I ask but he isn't interested in cooking."

"You're fifteen?" asked Gladys.

"Yes, ma'am. Two months ago."

Abigail examined Henry more carefully. *Fifteen? He did not look that old. Mike was bigger, even at twelve.*

"We've been on this side of the river for a couple of days," said Mary. "I cooked enough for the day this morning. Tomorrow we'll pack it all away. I'm eager to get moving. We're from Ohio where we had a small farm. We hope to be granted a much larger and more profitable farm in Oregon."

"And I want to continue my education," added Henry. "I completed the school near our farm," he bragged.

"But I read that there are few schools in Oregon," said Abigail.

"In that case, I'll continue my self-education, just as I was doing in Ohio. I packed several books. Maybe we can exchange books some time?"

"What will you do with a better education?" asked Abigail.

"Newspaper reporting. Maybe be an editor or even own a newspaper someday. My notebook and pencil are always with me. What do you want to do?"

"Get off this trail." *Strange Q for a girl!* "Get married, have kids, take care of everyone"

*****

AT THE MEN'S MEETING, Captain Bridgewater got straight to the point. "This trip will be long, tedious, and dangerous. People will die—perhaps even some of us here at this meeting. We must continue despite hunger and thirst, heat and cold, dry and wet. We will cross deserts and rivers, mountains, and valleys. Wagons will break down and we must repair them or share their load. I need your cooperation and all the help I can get. Has anyone ever been on the Oregon Trail before?"

"I use my wagon all the time and we camped ta git here," replied George Cromwell. "I know my wagon and how to camp." No one else said anything.

Captain broke off a stalk of Timothy grass and chewed it for a moment. "There are thirty-five wagons, counting mine. That's too many for me to supervise. We must divide into groups and each group needs a group leader. I realize I don't know you well and many of you do not know each other, but here's my plan. I've asked Michael Roberts, Fred Wells, Charles Field, and George Cromwell to be group leaders. You men please step forward. The rest of you, choose a leader and line up behind him."

No one chose to be in George Cromwell's group. Captain Bridgewater was not surprised. Already unpopular, Cromwell was a belligerent know-it-all.

Captain attempted to resolve the organizational problem. "This is a tentative organization and we may well change it in a few days. For now, I'll assign some of you to George's group." He made the group sizes be approximately equal."

"Next," said Captain, "we need to take inventory of the skills available on our train. Just tell me what you can do to contribute to the welfare of our train. I'll start. I have military experience. I've farmed and trapped fur. I'm a fair shot with rifle and pistol and I have one of each."

"I'm a hunter," injected George Cromwell. "I'm a good shot and can skin and butcher too. I taught my son here, Jeff, to do the same. We got guns and ammo and can keep ever'body with meat if Bridgewater leads us to any. But I 'pect somethin' in trade for the meat; I'm not giving it away. Me and Jeff are fighters, too, if Injuns bother us."

Fred Wells stepped forward. "I'm a farmer but I can hunt. I have a rifle and shotgun."

"I'm a farmer and carpenter," said Michael Roberts. "I can also hunt, skin, and butcher. I own a plains rifle, a pistol, and a shotgun. If I have food, you have food, no need to trade."

"Hummph," grunted George Cromwell.

"I'm a farmer and fiddler," laughed Ralph Richardson. "Probably a better fiddler—which is why I'm headed west. My wife is a good nurse. We'll need her help."

Charles Field coughed. "I'm a farmer and Methodist lay minister and will be happy to conduct worship services. My wife is a good singer and seamstress. I have consumption and I'm heading west for my health."

As the men talked about their skills and interests, they became more comfortable with each other. Most were farmers but the train included a wainwright, a teacher, and a shopkeeper. All were armed in some fashion and most were at least somewhat familiar with farming. Captain Bridgewater was pleased with the diversity of the group. He had chosen well.

A tall man, about the same age as Captain Bridgewater, but even taller, approached the group and shook Captain Bridgewater's hand.

"This is my good friend Daniel Murray," said Captain. "Daniel is leading a train that will be a couple of days ahead of us. We'll be eating his trail dust--unless I can catch him." Captain chuckled.

"My boys and I are going to California," said Daniel. "We'll be separating from you about half way through the trail. If any of you change your mind and decide to go to California instead of Oregon, you're welcome to join us. That is, if you can catch us!"

"Likewise to anyone in your train, Daniel. I'm sure we'll meet up at several different points along the trail."

*****

Captain Bridgewater dismissed the men, but Michael waved his arms over his head. "Everyone in my group, please stay for a few more minutes."

Michael's men gathered around him.

"I've no more idea about what we're doing than you do," Michael began. "Here is a little book you can read." He held up Marcy's handbook. "Basically, we'll all be learning as we go. Fortunately, Captain Bridgewater is knowledgeable and experienced."

"I am Angus Campbell," said a small young man. "Your book sounds interesting. Could I read it?"

Michael handed Angus the worn paperback. "My daughter and I studied it extensively. I hope it is correct. You should find it useful and interesting."

"Daughter? I thought you had two sons."

Michael shook his head and chuckled. "No, my daughter is my oldest and a bit of a tomboy. She's practical and insisted on cutting her hair and wearing trousers and a felted hat. I think Abigail made good choices, but my wife disagrees."

"My wife would agree with yours."

"Does everyone have a gun and know how to use it?" asked Michael.

"I got a shotgun," replied Ralph Richardson. "I can use it, but I'm not a particularly good shot. Don't count on me to hunt, but you can count on me to fiddle," he yukked.

"Captain tells me we'll be off to a late start tomorrow and it will seem an easy day as we learn what to do. Each day will gradually get more productive but will become harder and harder work.

"Make certain your water barrel is full. Also, be sure to load a few sticks of firewood in your wagon. I think we'll have plenty of water and wood for the next few days, but this is a good habit to cultivate."

"What about meals?"

"Cook a large breakfast and plan on eating it again at noon. You may not want to make a fire at noon. Captain Bridgewater's cook recommended to always soak dried beans during the day to cook for supper and to cook enough to have beans for breakfast as well. He is called 'Beans' Allen."

Everyone guffawed.

"See you in the morning," said Michael.

Angus remained by Michael's side after the other men left.

"Mr. Roberts," began Angus.

"Call me Michael, please. We'll be together for months on this long trail."

"Thank you, sir. I wish to explain my situation and, frankly, ask for your help."

"I'll certainly try."

"Michael, I am a shopkeeper from Ohio. My father is also a shopkeeper and quite wealthy. We lived in town, a small town, but still a town. My wife's family lived in the same town and was also well off. We are accustomed to having people and servants work for us. I am a good shopkeeper but know little about farming, camping, or hunting.. My plan is to open my own store in Oregon."

Michael looked at Angus more closely. He obviously was not a hardened farmer or outdoorsman; instead, Angus appeared to be the studious type. "Thanks for telling me. Good luck with your store. We'll need it in Oregon. I'll probably be a customer."

"There is more. Nancy and I are newlyweds. The Oregon Trail is our grand adventure. But, Michael, as I have recently learned, Nancy is not a good cook. Oh, she has been in the kitchen and watched others prepare food, but she is not a cook. She also does not know how to wash or mend clothes. She's just never had to do these things. Someone has always done it for her."

Michael shook his head. *Oh, the impetuousness of youth.* "I'll talk to my wife about teaching your Nancy these skills."

"Thank you, sir. Michael, for my part, I do not even know how to chop wood or shoot a gun. I am feeling pretty helpless—even useless."

Michael shook his head again. *Just as I thought.* "I'll teach you. Are you well supplied?"

"I think so. We have the recommended amount of food. I bought a new Sharps rifle, a Parker shotgun, and a Colt revolver."

"You found a Sharps? Those are hard to come by."

"I own a Sharps, but do not know how to use it."

"Tonight, your wife can help my Alice prepare supper. Then join us for supper."

"Thank you, Michael," Angus chortled. "I am famished."

*****

AS ALICE ROBERTS WAS PREPARING to cook their Sunday supper, Nancy Campbell came into the Roberts' encampment. Her face was bright red.

"M-M-Mrs. Roberts," Nancy stammered, "Angus said that we were having supper with you tonight and you would help me learn to cook. I brought some flour." She held out a sack of flour to Alice.

"First, please call me Alice. We're pleased to meet you and share supper with you. Yes, I'll be happy to teach you what I know about cooking. Cooking can be hard work and I'm glad for your help."

Alice studied Nancy. She appeared to be about Abigail's age, but shorter and smaller. *How old was she?* Nancy was pretty, with long blonde hair and bright blue eyes. Her trail dress and matching bonnet were frilly and must have been expensive. *She did not make that dress.*

"What a beautiful dress. Almost too pretty for the trail."

Nancy's smile showed pretty white teeth. "Thank you, ma'am. My mother's seamstress made it with a sewing machine."

"I've heard of those machines but have never seen one. May I examine the stitching?"

"Certainly." Nancy stepped near Alice and held out her dress.

"Oh, my! Such tight stitching. I wonder if I could get such a machine in Oregon and learn to use it. They say it saves hours of hand stitching."

"I don't know how to use a sewing machine but I watched seamstresses and it did not look difficult to use. I think Angus has two sewing machines in our wagon."

"Why two? Do you intend to learn to sew?"

"Angus is a shopkeeper and plans to have a store in Oregon. Our wagon bed is full of merchandise for the store."

Abigail entered camp with an armload of wood. Michael had already told Abigail about the situation with the Campbells.

"Hi, I'm Abigail. Welcome."

"Hi,. I'm Nancy . Thanks so much for offering supper. My husband is starving, poor man. Did you cut that wood yourself?"

"Oh, no. It was lying on the ground. I can use an axe, but normally it's not necessary. I just pick up wood that is already cut or broken. It is called *squaw wood*--Indian women gather it."

"Abigail, Nancy brought us some flour. Let's show her how to make biscuits. But first, build up the fire so there are good coals."

"You must think I'm a complete dunce," said Nancy. "But, back home in Ohio, we had a fine kitchen with a stove and servants to cook for us."

The Enchanted Journal

"Sounds wonderful. Why did you leave?" asked Abigail.

"Adventure," replied Nancy. "I know it sounds foolish and perhaps it was, but we wanted to get away and have an adventure on our own. Plus," Nancy blushed, "my parents did not want me to marry at sixteen. So, here we are."

"You are sixteen years old?" asked Alice. *You need a mother, child, not a husband.*

"Yes, ma'am. Please don't misunderstand. We were not forced to marry and I'm not pregnant. I love Angus with all my heart."

"Abigail, show Nancy how to mix the biscuits."

"You can do all this?" Nancy swung her arms around the camp. "How old are you?"

"Fifteen," replied Abigail. "But I've been working on the farm and helping mama in the kitchen since I could walk."

"Why do you wear trousers?" asked Nancy.

"Comfortable and practical," answered Abigail as she mixed the dough. "Here, rub some lard on the inside of this Dutch oven so the biscuits don't stick. We'll make enough biscuits for tonight and tomorrow's breakfast and lunch."

"These dried beans soaked all day and are ready to be boiled," said Alice. "Can you chop onions?"

"I'll try," said Nancy.

"Don't cut yourself. Show her, Abigail."

Alice pointed to the roast on a spit over the fire. "That roast pork will add flavor to the beans. Cut away a few slices and add them to the bean pot. "Put the onion chunks in the bean pot, too."

I've just gained another daughter, thought Alice. *And a younger one at that.*

*****

MICHAEL MADE A QUICK INSPECTION of the Campbell encampment. "Nice wagon," he noted, pointing to a green wagon with orange-brown wheels.

"It is a new Schuttler," bragged Angus. "Made in Chicago by the Peter Schuttler Company. They shipped it to Independence for final assembly. It cost fifty dollars more than other new wagons, but the wainwright said it will carry 3500 pounds."

"Better not load it that heavy. Your oxen have to pull it and you'll have to unload it regularly to cross rivers and go up hills. Are your oxen shod?"

"I do not know. Can you tell?"

Michael inspected the oxen. "Yes, they are proper shod. Oxen have cloven hooves and must have a two piece shoe for the rocky trail."

Michael glanced inside the Schuttler. "Is that a piano?"

"Yes, a new Steinway upright from New York. Nancy loves to play piano. She is quite a talented singer as well."

"Does Captain Bridgewater know about your piano?"

"Yes, he does not particularly agree with our packing a piano, but says he will enjoy the music until we offload it."

Angus got his axe from the wagon.

"Nice axe," said Michael, "new?"

"Yes, I have several."

"Why?"

"To sell or trade. Remember, I am a shopkeeper. My wagon is packed with merchandise: knives, pots, pans, blankets, beads, rope---many things."

Angus and Michael stepped a little way from the Campbell tent and into a somewhat secluded wooded area.

"Most of the time," Michael began, "You won't need to use an axe to chop wood. The women and children will pick up dead, dry wood."

"Good, but I still need to learn how to use the axe."

"Yes, you do. We'll start with cutting long logs into shorter ones. You could burn the long logs in two, but sometimes you must chop them into shorter pieces. Frankly, I usually burn them into shorter pieces. Put the long log on some kind of chopping block or other log—not on the ground. If your axe blade goes into the ground, it dulls quickly. Hold the axe with your left hand near the bottom and your right hand near the middle. Allow your right hand to slide down the handle as you swing the axe. Put your feet apart and swing so that if you miss, you won't hit your leg. Gauge your distance to the log by extending your arm and axe before you swing. If there is already some kind of crack in the log, try to hit it. I'll show you." Michael swung the axe powerfully and cut a large chip in the log.

"Now you try it, Angus."

Angus first swung his axe tentatively, but increasingly harder as he gained confidence.

"You've got it. Now keep in mind the most important detail about using the axe."

"What's that?"

"Don't let the axe hit you. Now, let's go to camp for supper."

"As I said, I am hungry," Angus laughed.

Chapter 5: April 4, 1859: Monday

Abigail milked the cows and goats early Monday morning just as though she were at home in Tennessee. Following a tip from Captain Bridgewater, she covered the milk bucket and hung it from the side of the wagon. If this trick worked, they would have buttermilk and butter that evening.

Alice Roberts wore a new trail dress and bloomers with a sun bonnet. Like Abigail, Alice wore a pair of light calf skin top boots for wading or mud. They would walk many miles every day.

Wearing a frilly dress and bloomers, Nancy came into the Roberts' site just as Abigail began to make coffee. She taught Nancy to roast and grind the beans.

"I'll show you how to make porridge," said Alice to Nancy. "First, crush this parched corn into a coarse meal." She handed Nancy the mortar and pestle. "I call it porridge, but some people call it corn mush, or hasty pudding.

"Dump the crushed corn in the pot and crush this loaf of brown sugar. We use brown sugar loaves. It is less expensive than fine white sugar and it keeps well, but you must crush it. Just a little sugar is needed and sometimes I don't add sugar. Add a pinch of cinnamon, some water and put it on the fire."

Soon Angus joined them for hot coffee and a breakfast of biscuits, porridge, eggs, and last night's leftovers.

"Eggs!" said Angus. "I love fried eggs. We had eggs but most of them have already broken."

"Protect your eggs by putting them in the barrel of corn meal," said Alice.

"How clever!" said Nancy. "I'll do that right away." Nancy and Angus returned to their own camp to pack for the trail.

"Be sure to carry all the water you can and some extra firewood," Michael cautioned as they left. He and Mike took down their tent while Alice and Abigail packed their wagon.

Captain Bridgewater organized the wagons into a long train arranged by groups. His wagon was in front of the train and was followed by the Roberts' wagon and group. The groups would alternate positions every day.

"So Captain," Michael teased, "if we're on our way, Frank must be a good cook."

"Well, he can cook beans and fry bacon. His johnnycakes and corn mush were acceptable this morning. He'll probably learn more from the ladies as we travel."

With a "Wagons Ho!" Captain put them on the move. Their long journey had begun.

After a few miles, Abigail wondered if they had made a serious mistake by joining the wagon train. She was accustomed to walking but not in so much dust. Their new oxen did not appear well-trained and were stubborn as they lumbered along. The more adventurous young men sometimes raced for a better position and kicked up even more dust.

Abigail sensed someone hurrying to catch up to her. She stopped and turned to see a short teenage girl with curly black hair and a big smile.

"Hi! I'm Maggie Alexander. We're part of your papa's group. Can I walk with you?" Maggie appeared to be bursting with the need to talk to someone.

"Sure. I'm Abigail Roberts. Where're you from?"

"Alabama. My papa is a farmer and says we can do better in Oregon, but I think he just wants the adventure of the Oregon Trail."

"We're from Tennessee," said Abigail. "I'm sure my papa wants the adventure. My mama was happy in Tennessee. I was too."

"Oh, look! A butterfly! Isn't it pretty?" Maggie tried to entice the Red Admiral from her shoulder onto her finger but it flew away to join a swarm. "There are so many butterflies. Almost one for every wildflower. And the colors! Every color I can imagine. Beautiful."

Abigail raised her eyes from the dusty trail. "You're right. I need to look around more."

"Your trousers look comfortable and practical. Sometimes I wish my mama would let me wear trousers, but I prefer to look like a girl."

"My mama is not happy with my clothes, hair, and hat. She thinks I'm trying to disguise myself as a boy, but I'm not."

Maggie giggled, "Anyone can tell you are not a boy, Abigail. Now, *I* could pass for a boy."

Abigail gave Maggie a quick glance as they proceeded. "No, not really. You remind me of my friend Lydia, back home."

"Speaking of boys," Maggie giggled again and looked around. "Have you seen any cute ones?"

"No, and I'm not looking for a cute boy, either. I just want to get to Oregon and get off this trail. I'm not looking for romance. Too much trouble."

"I just turned fourteen," said Maggie. "But to find a cute boy would be fun. There aren't many in our train, but other families may join us."

"I'm fifteen," replied Abigail. "Too young for a sweetheart."

"Did you have a sweetheart back home?"

"No, and I won't have one on the trail either."

"You're much more practical than I am," sniggered Maggie. "But I'll have more fun!"

*****

CAPTAIN BRIDGEWATER HALTED the caravan at noon. He summoned his group leaders with a long blast on his horn.

"We'll take a break now for ourselves and the animals. Be sure to let your animals drink and graze. Gather firewood and water. Pass the word along."

They ate leftovers from breakfast and did not light a fire in the heat of the day.

After their two hour nooner, the train continued to Westport and stopped there to regroup and prepare for the night.

The train stopped and George Cromwell galloped up to Captain. "Why we stoppin', Bridgewater?"

"We must get organized and learn how to manage ourselves."

"It'll take forever iffen we don't speed up."

"We have many greenhorns, George."

"Ya shouldna let greenhorns come. Most of 'em are in my group. I ain't got time to teach ever'one ever'thing."

"Should I have picked a different group leader?"

"Bah! Who else ya got? I kin do it." George rode off to his wagon and group.

The wagons circled close together to form a corral with all the animals inside. Families unloaded tents and cooking gear to prepare for supper and the night. The continual search for firewood resumed and campfires were lit. Buckets of water were hauled from the nearby stream and emptied into water barrels on the wagons. Guards were assigned to patrol the area.

*****

TERRILL JOHNSON SMILED at the children assembled in front of him. "Welcome to school!" Mr. Johnson had convinced Captain Bridgewater to allow him to conduct classes during lay-bys or short travel days.

The children groaned.

"Who knows where we are?"

"The Oregon Trail," said Henry. He smiled at Abigail, pleased with his knowledge.

"What state?"

"Missouri," said Henry.

"No, actually, we're in Kansas Territory now. Kansas isn't a state yet, but it will become one soon. We began in Independence, Missouri, but now we're in Kansas Territory."

Mr. Johnson unfolded a large map and continued, "This river," he pointed, "is the Little Blue. We will follow it to the Platte River, which is in Nebraska Territory. Now, tell me where you're from."

The students rattled off their home states. Most were from Ohio, Kentucky, Tennessee, and Louisiana.

"Now let's see how well you know arithmetic."

More groans issued from the students as Mr. Johnson handed out chalkboards.

*****

HAVING ARRIVED IN WESTPORT, Abigail was setting the campfire for supper when Nancy arrived to help. Nancy handed Abigail a bag of potatoes.

"Your mama said she would show me how to cook potatoes tonight. Angus said we should provide this beef as well." She handed Abigail another bag.

"Thank you. This will make us a fine supper."

"I'm the one who thanks you. We'd be starving without your help."

Gladys Jones walked past the Robert's camp, hesitated for a moment, smiled, and proceeded to her own camp.

Alice joined them, holding little Sue by the hand. "Ready for more lessons?"

"Indeed. I brought potatoes and beef."

"Excellent. Abigail show Nancy how to prepare the potatoes for boiling. Sue, see if you can stack these rocks while I make cornbread."

"We have butter for the cornbread," bragged Abigail. "Of course, Captain Bridgewater was right—the bouncy wagon churned the milk into butter."

Mike came into the site with his whittling knife and stick in hand. "When will supper be ready?"

"Soon," answered his mother. "Meanwhile, use this bucket to fill our water barrel and get water for cleaning up. Clean yourself up while you're at it. Don't run with that knife and sharp stick."

Mike groaned but put his knife away, took the bucket, and walked towards the stream.

"Nancy," said Alice. "Be sure to boil water before drinking it. Foul water can make you sick."

"Yes ma'am."

Angus came into camp carrying an armload of firewood. "Here is my contribution," he grinned. "Guess I would make a good squaw."

"Be sure to save some firewood for yourself."

"Oh, I did. We will have a nice campfire tonight. Not that we will need it." He smiled at Nancy.

Michael arrived. "Our train is doing well. There is much to learn, though."

In the distance, Abigail heard George Cromwell shouting at someone in his group.

"I am glad we are with you, Michael," said Angus.

*****

THE LOUD SCREECH from the darkness startled Michael from a deep sleep. He rolled out of his bedroll beneath the wagon and grabbed his gun, reluctant to stand. In the distance, Captain Bridgewater raised the horn to his lips and blew another awful squawk. It was four in the morning.

Michael woke his son. "Wake up, Mike. Time to get moving."

Mike groaned and kicked off his quilt.

Michael built and lit a cooking fire. He filled the coffee pot with water and placed it on a rock in the fire. Alice and Abigail were awake and moving toward the breakfast area. Michael would come back for coffee and breakfast after tending to his animals.

Nancy and Angus entered the Roberts campsite as Michael was shaking the tent. "Be sure to shake all the dew off your tent, Angus. Helps it to dry before packing it away." *How many thousands of little details would he have to teach Angus?*

"Yes, sir. Good tip, thank you."

"Now to tend to our animals." Angus followed Michael to the center of the circled wagons.

"We'll get them to water, and let them graze while we eat breakfast," said Michael.

*****

AS THE ROBERTS WERE PACKING for the day's travel, Captain Bridgewater rode up to Michael. "Sorry, Michael, but it is your group's turn to go to the rear of the train. It will be dusty, so you might want to move to the side of the trail instead of staying in the dust. Watch out for snakes."

Snakes! Abigail shuttered. She hated snakes. Abigail picked up a long stick.

Michael noted Abigail's snake stick. "Don't try to kill the snakes, Abigail. Listen for the rattle and stay away from them."

"Yes, sir." But Abigail held on to her snake stick.

At seven o'clock, Captain Bridgewater signaled to move out. His wagon, with Beans Allen driving, led the way. George Cromwell's group followed with George and Jeff on horseback beside the oxen. Captain Bridgewater moved ahead of the caravan to scout the way.

After a few miles, a simple sign showed two arrows. Captain Bridgewater rode up and down the train, telling the group leaders, "Trail splits here. We go right. Santa Fe travelers go left. This is a good section of trail and won't be so dusty now."

Off to their left, a caravan of prairie schooners was disappearing into the dust.

*****

CAPTAIN BRIDGEWATER HABITUALLY gave geography lessons to whomever was nearby. Besides being instructive, it helped him remember as well.

"That hill," Captain Bridgewater said to George Cromwell while pointing to a tree covered high rise in the middle of the prairie, "is Blue Mound."

"Ain't blue ta me."

"It looks blue at certain times of the day and season. Remember Blue Mound, it is a well-known landmark. We won't take time to explore it, but we will encamp within sight of it as soon as we find water."

"We should git on. Don't want to git caught in snow in the mountins."

"We're doing fine, George. Don't be so impatient. These people must learn how to travel."

Captain also enjoyed giving history lessons. "Legend is that the first person to die of an accidental gunshot on the trail was near Blue Mound. Supposedly, the man's name was Shotwell—seems a strange name, don't you think? Anyway, this Shotwell was taking his gun out of his wagon, muzzle first. Somehow, his gun went off and shot him through the heart."

"Sounds like somethin' the greenhorns in my group would do."

"Tell them the story. Maybe you'll save someone's life."

Captain found water, grass, and wood a few miles ahead near Lawrence, Kansas, and between the Kansas and Wakarusa Rivers. "We'll spend the night here," Captain said. "But not in the town of Lawrence. It is too political and too rough. Besides, Lawrence does not have good supply stores.

*****

GLADYS JONES WALKED through the Roberts' camp; Michael was her group leader. She noticed Nancy and Angus again having supper with the Roberts' family.

"How nice to have supper together," Gladys said. "Are you related?"

"Just friends," replied Michael, "enjoying each other's company. Did you have a good day on the trail?"

"Fair to middlin'. Anything special tomorrow?"

"Just more walking, I'm afraid. At least the trail is easy for now."

Gladys continued to her camp.

James had their tent pitched when Gladys arrived. "Been visitin'?"

"Our group leader and that young couple. That girl's too young to be married. Bet she's pregnant. I think she can't cook, either. You watch, they'll always eat with someone else."

"They seem a fine young couple."

"You're just sayin' that 'cause the girl is pretty."

"No, they're good people, just young. Remember when we were young?" James reached to touch Gladys' arm.

Gladys snatched back her arm. "Well, we're not young anymore."

"Angus seems well educated and will do anything he is told to do. He just doesn't know what to do unless he is told."

"That shopkeeper has scads of dough, I can tell. That's how he got that girl—she's too pretty for the likes of him.

*****

AFTER SUPPER, as they were cleaning up, Abigail said to Nancy, "Mrs. Jones doesn't like my trousers. She told me again today that they weren't proper and I should wear a bonnet."

"That woman's a snoop," said Nancy. "In a few days, she'll know everything about everyone in the train. Then she'll start making things up and gossiping. Wonder what she's saying about me?"

*****

DURING BREAKFAST the next day, Abigail said to Nancy, "Mind if I walk with you today?" They had most meals together and were fast becoming friends.

Nancy glanced at Angus, who chuckled and nodded his head.

"I'd like that a lot," replied Nancy. "The wagon bounces so much and Angus doesn't talk."

"Hard to talk in that noisy wagon." Angus laughed.

"Be sure to grease the axle," Michael said.

"Show me how, please."

After breakfast, cleanup, and loading, Abigail, Nancy, Angus, and Michael proceeded to the Campbell's wagon and Michael showed Angus where to apply grease.

Nancy said, "Let me get my trail hat." She disappeared and emerged from the wagon with a fresh bonnet.

Abigail lampooned Nancy's frilly bonnet by pulling her own felted hat snug on her head and tightening the stampede string. It was a windy day already and would probably get worse.

Angus pulled his wagon behind Michael's just as Captain Bridgewater blew his horn to get moving.

While they trudged along, Abigail said to Nancy, "I love to hear you play piano and sing. How did you learn?"

Nancy blushed. "Thank you. My mother taught me from a young age. I can't remember not playing the piano. My mother says I am a musical prodigy—that means someone who is naturally endowed with exceptional abilities."

"I know."

"Oh, I'm sorry Abigail. I did not mean to question your education. You are exceptionally smart. How were you educated?"

"In the one room country schoolhouse that people always belittle. But my mother challenged me to read and study. My education is not complete. In Oregon, I'll go back to school. I hope Mr. Johnson will take me into his school."

"I'm sure he will," said Nancy. "Even though my mother said music came naturally to me, I studied and practiced hard. We had servants, so I did not do household chores; instead, I played piano all day. Perhaps I should have learned to cook and sew!"

"Don't worry, you'll learn on the trail. My mother and I will teach you."

"I must!"

"How did you and Angus meet?" Abigail was curious, especially since Angus was four years older.

"Angus and I grew up together and our parents were friends, but he paid little attention to me until he came back from college."

"Angus attended college?"

"Oh, yes. Well, seminary. His parents wanted him to become a minister, but he became disillusioned with religion while in seminary. Strange, don't you think? Seems the opposite should have happened. Don't misunderstand: Angus is a strong Christian, but with unanswered questions. Anyway, Angus returned to work in his parents' store after two years in seminary and thoroughly enjoyed being a shopkeeper. He wants to open his own store in Oregon."

"Seminary?" said Abigail. "So that's why his talk is sometimes a bit stilted."

"Yes, the seminary urged him to avoid contractions. Said it was not proper for a minister to use in sermons. I'm trying to get him to sound more relaxed and casual though. Please don't mention this."

"I won't."

"One day," Nancy continued, "I entered Campbell Dry Goods store with my mother and Angus did not recognize me. My mother had to introduce us!" She giggled at the memory. "I was fifteen, and he was nineteen. He called on me, but his parents thought it unseemly to be calling on someone so young. They still wanted Angus to become a minister. He persisted, and we were married three months ago when I turned sixteen."

"What a beautiful love story!"

"And what about you, Abigail? Do you have a sweetheart?"

"Oh, no. And no prospects either."

"Oh? What about Henry Wells? He obviously likes you."

Abigail blushed. "I'm glad to have Henry as a friend, but that's all he'll ever be." *Henry! That's who Angus reminded her of: Henry! Angus was a grownup version of Henry. How did Angus ever attract such a beauty as Nancy?*

"Henry seems quite nice and obviously intelligent. He'll grow and will make something of himself. You'll see."

"I don't want a trail romance. I just want to get to Oregon and quickly. Maybe I'll feel differently once we get there."

Sandlin

The Enchanted Journal

Part 2

Life on the Trail

Sandlin

The Enchanted Journal

Chapter 6: April 7 – The Routine

A ROUTINE QUICKLY DEVELOPED. Captain Bridgewater woke everyone at four in the morning with his horn. The men led the animals to fresh grass and water while the women cooked breakfast. Their simple but filling breakfast usually included coffee, biscuits, salt pork, and beans. Sometimes johnnycakes replaced the biscuits. Milk or buttermilk and butter were often available. A barrel served as the table. People sat on the ground, barrels, stumps, logs, or rocks to eat. Everyone carried their own tin cup and a fixed blade knife for eating. Tin plates and spoons were distributed as necessary. By seven o'clock, the wagons were repacked and rolling.

Around noon, if a suitable campsite was available, the wagons stopped for lunch—the nooner—and a rest. Tents were pitched only if rain was expected, but rain showers often developed so quickly that everyone crowded into the wagon. The noon meal was usually the same as the breakfast meal.

Sometimes the women made dough during the nooner and baked bread that evening in a Dutch oven. Saleratus made the bread rise, but some complained that the saleratus tasted bitter.

After about two hours, the nooner ended, and the journey resumed until six o'clock or so—again, provided a suitable campsite was available.

After making evening camp, Terrill Johnson and his wife, Ellen, often conducted their school for the children, particularly during lay-bys. Terrill taught geography, history, and arithmetic to the older children. Ellen taught reading and arithmetic to the younger children. The Johnson's own children, Cathy, age ten and Mark, age six, attended classes. Sometimes parents attended the classes with their children, especially when Terrill taught the geography and history of their location.

George Cromwell almost always went hunting in the afternoon, usually accompanied by his son, Jeff, and sometimes a few other men.

Maggie often sketched the local sights or finished a sketch she had started previously. Her sketch pad was filled with drawings of mules, oxen, wagons, campsites, rock formations—the illustrated story of the trail.

After supper, Nancy played piano in her covered wagon, sometimes accompanied by Ralph Richardson on his fiddle. When Judy Field joined them, everyone stopped to enjoy the concert.

*****

The Enchanted Journal

"ABIGAIL," SAID HER MOTHER, "you and Mike get water for washing clothes, and try to find berries for a pie. Stay in sight of the wagon, though. Nancy and I will start washing clothes."

"Yes, ma'am."

Although they had been travelling only a few days, their clothes were already grubby from the constant dust. They had few changes of clothes and did not change every day. Most days the clothes received a good shaking instead of a washing.

Abigail picked up two buckets and a carrying stick to go across her shoulders. Mike grabbed a smaller bucket.

*****

JEFF CROMWELL WATCHED AS ABIGAIL walked briskly past their campsite on her way to the stream. He rose and turned toward the stream as Gladys Jones crossed in front of him.

"Jeff, you leave that girl be." His mother was well aware of the rumors and accusations that had contributed to their need to leave Kentucky.

"Aw, Ma," Jeff groaned. "She might appreciate some help."

"You leave her be," Ester repeated. "We don't need none of your trouble on this trail."

"Listen ta yer ma, boy," George advised. "We're barely a few days from Independence, where ya roamed. We'll be to a fort soon enough ta satisfy yerself." He grinned.

"Can I at least have a shot of your whiskey?"

"Just one." George handed Jeff his bottle.

"Another thing," said George. "Don't go git yerself a squaw at the fort. You know how I feel 'bout Injuns."

"Indians are people," insisted Ester. They had this argument regularly.

"No, they ain't," argued George. "They's cursed savages, same as Africans. Says so in yer Bible."

"Show me." Ester grinned as she handed George her Bible, knowing he could not read.

"Heard a preacher say so, oncet."

"When was that, George? You haven't been to church in a coon's age."

"No doxology works out here."

"Let's eat supper," Ester said. "We're having venison steaks from that deer you shot."

George Cromwell loved to hunt and was an excellent marksman. He tried to hunt every day and usually was successful. He sometimes shared his kills with the other pioneers, but more often insisted on a trade.

Although a small woman, Ester was not intimidated by her brute of a husband. At twenty, their son Jeffa was nearly as big as his father and would equal his size and belligerence soon.

"After supper," George said, "I'm goin' ta talk ta Bridgewater. The way we're goin', mountin snow will catch us."

"I'll go with you, Pa." Jeff did not want to help his mother clean up. Besides, they would go past the Roberts camp and he might see Abigail.

*****

"ONE THING FOR SURE," said Gladys Jones to her husband. "Those Cromwells are no good."

"George is an ornery cuss, all right. He argues with everyone; I'm glad we're not in his group. He hunts but doesn't share—even with his own group. He insists on selling or trading. I had to buy this venison from him today."

"The Cromwell son looks like a lawbreaker. He's after that tomboy . She tries to disguise herself but don't fool no one. She'd best watch herself."

"Mrs. Cromwell seems a good Christian woman."

"Hah! If she was, she'd get away from the Cromwell men. They both drink whiskey."

"At least she has her Bible to comfort her. I saw her reading it today. I think George can't read."

"I doubt that grumpy old man would read the Bible even if he could."

The Enchanted Journal

James cocked his head as a tune from Nancy's nearby piano drifted into their camp.

"Good thing that clotheshorse can play piano. I'm sure she can't cook. I bet Captain Bridgewater is listening. They say he has an ear for music and an eye for a pretty girl. That's why he let her bring a piano on the trail."

*****

ABIGAIL AND MIKE had to make two trips to the nearby stream to fill the large washing pot sitting on the fire. On their third trip to the stream, they collected rinse water. With the wash pots filled, they each took a small bucket and searched for berries.

Alice showed Nancy how to wash the dirty clothes by hand using homemade lye soap and stirring the pot with a stick. Clothes would not be washed every week, but today provided a good opportunity. As Nancy spread the last of their washed clothes to dry, Abigail and Mike returned. *This was not a coincidence.*

"Any berries?"

"Only a few. But I found an old journal."

"A diary? How interesting! Who wrote it?"

"A girl my age, but she wrote it seventeen years ago."

"You can read it later, but for now, please help me prepare supper."

*****

CHORES ACCOMPLISHED, Abigail found a candle and entered the tent she shared with her mother and Sue to read more of Milli's journal.

1843

Today, I turned fifteen years old as we arrived in Independence, Missouri! My brother, Matthew Jr. (Matt), is twelve and causes many problems with his curiosity, mischievousness, and disobedience. My youngest brother, Sam, is eight years old and easier to deal with, but cannot help as much with chores as Matt. Sarah, my baby sister, is only three, so she rides in the wagon most of the time. The rest of us will take turns walking to ease the load on the mules and stretch our muscles. Besides, the wagon bounces a lot.

Our equipment includes a coffee mill and pot, tin cups and plates, cutlery, bread pan, rolling pin, churn, axe, shovel, and water barrels. We will cook over an outdoor firepit using a cast-iron spider skillet, Dutch oven, folding camp grill, trammel hooks, and trivets. We have a large tent for shelter and sleeping. Of course, Papa packed his fishing line and rifle.

We each have three changes of clothes, two blankets and a comforter. There is little room in the wagon for anything else other than food—and we have a lot of food! Papa says we have enough food for the entire six-month period because there is little opportunity to resupply along the way.

Our guide is a former trapper, Bill Shaw. Most people in our wagon train are farmers wanting more and better land. Some are simply *adventurers with no definite plans—particularly the young men. One man plans to open a dry goods store in Oregon. We have a missionary family and several school teachers. There is even a banker! Fortunately, a doctor travels with us; he plans to open a practice in Oregon.*

ABIGAIL TURNED THE PAGE to read more of Milli's first days on the trail.

1843
After ferrying across the Missouri River yesterday, we rose early to begin our journey. Mama fixed coffee, johnnycakes, and salt pork for breakfast and made extra for lunch.

We are on the trail but usually walk beside the wagons. Walking is more comfortable than the rough riding wagon.

Midday, we stopped for about two hours—this is called the 'nooner'. Mama did not cook; instead we ate more breakfast from this morning.

We are settling into a routine: wake early, breakfast, repack, walk, nooner, repack, walk, make camp, supper, sleep. Fortunately, the weather has been fine and the trail is easy except for the dust.

Unlike our previous life, nothing follows an exact pattern. We were accustomed to
    Wash on Monday
    Iron on Tuesday
    Mend on Wednesday

Churn on Thursday
Clean on Friday
Bake on Saturday
Rest on Sunday

But now, each day's schedule and activities depend on the weather, water, grass, and wood. Even the church schedule varies, although we attempt to keep the Sabbath holy.

We've been taught that deeds of necessity may be done on the Sabbath and mother says it is necessary that our dirty clothes be washed. She reminds us that cleanliness is next to godliness.

We stop before dark to make camp. I help Papa and Matt pitch a tent for Mama, Sue, and me. Papa, Matt, and Sam sleep under the wagon unless it is raining. Our meals do not vary much. For supper, Mama cooks salt pork, potatoes, beans, and cornbread. She makes extra beans to have for breakfast. Judging by the size of the bags in the wagon, I think we will eat a lot of beans!

Milli's journal ended here and Abigail was disappointed. *I wish there were more entries. I'd like to know more about how Milli's train handled the trail.*

*****

THE MORNING AFTER FINDING MILLI'S JOURNAL, Abigail glanced again at Milli's journal while Captain Bridgewater organized the emigrants to cross a flooded creek. *I didn't notice this page last night. Must have skipped it.*

The Enchanted Journal

1843

I was not prepared for the number of graves along the trail. Today, I counted six, and we are just getting started! Those poor people must have been ill before they began the trail. Or perhaps there were accidents. Four graves were just piles of rock; two had simple wooden crosses.

We are near two remarkably large boulders that I call 'The Eggs' because they are almost identically sized, shaped, and smoothed. I suppose water flow has shaped them over many years, perhaps hundreds of years. The creek is flooded but not quite touching the Eggs.

Captain Shaw was organizing us to cross the creek when our scout returned with good news. He found a much better place to cross the creek only a mile upstream. I was glad to not attempt a crossing at the Eggs—for some reason, they frightened me.

Abigail looked up from Milli's journal and shuddered at the Eggs near the water. She searched for Captain Bridgewater and found him near his wagon, studying the creek, while chewing on a blade of Timothy grass.

"Captain Bridgewater?" Abigail said awkwardly. "Excuse me, please, sir. I have a question."

"Yes, young lady. What can I help you with?"

"Sir, do I understand we are about to cross this large creek here? The water just looks so fast."

"We sure are. Don't be afraid. Notice the tracks from other trains crossing here. We must cross many creeks before getting to Oregon—even some rivers. You'll get used to it."

"Well, it's just that I believe a much better location is about a mile upstream of us."

Captain Bridgewater smiled. "And why do you think that my dear? Are you familiar with this area?"

"I've not been here before, but I found a journal claiming the best crossing is a mile upstream." She opened the journal and pointed to the passage. "See, this family had the same problem years ago."

"Could I read that journal?"

Abigail handed it to him. "There are only a few pages, and it was years ago, but they were in our same location."

Captain read Milli's description of the Eggs and flooded creek. "Hmm, it will only take me a few minutes on horseback to check. I'll go upstream a bit."

Captain Bridgewater soon returned. "Well, I'll be blessed," he said to Abigail. "That journal is correct. We'll move upstream."

Later that day, on the other side of the flooded creek, Captain Bridgewater found the Roberts' camp. He approached Michael Roberts. "Michael, your daughter was a great help to us today. Could I speak to her?"

"Of course." Michael shouted, "Abigail!" and she appeared, carrying an armload of firewood.

"Abigail," Captain Bridgewater said, "I thank you again for your advice. I wonder what other useful information might be in that journal. Might I study it tonight?"

"Of course. I'll get it, but there are not many pages."

"Thank you. There are few maps or notes and every bit of information helps. I'll return it to you tomorrow." Captain ambled away.

Abigail turned to help her mother prepare supper and Nancy arrived carrying a bag of beans. "I'm so embarrassed to depend on you. We at least want to share our supplies."

"Tonight, we'll make cornbread, and I'll show you how to make soup from portable soup," said Alice, holding up a brownish lump. "This is portable soup. I made it by boiling beef and drying it before leaving Tennessee. It keeps especially well. All we need to add is water, but I prefer to add potatoes, beans, and onions as well.

The Enchanted Journal

Abigail found some wild onions today, so we'll use those instead of dried onions."

"You know we'll always have beans," said Abigail, laughing. "They're good for your heart."

*****

"FRANK, I BELIEVE I'LL CALL YOU 'BEANS ALLEN'," said Captain Bridgewater as he sopped his supper plate with a piece of johnnycake.

"You won't be the first," said Frank Allen, chuckling.

"Well, at least your beans are tasty."

"And we have many kinds of beans, so you won't get tired of them."

"We'll see about that."

Captain Bridgewater called for an assembly by blowing three quick squawks on his horn. "Our aim is to get to Oregon as quickly as possible. However, sometimes we must stop and rest. To the extent it is possible and safe, we will rest on Sunday. We will also try to relax and enjoy ourselves on Saturday nights such as this one. Mr. Richardson, how about a tune?"

Mr. Richardson placed his fiddle on his shoulder and played "Oh, Susannah!" Frank Allen disappeared for a moment and returned with a harmonica. Someone produced a juice harp and joined in.

Angus turned to Nancy. "Would you care to dance?" They led a group of the younger pioneers in a lively two-step.

Fred Wells proved to be a good singer as he led everyone in singing "Sweet Betsy from Pike."

> *"Did you ever hear tell of sweet Betsy from Pike,*
> *Who crossed the wide prairies with her lover Ike,*
> *With two yoke of cattle and one spotted hog,*
> *A tall shanghai rooster, an old yaller dog?"*

*****

55

DESPITE HER VOW, Abigail had worn her new calico dress to celebrate their first Saturday night on the trail. She joined her mother and father near their wagon.

"My, don't you look spiffy!" said her mother as they ambled toward the music.

Most of their fellow emigrants had gathered around Mr. Richardson and his fiddle. Searching the crowd, Abigail realized, to her dismay, that she was the oldest unmarried girl in the train.

Mr. Richardson slowed the pace with a waltz, and Alice and Michael strolled to the dance area. Abigail loved to see her mother and father in each other's arms and waltzing. *Such fine parents and so in love. I'm a lucky girl.*

Jeff Cromwell approached Abigail with a grin, his decayed eyetooth stained by tobacco. "Ah, so you *are* a girl! And a fine one at that. I wondered about you. Would you dance with me?" He extended his hand.

"No."

"What?"

"No. I will not dance with you. Leave me alone. Skeedaddle."

"C'mon. Dancing is easy. I'll teach you."

"I know how to dance, but I'll not dance with you. Leave me alone."

Jeff stomped away, joined the crowd of onlookers, and took a sip of whiskey from his hip flask. To Jeff's astonishment and anger, little Henry Wells asked Abigail to dance. She accepted, and they began twirling around.

After Abigail returned to her place, Michael strolled to her with a smile. "Are you too old to dance with your father?"

"Of course not."

They eased into the center of the dance area.

"Abigail, what was going on between you and Jeff Cromwell? Is there a problem?"

"Jeff scares me, Papa. He's evil."

"I trust your sense of judgment about men. Jeff is rough and crude. I'll speak to Jeff and his father."

"No, please don't. That would make things worse. I'll just stay away from him. Please understand."

The Enchanted Journal

"All the same, I'll keep my eye on Jeff."

Captain Bridgewater proved to be a good and popular dancer and was much in demand. He danced the two-step with Abigail, Maggie, and Alice. Nancy tried to teach him the polka and he laughed as he stumbled about.

Gladys Jones nudged her husband. "Do you notice how Captain Bridgewater dances with all the women?"

Most people stayed awake later than usual but soon all tired and headed for their tents and beds.

*****

ABIGAIL OPENED Milli's journal as she slipped into bed. *Was this a new entry? How could she have missed it this morning?*

While waiting at the Eggs, I met an interesting boy—well, a young man, William Anderson. He is two years older than me and seems quite nice. William is handsome and strong. The Anderson wagon is just ahead of us on the trail, so I will see William again tomorrow.

So Milli had met a handsome boy! Abigail wondered if Milli's trail journal would turn into a romance novel.

And what about her? Would her adventure follow Milli's? Abigail did not think so; besides, she was not interested in romance. She just wanted to get to Oregon. She blew out her candle and snuggled into her quilt.

*****

SUNDAY MORNING, Captain Bridgewater returned the journal to Abigail. "Thank you for dancing with me last night. Makes me wish I were twenty years younger!"

Abigail blushed. "You are a good dancer."

"My sweetheart and her mother taught me well."

"You had a sweetheart?" As soon as the words left her mouth, Abigail was sorry she asked.

"Yes, long ago," Captain's voice had a touch of melancholy. "Isabella—she was called 'Bell'--died of smallpox. Her death devastated me, and I have been on the road ever since. But my travels will end in Oregon."

"I hope mine will too."

"You said this was the journal of a girl like you, but it reads like a wagon master's journal to me. Thank you for loaning it to me. I wish there were more pages."

Abigail gave Milli's journal a quick glance and put it away in the wagon. It was time for church service. She walked with Captain to join the small crowd and hoped Jeff Cromwell would not be there, but those thoughts made her feel sinful. Jeff was not in the crowd, but his mother was. Abigail breathed a sigh of relief.

"Allow me to introduce Reverend Charles Field," announced Captain Bridgewater to the assembled pioneers. "Reverend Field will serve as minister for our train and will lead us in worship today. But first, let me say a few words about worship and observance of Sunday.

"God instructed us to rest on the seventh day, and we will attempt to do so. However, we may take our day of worship a day or so sooner or later, according to our situation. Also, we cannot stop all activity on those days of rest. There is simply too much to be done. I pray God understands. And now, Reverend Field, meet your congregation."

"Thank you, Captain." Charles Field stepped to the front of the group and cleared his throat. "I'm actually not a reverend, I'm a Methodist lay minister on my way to Oregon, just as you are. That said, I'm pleased to lead you in worship. I admit to knowing only the Methodist manner of worship. If anyone wishes a different type of service, you are welcome to organize a service before or after this

The Enchanted Journal

one. You are even welcome to replace me occasionally," he said with a chuckle and cough.

Gladys whispered to her husband. "I'd feel better if he was Baptist like us. He's very sick and won't last long."

"Mr. Richardson, Mrs. Field, would you lead us in singing?"

Mr. Richardson easily switched from fiddling Saturday night dance songs to well-known religious songs. Judy Field began "Just as I am" in a clear alto voice. Abigail and her mother added their own altos as her father's baritone joined in. A soft but exquisite soprano came from the rear of the congregation. Abigail recognized Nancy's voice and listened as it grew more confident and euphonious.

Reverend Field opened with a prayer and readings from the Bible. He gave a brief message and closed by praying for a safe journey. Judy Field led the congregation in singing "Sweet Hour of Prayer." Nancy's soprano now resounded from the congregation and people turned to identify her.

Captain stood and announced, "We'll consider this our nooner, and be on our way afterward."

Abigail opened Milli's journal, wondering what to expect. A page had been added.

1843

We crossed the flooded creek with no losses and no damage. What a blessing to have discovered a better crossing than the 'Eggs'. We continue westward.

I walked a few miles alongside William Anderson. He insists on calling me 'Miss Milli' even though I am younger than him. I call him 'William.' I enjoyed William's company; it made for a pleasant day. He is smart and always polite.

Four graves were beside the trail, but not in a group. None showed fresh dirt.

How could this be? Abigail thumbed through the journal. This was the last page, but she would check again tomorrow. The new pages were just too strange. Was Milli trying to tell her something? Why? Was God telling her something? What?

*****

CAPTAIN BRIDGEWATER'S CARAVAN passed near an Indian village as its inhabitants dismantled it. Squaws and children scurried around like ants without the chaos. Although some teepees were still fully erect, the sewn skin coverings were being removed. They had already reduced some teepees to long poled skeletons.

Captain Bridgewater rode to Michael and Abigail as he returned from his conference with the chief.

"They're moving on," explained Captain. "They need pasture for their horses. In a few miles, they will turn off, but we will keep going for about eight more miles to our pasture, water, and wood."

"Captain, why don't the men work?" asked Abigail indignantly. "I've been watching, and the women and children do all the work while the men just lounge around." She pointed to the rapidly disappearing village where the squaws were tying one end of the teepee lodge poles to their ponies while the other end of the lodge poles drug the ground. The squaws interwove a trellis of rawhide and frames to the lodge poles. They placed robes, blankets, and clothing on the trellis.

"The men think it is beneath them to do women's work."

"Don't you start a problem with my wife!" laughed Michael.

"They don't have wheels," said Captain, "so they use these sledges—travois—to move their belongings."

They added papooses strapped to boards and little puppies on top of the travois. The entire camp, except for the braves, moved purposefully and rapidly to move to the new camp.

They loaded one travois with extra buffalo robes and several squaws placed an invalid older squaw on the robes.

Even the larger dogs did their share of work pulling scaled-down travois loaded with smaller and lighter camp items.

With the village dismantled, the squaws drove the ponies and dogs down the trail.

"Why them Injuns ahead of us?" George Cromwell yelled.

"They go a little faster than our oxen, so let 'em go first," said Captain. "If we go first, they'll catch up to us and beg for food."

"Ain't no Injun gittin' my dinner!" George wheeled his horse around and returned to his wagon, shouting to everyone, "Bridgewater's lettin' Injuns go first!"

"Abigail," said Captain, "while we're waiting, could I have another look at that journal you found?"

1843

There are so many buffalo that I cannot count them. They trample along as though marching, and I can hear the roar of their bellowing from a great distance. When the buffalo cross a stream, they befoul it such that the water cannot be used. We use dried buffalo dung (chips) for fuel when trees are not around. The buffalo chips burn hot and do not smell as bad as I thought.

I walked alongside William Anderson again. He is eager to kill a buffalo and got his chance with Papa and several other men. Now we have fresh meat to share for a few days. The buffalo hump and tongue are particularly prized.

*****

CAPTAIN BRIDGEWATER RODE UP to the Roberts' wagon during the nooner. He handed Milli's journal to Abigail and grinned. "I have a feeling buffalo are nearby. How about some buffalo, Michael? Grab that new gun of yours."

Michael was soon alongside Captain Bridgewater and a few others, including George and Jeff Cromwell. Abigail relaxed when Jeff left camp.

Fred Wells and his son Henry rode up. "Got room for Henry and me?"

George Cromwell glanced at little Henry. "No mama's boys," he scolded.

"Of course, you and Henry can come, Fred," said Captain. "Stay in my group."

"Just don't mess up my hunting," retorted Cromwell.

"There's not a lot of buffalo in this herd, but we can kill a few," said Captain. "I remember a time when there were so many you couldn't find the start or end of a herd. We'll use all the meat we can harvest today, but some people cut out the prime parts and leave the rest to rot. Indians may come afterward and harvest the rest of the buffalo and its hide." He chortled. "The Indians will offer to sell us the hide from the buffalo we shot."

"Only good Injun is a dead Injun," quoted George Cromwell.

"We may see Indians. Give them a chance to be peaceful. Do not automatically start shooting at them."

"They'd best leave my buffs be then." *NO.*

"The Indians consider the buffalo to be theirs and that we are the trespassers."

"Thet ain't right."

Captain turned to the right, but George and Jeff Cromwell turned left. Two shots rang out, then more.

Captain said to his group, "We'll creep up on the herd to about a hundred yards. Closer might be dangerous if they stampede. Pick a young, tender buffalo, preferably a cow old enough to have a hump. Don't shoot them in the head; shoot them broadside through the lungs. Every man shoots one buffalo. We'll take the tongue, hump, shoulders, and rump back to camp.

The Enchanted Journal

The hunters crept up on the shaggy beasts whose giant heads swayed in rhythm as they tread. The hunters stopped about a hundred yards from the herd, kneeled, and braced themselves for a killing shot. Every man shot a young buffalo; most kills took a single well placed shot.

More shots came from the Cromwell's direction.

"We'd best not shoot any more buffalo," said Captain. "Sounds like the Cromwells have shot many—unless they're in a gun battle with the Indians. Let's pack what meat we can and find the Cromwells."

Captain found the Cromwells and, as he expected, they had killed a dozen buffalo. "You really enjoy killing, don't you, George," said Captain. "Most of this meat will be wasted."

George Cromwell grinned at Captain. "We got 'em, didn't we?" He stood by a massive bull and poked out his own chest.

"We can't carry more. Pack what you can back to camp. Maybe we can get others to help you in return for some of the meat."

George showed how to get the prized hump meat. He skinned down the buffalo's back to get at the tender meat under the surface, before cutting off the front legs and shoulder blades to further expose the hump meat. Within fifteen minutes, George had cut away five or more pounds of prime hump meat and packed it in a bag on his horse.

On the way to their encampment, Captain said, "We might as well stay where we are tonight. We can feast on fresh buffalo and dry and smoke the rest while we have wood. The animals can rest and feed before we push for Alcove Spring. Should take us three or four days to get to the Springs. Be sure to collect extra wood and water here."

*****

ABIGAIL WAS NOT SURPRISED to see Milli's note about buffalo. *So that's why Captain wanted to hunt.* How could this happen? Who wrote the new pages? Where was the pen? The ink? Would the unexplainable continue? She opened the journal.

1843
We are drying and smoking strips of buffalo meat for our journey.
Today, I counted seven graves on the trail. All were simple piles of rocks. Two showed fresh dirt on the rocks and were small.
Tomorrow we will float the Kansas River. Captain Shaw says it will be our first difficult test. The procedure is to partially unload each wagon so it will float and use double teams of oxen so that one team always has their feet on the river bottom. Riders on horseback will urge the oxen onward. I am nervous about this crossing, but William says he will watch out for me.

Abigail added her own thoughts beneath Milli's.

I don't understand how new pages are added to Milli's journal or what she or her journal is trying to tell me. However, we are also near the Kansas River and will cross it tomorrow. Milli has made me nervous.

Chapter 7: April 15–Kansas River

"THIS IS TOPEKA," said Captain to George Cromwell, whose group had rotated to the front of the train. "There are a few rough cabins over that way, but it's really not a town and has few supplies. The Pappan brothers operate a ferry service here, and we'll use their ferry to cross the Kansas River."

"How much?" grumbled George.

"A dollar a wagon."

"What iffen I don't pay?"

"You can move downstream and try to float across, but I don't recommend it. The Pappan ferry is much safer."

"I wonder 'bout ya, Bridgewater. We paid ya ta lead us and now yer makin' us pay again. Do ya get part of the toll? Ya always take the slow route and say it's safer. Just how much 'sperience do ya really have?"

"Much more than you, Cromwell." He assembled the group leaders with a short toot on his horn and explained the situation.

"I'm not payin' or waitin'," said George Cromwell to the other group leaders. "I'll move downstream, ford the river, and keep goin' on the other side. If ya push hard, ya might catch up ta us in a couple of days. Anyone with me?"

Two families, the Horners and the Greens, joined the Cromwells. All others used the ferry.

As the wagons lined up at the ferry, Indians surrounded them, wanting to trade. George Cromwell pulled out his revolver and chased them away.

Captain said, "I'm trading for pemmican while we wait."

Alice Roberts followed Captain's example and traded for pemmican. She showed the ball of pemmican to Abigail and Nancy. "It's dried buffalo meat pounded into flour mixed with dried berries and marrow. I've heard of it but didn't have any. They say it will last almost forever. Now, we can have pemmican with our hardtack."

Everyone hated the hardtack meals, which were forced by weather not permitting cooking.

"I'll get Angus to buy some, too," said Nancy. As a shopkeeper, one of Angus' skills was trade and negotiation.

"Good idea," agreed Alice. "I want to learn to make pemmican myself, but, for now, we'll trade for it."

While they waited their turn on the ferry, George Cromwell and his small group passed.

Maggie moved off to one side of the caravan, pulled out a sketch pad, and began drawing the ferry on the river.

The Enchanted Journal

*****

GEORGE CROMWELL DROVE his wagon downstream from the Pappan ferry, with the two other wagons following.

"I can't believe ever'body else is payin' a dollar and waitin' in line," George griped to Jeff, riding alongside him while Ester drove the wagon. "We'll git so far ahead thet they cain't catch us."

"Do you have a map?" asked Ester.

"Don't need one. Just follow the tracks."

George found a place he liked about a mile downstream of the ferry. "We cross here," he said.

"There are no wagon tracks here," objected Ester.

"So yer a guide now?" George rebuffed. "Jeff, check it out."

Jeff eased his horse out into the river and crossed to about the mid-point. "Looks OK, Pa."

"We'll lead the way," George said. "Jeff, ride upstream and ahead of the oxes. I'll ride downstream."

"Shouldn't we unload and float across?" asked Patrick Horner.

"No need. Ya saw how deep when Jeff rode out there."

From his horse on the left-hand side of the oxen, George shouted, "Get up!" and whacked the lead ox with his goad stick. From the driver's seat, Ester snapped the harness and echoed, "Get up!" The wagon jerked and creaked as its oxen took the slack from the yokes and rolled from the sandy bank into the shallows.

Patrick Horner rode his mule beside his lead ox, yelling "Get up!" and prodded it into the water. His wife slapped the harness on the back of the oxen. Their wagon wheels deepened the tracks made by the Cromwells' wagon in the sand.

"Our turn," said Hiram Green. "Everyone in the wagon and hang on tight." Having no mule, Hiram was in the driver's seat. He cracked his whip and slapped the reins. "Get up!" and the Greens' wagon entered the river aligned with the Horners' tracks.

"Water! Water's comin' in!" yelled Mrs. Green when the water level reached the floor of the wagon bed.

"Drops off here!" hollered Jeff from his lead position.

"Get up!" George prodded his lead ox onward as his wagon floated in the swift current. The oxen kept their feet and pulled the floating wagon to the shallows and up the sandy bank.

The Horners' wagon floated downstream about two wagon lengths at the drop off, but its oxen, prodded by Patrick beside them, continued to pull towards the bank.

The Greens' wagon reached the drop off, and water splashed over its shallow sideboards. "Haw," yelled Hiram. He cracked his whip and pulled the reins to turn downstream.

"No! No!" George bellowed. "Don't turn 'round."

The wagon tilted as one set of wheels fell into the drop off. Water flowed into the wagon bed and the wagon sank. Mrs. Green screamed, "Help! Help us!"

"Aren't you going to do something? shouted Ester.

Already well up the bank, George and Jeff jerked their horses around and entered the shallows.

A wheel on the drifting wagon snagged something on the river bottom, and the wagon tipped on one side, dumping passengers and contents into the raging river. The wagon twisted away from its oxen. Free of oxen, it sped downstream in the swift current. The wagon crashed into a large rock, flipped over and over and broke into pieces.

Ester glared at George but said nothing.

"What could I do?" George said. "Thet wagon is already out of sight. We'd never catch it. Besides, they're all dead now. Jeff, better go back and tell Bridgewater or whoever has already crossed. We'll keep goin'. Ya can catch up easy."

Jeff turned and trotted his horse toward the ferry.

*****

JEFF REACHED THE FERRY to find Captain Bridgewater waiting to cross, but Michael Roberts had already crossed. Jeff rode towards Michael while searching for Abigail and found her near her father. Jeff smiled at Abigail, but she showed no reciprocation.

"Problem?" asked Michael as Jeff reached him.

The Enchanted Journal

"The Greens' wagon got swept away by the river. I tried to save them," Jeff bragged, staring boldly at Abigail, "but couldn't."

"Where are they now?" asked Michael.

"I don't know. Their wagon broke into pieces, and I couldn't find them. They must be far down river by now. Drowned, I suppose."

"Fred," Michael yelled. "Watch things over here. I may be gone a while."

Michael turned to Angus. "Angus, come with me. Abigail, pass the word around. Be sure to tell Captain after he crosses."

"Jeff, let's go find your father." Michael mounted his mule.

Jeff turned his horse around and retraced his footsteps to his father and their fatal crossing point.

*****

"GREENHORNS!" SPAT GEORGE CROMWELL when Michael questioned him. "Why did Bridgewater give me all the greenhorns?" George was already a mile from the crossing and searching for the trail.

"Never mind the trail; we must search for the Green family."

"Ya never find 'em, I tell ya."

"We must try," insisted Michael.

"I agree," said Patrick Horner. "You would want us to search for you, wouldn't you, George?"

"Besides that," said Michael, "you're heading in the wrong direction to get to the trail."

George jerked his oxen around, cracked his whip over them, and returned to his crossing point.

Captain arrived. "Let's search downstream," he ordered. Captain, George, and Jeff led the way on their horses. Michael and Patrick followed on their mules. The wagons remained behind.

After a couple of hours of searching in vain, the men returned to the wagons empty-handed except for Mr. Green's hat. Charles Field had joined the search party anticipating a funeral.

"At least let's bury his hat," said Charles through his coughs. He had brought a shovel and began digging in the soft sand near the river.

"George," began Captain. "I'm holding you responsible for their deaths."

"Me? Yer the one responsible. Ya let thet greenhorn join our train, even though his overloaded wagon didna have enough sideboard. He didn't even caulk the wagon bed. This ain't my fault. It's yourn."

"You should have set an example and used the ferry. At the very least, you should have unloaded the wagons and floated across the river instead of attempting to ford it with a full load."

Michael, Charles, Angus, and Patrick nodded their heads.

"I'm returning to the ferry to join the others," said Captain. "Patrick, what about you?"

"I'm rejoining the train," replied Patrick. "But I don't want to be in George Cromwell's group."

"George is no longer a group leader," said Captain.

"What? Ya cain't do that!" shouted George.

"I appointed you a group leader, and I can remove you. For the time being, I'll take over your group. You abandoned the train and left most of your group behind. Are you rejoining the train or continuing on your own?"

"I paid ya ta join yer wagon train and I'm still in it," George retorted. "But ya havna heard the last of this."

*****

GONE, Abigail thought while waiting at the ferry. Abigail didn't know the Green family well, but she cried for them.

Nancy came to the Roberts tent and wept with Abigail. "This could happen to any of us," Nancy said. "I'm frightened."

"Abigail," her mother said. "Check with Fred to see whether we should move on or stay here tonight."

"I hope the Cromwells do not return to the train," said Abigail to Nancy as they searched for Fred. "His father is bad enough, but Jeff gives me the creeps."

"Me too," agreed Nancy. "He is always staring at me. I won't go near him."

They found Fred. "Captain said we will stay here tonight," advised Fred. "Go ahead and make camp."

That night, seeking a different subject, Abigail said, "Mama, Marcy's book tells how to make pemmican." Alice found the page and showed it to her mother.

> *The pemmican, which constitutes almost the entire diet of the Fur Company's men in the Northwest, is prepared as follows: The buffalo meat is cut into thin flakes, and hung up to dry in the sun or before a slow fire; it is then pounded between two stones and reduced to a powder; this powder is placed in a bag of the animal's hide, with the hair on the outside; melted grease is then poured into it, and the bag sewn up. It can be eaten raw, and many prefer it so. Mixed with a little flour and boiled, it is a very wholesome and exceedingly nutritious food, and will keep fresh for a long time.*

"Not exactly the way the Indians explained it to me," said Alice. "But it is a start. Thank you."

*****

Abigail anxiously opened Milli's journal. Had Milli floated across the Kansas River? Abigail's own writing from the day before had disappeared and been replaced by Milli's! Another new page! *This is Milli's journal, not mine. I'm not permitted to write in it!*

1843
Today, while attempting to float across the Kansas River, we lost two wagons and three people. Captain Shaw said they had not caulked the wagons as he instructed. How can inexperienced people not listen to the voice of experience?

We added three graves to the four already on the trail.

We crossed safely, as did the Andersons. I could feel William watching me and knew he would protect me. Our next lay-by is at Alcove Spring.

I'm so glad we had a ferry and used it, thought Abigail. *I must keep in mind that the trail was much more primitive in Milli's time.*

The Enchanted Journal

Chapter 8: April 20—Alcove Spring

ALCOVE SPRING WAS A FINE SPRING of cold water with large oak, cottonwood, walnut, and sycamore trees growing in a half-mile-wide band along the river. Captain Bridgewater smiled at his luck and found a grassy camping place surrounded by wildflowers.

"Rain's a-coming," Captain Bridgewater said to Michael as he arrived. "We'll lay-by here. Circle the wagons." He rode on to spread the news to everyone.

George Cromwell spat a fat gob. "This is a fine place, Bridgewater, but we could go on for several more hours."

"The Big Blue River is nearby and would stop us. We need to rest and regroup before crossing it."

"We'll never git to Oregon this way." George jerked his horse around and rode away but added his wagon to the circle.

"Abigail, Mike," called Michael. "Help me tie down the wagon covers and flaps. We don't have time to pitch the tent." Besides the covers over the hoops, Michael had added flaps all around the wagon. He and Mike—sometimes everyone—slept under the wagon.

With the wagon secured, Michael handed Mike a coil of string and fish hooks. "Mike, make yourself a fishing rig and see what you can catch for supper. I'll put out a few snares and try to catch a rabbit or two."

Sandlin

? No fish in springs

Mike loved fishing, and the rain did not bother him. He ran to the springs.

Inside the wagon and out of the rain, Abigail picked up Milli's journal and began turning pages. She found the latest entry.

1843

Last night, we lost some cattle and had to round them up before rejoining the train. We thought Indians had taken them, but they just strayed away.

I counted just three graves today. Made me feel better to not see as many as on other days.

We stopped at a pretty place named Alcove Spring that has good water, wood, and grass.

It is raining hard now, and we are crowded into the wagon but going nowhere.

When the rain stops, we will build our campfire and cook supper. There are fish in the spring, and William hopes to catch some. A bit of fish would be a welcome change in diet from dried buffalo.

Last night, we had a bit of entertainment from the fiddle of our neighbor. Another neighbor joined in with his mouth organ. Soon we were singing. I learned two new songs: "Wait for the Wagon" and "Uncle Sam's Farm." William Anderson is a talented singer, and I enjoyed hearing him and singing with him.

Mike returned with two, three-foot long catfish as the rain stopped.

not likely from fresh, clean water

"Abigail," said her father. "Go invite the Campbells for supper. Mike, clean those catfish."

Relieved her path would not take her past Jeff Cromwell's wagon, Abigail strode past the Jones' camp as Gladys followed her with her eyes.

"We're having fish tonight, Abigail said to Nancy. "Mike caught two big ones. Get some lard and come help fry them."

"Wonderful! I love fried fish."

*****

THE RAIN RELIEVED THE DUST, and after a day's layover, the mud dried. Now well rested, the Bridgewater train left Alcove Spring and returned to the trail.

A few miles later, Abigail could not believe her eyes. A trail from the east joined their westward path and was jam-packed with men, women, and children pushing and pulling large wheelbarrows! Unlike their own wagon train, Abigail could not detect any wagons or oxen—only wheelbarrows.

"Look, Mama!" said Abigail. "I don't mind walking--at least I'm not pushing a wheelbarrow!"

"You see, someone always has it more difficult than you do."

Captain's horn squawked as he summoned his group leaders. He pointed to the trail from the east and its emigrants. "These are Mormons on their way from St. Joseph to Salt Lake City. At this junction, sometimes people give up getting to Oregon and turn off to St. Joseph instead. If anyone in your group wants to go to St. Joe, let them. No refunds though."

"Why we lettin' a bunch of morons git in front?" complained George Cromwell.

"Not morons, George. Mormons from the church of Latter-Day Saints."

"Iffen they ain't got good sense to git a wagon instead of a wheelbarrow, they's morons."

"Those poor people can't afford a wagon, and the LDS church ran out of money to buy wagons and oxen for them. Brigham Young designed those handcarts and told them to walk to Salt Lake

City. Thousands have walked since 1856. They've learned how to do it now, but the first handcart companies had many problems and many deaths. We might as well take an early nooner and let them get ahead."

"What!" George was furious. "We be too slow now. The morons will slow us to a crawl."

"Actually, the handcart companies go farther every day than a wagon train. That's why we might as well put them in front. Remember, we are walking too and oxen are slow."

"I tried ta git ya to use mules."

"The Mormons don't have to graze and water oxen or mules. Tell everyone what's happening while I find the Mormon leader and exchange information."

*****

TERRILL JOHNSON ORGANIZED his open air classroom. "Here's your geography lesson for today. The Big Blue is the largest tributary of the Kansas River and flows hundreds of miles. After we cross the Big Blue, we'll come to the Little Blue. We'll follow the Little Blue to the Platte River and the Platte to Fort Kearny.

"I know you are curious about the people in front of us with the wheelbarrows. The people are Mormons and the wheelbarrows are called handcarts. Here's what they are doing and why." Terrill supplemented Captain's story with facts from his textbooks.

"What about wives?" asked Jeff, while staring at Abigail. He rarely came to Mr. Johnson's classes, but curiosity about Mormons brought him to this one. "Is it true that Mormon men have many wives?" He leered at Abigail.

"Yes, the LDS church approves of polygamy," admitted Mr. Johnson.

"Well, maybe I'll become a Mormon," laughed Jeff, glancing again at Abigail.

"The Mormons have many restrictions," said Mr. Johnson. "No coffee, tea, tobacco, or whiskey. Sunday is spent at church. You'd serve a two-year mission."

"That's a lot of trouble just to have a few extra wives."

The Enchanted Journal

*****

AFTER SUPPER, Abigail was about to open Milli's journal and read her continuing story in the combined light of dusk and fire when she noticed Angus absorbed in a book. "What are you reading, Angus? You seem so serious."

Startled, Angus looked up from the page as though confused, then found his voice. "*Philosophy of Religion* by William Calmes Buck. He is Baptist, but his book is quite thought-provoking. I particularly like how Dr. Buck develops a premise into doctrine through logic, his knowledge of Hebrew and Latin, and definitions. His writing requires my complete concentration. I apologize for isolating myself." He smiled at Nancy.

"See," said Nancy, "sometimes he does this."

"I do not understand," began Angus, "why God would tell some people one thing and other people another thing. Take, for example, baptism. Dr. Buck insists on total immersion and is adamantly against infant baptism. Are religions that anoint or sprinkle wrong? What about children who die young? I am trying to figure this out. What do you think, Abigail?"

"Hmm, no one has asked me before. They sprinkled me as an infant and I have never been immersed. I consider myself a baptized Christian, but Dr. Buck might not."

Angus returned to his studies while Nancy moved to her music, and Abigail opened Milli's diary.

1843

Four new families joined our train at the junction from St. Joseph. I met Naomi Christensen; she is a Mormon but seems quite nice. She told me that 'Naomi' is a Hebrew name that means 'gentle and beautiful'. She certainly is a tall and beautiful blonde, but I am not so sure about the 'gentle' part. Naomi is on her way to Salt Lake City to marry an Elder in the Mormon Church she has never met. Such a strange practice! Naomi is only a year older than me!

Today, I counted six gravesites on our way to the Blue River. One grave had been disturbed. Captain Shaw told me that Indians sometimes disturb graves searching for clothes and valuables.

[margin note: ? Strange unlikely]

Now we are encamped on the beautiful Blue River with plenty of wood and water. Our oxen and cattle are enjoying the lush grass. The river is full of fish, and everyone caught some. William Anderson caught many fish and gave some to us. They were delicious! William is quite nice to us, and I enjoy being around him.

A small tribe of Indians—men, women, and children—called on us and demanded a toll for passing through their land. We gave them a calf and some bread. After eating, they performed a war dance around a large fire. They yelled fiendishly and waved scalps recently taken from their enemies. If they were attempting to frighten us, they certainly succeeded!

[margin note: Guess who taught them this.]

Is Milli's journal a message from God about Mormons? I don't know any Mormons, but at least Naomi was in a wagon and not pushing a handcart. Wonder if her family was wealthy?

*****

The Enchanted Journal

BEFORE THEY LEFT Rock Creek Station, Captain gave firm instructions. "There is no water for 20 miles after Rock Creek, so fill all your barrels and buckets. Also, put extra firewood in your wagon. We must make 20 miles today, so our nooner will be short. There's no water or grass anyway." As though his words reminded him, he searched and found a long stalk of Timothy grass to chew. "Wagons Ho!" They moved out.

"Look, Abigail," said Mike as they topped a rise alongside their oxen. "Prairie schooners in front of us and prairie schooners behind us." Long files of the white topped wagons stretched as far as they could see.

"Yes, and they all kick up dust."

Abigail sprinkled water on a large bandanna and tied it around her face.

"You look like a bandit," Mike laughed.

"Perhaps, but this helps keep dust out of my nose and mouth."

Mike copied Abigail's mask. "You're right, it does help."

"I'll be glad to get to the Platte River and see some grass again."

1843

Dust! Dust! Dust! How I hate the dust! And now, Captain Shaw says we will have no water and no firewood along the way today. We have filled the barrels and all the pots we have, and I drank as much water as I could hold.

I wonder how many graves are in this dry section of trail? More than usual, I expect.

Today, Naomi Christensen walked with me and told me some of her Mormon beliefs. She considers Mormons Christian, but her views do not match my Methodist beliefs or those of my

Baptist friends. Which view is correct? I don't know or have the basis to judge so I will 'judge not' and hope that I will not be judged.

William Anderson swings a powerful axe; he helped me put extra firewood in our wagon. I introduced William to Naomi. They seem to get along well.

Many times, Milli's day matched Abigail's. *Of course, it does*, she thought. *Long, hard, boring days. Except I don't have a William to share it with. Will Naomi convert Milli or William to Mormon?*

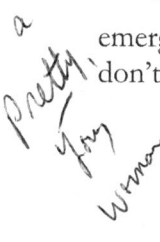

Chapter 9: April 28–Platte River

THE PLATTE RIVER WAS WIDE, shallow, turbid with low banks, few bushes, and fewer trees. Although the trail followed the Platte, the ground near the river was often wet and soft, so the wagons could not travel along the banks.

"Look at that, Abigail," said Captain pointing ahead and to the left. "Like the ocean." Vast open fields of grass touched the bellies of their horses. There was not a tree or bush in sight except for the few lining the river.

"You've seen the ocean?"

"Indeed I have. And I'll see it again when we get to Oregon."

"Look to the right and see the Platte River with mountains behind it. We'll stay on this side of the river."

Captain pointed to the ground and a small volcano-looking mound. "Watch out for those holes. Prairie dogs live there. They make villages of connecting burrows."

He pointed a short distance ahead, where many small animals stood on their haunches by their burrow holding their little paws in front of them.

"Are those really dogs?" Abigail asked.

"No, prairie dogs are similar to a rat or squirrel. They won't harm you, but prairie dog holes can cripple your mule."

"Can we eat them?"

"I have but don't recommend eating prairie dogs except in an emergency. Kind of like eating a rat. They have ticks and fleas so don't handle them."

81

"Ugh!

"We'll be at Fort Kearny in a few days. I'll show you around. Let me know if there's something you want to see or do there but don't go wandering off by yourself."

"I'll be glad to get to Fort Kearny. I'm writing a letter to my best friend back in Tennessee and need to mail it."

"You know your letter will take several months to get to Tennessee, don't you?"

"Yes, sir. I figure at least two months. That's how long it's taken us to get this far away."

*****

THAT NIGHT, her letter to Lydia written and sealed, Abigail turned to Milli's journal. No longer surprised to find additional entries, Abigail was enjoying Milli's story and curious about its development.

1843

We encamped on the Platte River overlooking a vast sea of prairie grass. Papa thinks buffalo are near and is organizing a hunt. Mr. Anderson and William will join Papa. Papa says William is a good worker and hunter. Papa approves of William and this pleases me very much.

Naomi often walks with me but has ceased witnessing about her Mormon beliefs. I told William that Naomi would get married soon. He laughed and said, "Mormons!"

The trail has changed from being too dry to being too wet! Every afternoon, a thunderstorm and driving rain attack us. Sometimes hail

The Enchanted Journal

accompanies the rain, and all we can do is crowd into the wagon. Today, the storm went away but returned. Fortunately, we had prepared our tent well and passed a stormy night with violent winds but [*and*] got little sleep. The storm almost blew our tent away, but it kept the driving rain off us.

Several people are sick from drinking foul water and have watery bowels. Mama says we are not to drink the water unless it has been boiled, so we drink a lot of coffee and tea.

Every day I see more graves. Sometimes there is a grave nearly every mile of the trail! I am going to stop counting the graves as it is too depressing.

*****

"CAPTAIN BRIDGEWATER SPENDS a lot of time with that tomboy, don't he?" observed Gladys Jones to James, shaking her head.

"You mean Abigail? She's a hard worker. Smart, too. Everyone likes Abigail."

"She should wear a dress and not be with Captain Bridgewater so much. Ain't proper. He's old enough to be her father. They say he has a woman in every town and trading post." [*gossip!!*]

"I doubt that Gladys. Captain seems a fine upstanding man although a bit melancholy sometimes."

"We'll find out at Fort Kearny. You watch. When do we get there?"

"Captain says two more days."

"I seen that tomboy showing Captain Bridgewater a book and standing close by him. Ain't proper. Captain Bridgewater eats with the Roberts sometimes even though he has his own cook."

"Captain says Beans can't make good biscuits!" James laughed. "He says Alice Roberts makes the best biscuits he's ever tasted."

"They say Captain Bridgewater has a woman on every train, too. You mind my words."

*****

ABIGAIL PUT DOWN HER LOAD of firewood and inspected their camp. The wagons were circled and their animals inside the corral. Michael and Mike had pitched the tent and Alice was unloading pots, pans, and food for supper. Abigail built the fire for their evening meal. It would be the same as last night's supper: stew with potatoes, salt pork, beans, and onions—a simple one pot meal. Alice would make biscuits and coffee.

Little Sue was also studying the camp, a quizzical look on her face.

"What are you thinking about, Sue?"

"Same place."

Abigail laughed out loud. "Yes, it looks just like our camp last night doesn't it? The prairie is the same and we make our camp the same. You'll sleep on your mattress in the same tent. But we've moved along about fifteen miles. Are you ready for something different?"

Sue smiled. She sounded the word carefully. "Different."

"Soon we'll be at Fort Kearny and you'll see buildings and new people."

"Different."

Chapter 10: April 30–Fort Kearny

THEY MADE CAMP outside of Fort Kearny but within easy walking distance. Terrill Johnson began his school lectures with a geography lesson about their location. He used a map to show where they were and where they were going before giving a history of the area. Often, parents would attend the first part of Terrill's lessons.

"As you will see," Terrill began. "Fort Kearny is not a true fort. It is a small town built to service and supply emigrants like us."

"Why do they call us emigrants?" asked Maggie, looking up from her sketch of the fort. "We aren't foreigners."

"Excellent question," replied Terrill. "When people first took the Oregon Trail, Oregon was not a state. So those people were leaving the United States to go to a place that was a different country. That's the definition of emigrant and the name stuck and is still being used even though it is no longer correct. Who knows when Oregon became a state?"

"Just this year," Abigail answered.

"Yes, February 14, 1859. Oregon is now a state. What is the state capital of Oregon?" No one answered.

"It has changed a few times. First, the capital was Oregon City, then Salem, then Corvallis, and now is Salem again."

Henry was busy writing in his notebook.

"We plan to live in Oregon City," said Mike.

"I do too, Mike," said Terrill. "Getting back to Fort Kearny, it is an important way station built in 1849 and named after General

Stephen Watts Kearny. The fort's commander may sell goods at low cost to the emigrants."

"I haven't been to the town yet but Captain tells me it has a half dozen or so wooden buildings and a couple dozen adobe buildings. Fort Kearny provides a mail service if you want to send a letter back home."

Abigail had letters from her mother and father and her own letter to Lydia to mail to Tennessee.

Terrill unfolded his map. "From here, we go towards Ash Hollow. We must go up a major hill and down a major hill before getting to Ash Hollow. It should take us less than three weeks." Terrill always reviewed the plans and map with Captain Bridgewater before passing the information to his class.

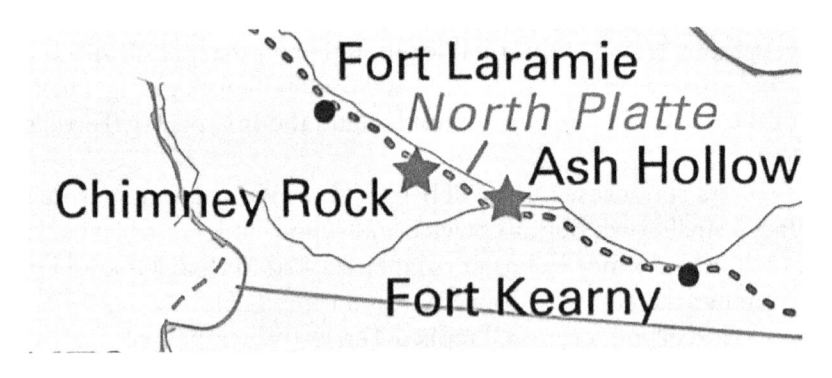

Fort Laramie
North Platte
Chimney Rock **Ash Hollow**
Fort Kearny

"Now for a little arithmetic." The class groaned and the parents slipped away.

*****

"SEE THAT TWO-STORY BUILDING," said Captain Bridgewater to the Roberts family as they entered Fort Kearny. "It is for the commanding officer and his wife. It looks plain but is well-furnished and comfortable inside."

Wood-framed buildings surrounded a large open square. Roads with mud homes extended from the square. They had planted a few bushes around the square, but there were no trees.

The Enchanted Journal

"You know the commander?" asked Michael.

"Yes, I served with Major May in the Mexican War. His motto was 'Remember your regiment and follow your officers.' In fact, I'll be having dinner with Major May and his wife, Kathleen, tonight. My friend Daniel Murry—remember meeting him?—will also be there. Gives me a chance to catch up on local news and pass along my views of the trail.

"The soldier's barracks is the long building on the opposite side of the square. They cram about two hundred men into the barracks. The other wooden buildings are for officers, the hospital and the sutler's store. We'll get our supplies at the sutler's store. You can mail letters at the sutler's store. Be sure to ask if there is any mail for you. Probably none, but ask."

Captain gave Mrs. Roberts and Abigail a stern look. "Do not, under any circumstances, go wandering around by yourself. There are few women here, and these men are not gentlemen."

"Thank you, Captain," said Mrs. Roberts. "We understand."

"If you'll excuse me," begged Captain, "I must go to the blacksmith's shop."

*****

THE BLACKSMITH'S SHOP was staffed by its owner and two apprentices. Off to one side, a smaller do-it-yourself area could be rented. There, Daniel Murray and his two sons were making a cooking tripod.

"Daniel!" said Captain Bridgewater.

Daniel and his sons looked up from their pounding. "Thomas! So you caught up to me after all. But I'm leaving in the morning, so you'll still be eating my dust."

Thomas chuckled at their old joke. He extended his hand to the taller of Daniel's sons. "David, good to see you again. You get bigger every time. You'll soon be taller than your father. And Glenn, you're not much behind David." Thomas shook Glenn's hand.

"Glad to see you again, Uncle Thomas," said David.

"Me too," added Glenn.

Sandlin

"Daniel," said Thomas, "you have some fine looking sons, that's for certain. Young men now. I wish the four of us could get off on a little adventure before I settle in Oregon, but that's not likely to happen."

"Never can tell. What brings you to the blacksmith shop, Thomas?"

"Need to repair a chain."

"Let me show David and Glenn how to fix that. Glenn, stoke the fire. David, grab your tongs."

"Thanks, Daniel. You always were the better blacksmith."

"See you tonight at Major May's dinner, Thomas."

*****

So Fort Kearny did not exist when you passed through here, Milli. You had to carry more supplies than we do. What did you do in this location?

1843

We are near the head of Grand Island along the Platte River with plenty of grass, wood, and water. Several small trails come together here so we can see other caravans.

Naomi joined us for supper. She talks a lot, especially to William. I can scarcely get in a word if she is around.

Indians come to see us regularly, and we often feed them. They are friendly, and I feel sorry for them. These are not the 'noble savages' described in newspapers. I would describe them as filthy beggars. All the same, Papa says they will steal our horses and mules, so we watch them carefully.

The Enchanted Journal

*****

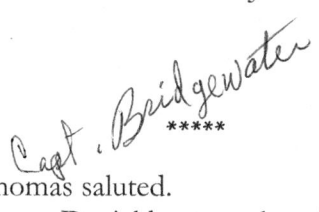

"MAJOR MAY!" Thomas saluted. [handwritten: Capt. Bridgewater]

"Thomas, welcome. Daniel beat you here." He pointed to Daniel seated at the table with a glass of wine. Daniel grinned and held up his glass.

"He usually does," replied Thomas. "Once again, I'm eating his trail dust."

"Speaking of the trail, tell me the latest," said Major May.

"We lost a wagon and two people crossing the Kansas River," said Thomas. "Three wagons did not want to pay the toll and tried to make it on their own. One of them did not."

"Foolish," said Daniel. "I remember when the ferry was not there, and there was no choice, but now there is a choice."

"Still no water for twenty miles after Rock Creek," reported Thomas.

"Any Indian problems?" asked Daniel.

"We've never had a direct attack on the fort or nearby Dobytown. Safety in numbers, you know."

"How many soldiers do you have now?"

"Almost three hundred plus support people. Dobytown has about a hundred people."

"My train has almost a hundred people," said Thomas.

"Mine too," added Daniel.

"What about the Mormons?" asked Thomas. [handwritten: Never heard of this before!]

"Thankfully, the Mormon Rebellion ended last year after President Buchanan sent troops to the Utah Territory. Brigham Young was replaced as governor by Alfred Cummings and Army forces are in place. I doubt you'll have problems with the Mormons."

Major May asked, "How are your boys, Daniel?"

"Almost grown. David is seventeen, and Glenn is fifteen. They are fine, strong young men. In California, I'll insist they get caught up on their education. After that, who knows?"

"They may want an adventure as we did," said Major May.

"Lord have mercy on them," said Thomas. "Let's hope they are smarter than we were."

"And you, Thomas, still a bachelor?"

"Yes, sir. Too old and set in my ways by now."

"Let's toast the good old days and thank God for getting us through them."

*****

THE TRAIL WAS RELATIVELY STRAIGHTFORWARD after leaving Fort Kearny. Captain Bridgewater kept his train on the south side of the Platte River as they moved toward Cold Spring.

There were many buffalo in the lush prairie grass, and the men enjoyed hunting. Everyone was eating fresh buffalo meat with every meal, and Alice Roberts was teaching how to make pemmican.

Captain Bridgewater rode far ahead of his caravan—ostensibly to scout, but also to collect his thoughts about the journey and the people he was leading. What is coming up, and who could he depend on?

I shouldn't have allowed that pregnant woman to join my train. But they insisted she was healthy and could manage. Now a grieving widower rides with us. Wonder if he'll stay?

George Cromwell made a foolish choice, and the Greens didn't have enough experience to overrule him. I should've argued more—even insisted that no one leave the train.

Captain stopped and savored a breath. *Not all farmers are a Jack-of-All-Trades, but Michael can do anything. Plus, Alice is especially capable--not to mention pretty. They are smart and well educated. And Abigail…*

I've never met anyone like Abigail. Abigail would be one of the first people I'd choose to take on a demanding task. She won't always be a tomboy, either—she is so pretty she can't hide it. And that journal! It has been helpful and will continue to be so. How does it work? It truly is enchanted, but I'm not telling anyone about it. Too many superstitions.

George would make a scene if he knew about Milli's journal. Might even call it witchcraft, I don't know. And his brute of a son will be a criminal—most likely already is. I'll bet the Cromwells are escaping from something. Unless Jeff delays his lawless career until our journey ends, I'll be forced to shoot him.

The Enchanted Journal

Poor Minister Field is terribly sick with consumption. I'll be surprised if he survives the trail. If he dies, we'll take care of Judy. She is so accustomed to caring for Charles and doing most of the camp chores that she will be all right. Might even be a trail marriage involved—every journey sees at least one trail marriage. Wonder who it will involve this time? Gladys Jones will have a list of candidates!

Isabella and I should have married but she was too young and God has cursed me for wanting adventure before marriage. Now I have my adventure, but want to settle down. Bell and I were the same ages as Angus and Nancy, but much more capable. We could have survived the challenges of the trail. I'm glad Nancy has her piano—reminds me of Bell, she played piano so beautifully and expressively. I'll be down-hearted when we offload Nancy's piano, but she will be broken-hearted. At least Richardson is a good fiddler. A little music sure enhances the evening.

The kids say they don't like the Johnsons' school, but I think they secretly enjoy it. Sometimes adults even attend history and geography lessons. They could read the trail handbooks—Michael has Marcy's Handbook—but many of my people can't read well. George Cromwell can't read at all. I had to read my trail contract to him.

Ah, water! A good place for a nooner. Captain Bridgewater stopped his horse to allow the train to catch up to him, but he forced his thoughts back to the trail and upcoming sights and locations. *We're making good time, but the trail will get even more difficult. These poor people can't even imagine what is about to happen.*

I must prepare everyone for a long hard pull at O'Fallon's Bluff—maybe even a sandstorm. We'll cross the South Platte and take a lay-by to prepare for Windlass Hill. Another lay-by after Windlass Hill at Ash Hollow—a pretty place but overused now.

Got to tell Terrill Johnson to prepare classes about the famous rock formations: Courthouse, Jail, Chimney, Scotts Bluff. His books should include basic information.

And then Fort Laramie. I need flour and vegetables. Wonder if Colonel Carrington and Margaret are still there?

Captain dismounted as the wagons circled for the nooner. *Wonder what Beans will cook?* Captain smirked.

*****

ABIGAIL TOOK ADVANTAGE of the nooner to read more in Milli's journal.

1843
We are near the junction of the North and South Platte rivers. Captain Shaw says that Fort Laramie is about 200 miles ahead. We have come 450 miles from Independence.

I was enjoying walking and talking with William, but Naomi joined us. She often joins when I am with William, but she takes over the conversation and talks only to William. I'm getting tired of her.

*****

May 10–O'Fallon's Bluff (mile 443)
THE WIDE TRAIL ON THE SOUTH SIDE of the South Platte River narrowed at O'Fallon's Bluff. The bluff extended twenty miles as a series of sandy hills.

Water was alkali, and there was little grass. A few scattered wildflowers broke up the monotony of the scene. As if the hills, water, and grass weren't bad enough, a strong westerly wind created a blinding sand storm.

The wind was too strong to walk against, and Michael crowded everyone into the wagon. "Wet your kerchiefs and make a mask," he instructed. "Keep your head down. Close your eyes as much as possible."

Michael climbed onto the driver's seat wearing his wet kerchief mask and his hat pulled down tight. He squinted his eyes, looked down at the rear oxen and urged them into the sand storm. It would be a long day.

Michael glanced up at Angus Campbell's Schuttler. *What a fine wagon. Nancy sat back in the wagon with a wet scarf around her face. Angus is doing well and Nancy is learning.*

Gladys and James Jones were behind Michael and out of sight but he could imagine the scene. Gladys would be sitting immediately in back of James and talking his ear off. *That woman never stops talking. Wonder what she learned—or thinks she learned—at Fort Kearny? Abigail says Gladys asks many questions about Captain. What is she saying about him? About me? Doesn't matter, it's just gossip and her entertainment.*

Michael looked forward to the South Platte River and a welcome break from the dust and sand storm.

*****

CAPTAIN STOPPED at the South Platte River and blew his horn to gather his group leaders. "We'll cross right here and right now. The river is wide but shallow. Watch out for quicksand—don't stop moving. See that freight wagon?" He pointed to a large wagon stuck up to its axles in the sands. "It can't be pulled out. We'll camp on the other side and lay-by to prepare for another steep hill to climb and an even steeper hill to descend."

Once across the river and having made camp, Abigail read Milli's journal for news and information about the South Platte location. *What did Milli and William do today? And that Naomi! What was going on between Naomi and William?*

1843
There are many buffalo, and we must beware of them running across our path because our trail lies between the bluff and the river. The buffalo

want to get to the river in the afternoon, and our guards make sure that the buffalo cross the trail behind us.

We crossed the South Platte safely and encamped on the other side.

There is no wood here but good water and grass. We must cook on buffalo chips, but there are many chips, and we collect them every day.

Naomi invited William and me to sup with her family, but she mainly talked to and about William. I asked questions about Salt Lake City, but no one wanted to talk about it. Something is not right there. Her family seems nice, but I felt unwanted.

William walked me to my tent, and I told him I questioned Naomi's feelings for him. He laughed and said she was just being friendly. If he falls for her, he will regret it when she leaves next month. Not to mention Naomi is about to marry!

Poor William! I thought he was smarter than this.

Chapter 11: May 17–Windlass Hill

"WHY IS THIS CALLED WIND LESS HILL?" George Cromwell asked. "I kin feel the wind blow, and this looks more like a cliff than a hill."

"Not 'wind less,' but windlass," answered Captain. "A windlass is a machine to help move heavy loads. We don't have a windlass but will wish we did down that hill."

"Ya mean ta tell me we're goin' down that cliff?"

"Yep, or else go many miles out of our way. This is the steepest hill until the Rocky Mountains. We'll unload the wagons and ease them down with ropes. It will take all day, but we'll spend the night at Ash Hollow, which is a little farther."

"Are ya sure ya been this way before? Ever' so offen I wonder."

"I've been here, George." Captain put his horn to his mouth and blew three short squawks.

Everyone gathered around Captain for instructions.

"We have to slide the wagons down this hill. Almost completely unload your wagon and unhitch the oxen. We'll lock all four wheels in place, tie ropes to the wagon, and wrap the ropes around rocks and trees. With everyone holding on to a rope, we'll let the wagon ease down. Then we'll lower another wagon. We'll need all day to descend. As a reward, Ash Hollow is at the bottom of the hill, and we will lay-by there for two nights."

"How do the oxen get down?"

"Lead them down one at a time—slowly."

"What about the gear from the wagons?"

"Strap some of it to the oxen, hand carry the rest."

"Ya mean we must git up and down thet thing many times, Bridgewater?" complained George Cromwell.

"Exactly," answered Captain.

"Well, I don't like it."

"I don't like it either," replied Captain. "But it's what we must do. Others have done it before us—look at the tracks skidded into the rock. The trees show rope burns. We can do my wagon first."

Frank Allen drove the Bridgewater wagon to the edge of the hill, unhitched the oxen, and unpacked the wagon. Captain, Michael, and Fred prepared it for sliding. Despite their disagreements, Captain was pleased to have the weight and strength of George and Jeff on the ropes.

"We'll gradually release the ropes and lower the wagon. When all of your rope is extended, unwrap it and find a lower tree or rock," explained Captain. "Locate your next tree before you need it. Ready? Give it some slack."

The wagon slid sluggishly down Windlass Hill. Captain's rope became fully extended first. "My rope is all out. Moving to another tree. Hang on." Captain eased farther down, found his second tree, and wrapped his rope around it. He glanced farther downhill at his next tree. "Let it down a little more."

Next Fred, then Michael, changed to lower trees as the wagon slid down the hill.

"Mine's out," yelled Frank. "Movin' down." He unwrapped his rope from the tree and scampered but tripped and fell onto the hard rocks, sliding. "Gosh darn it!" Frank skidded beneath the rear wagon wheel, yelling "Stop! Stop it!" as he tried in vain to grab the spokes and stop the two-ton wagon. A front wheel broke and crashed to the rocky path tilting the wagon precariously. Frank screamed "Aiiee" and grunted "Ugh!" using the last breath of air from his crushed lungs. The killer wheel broke away from its axle and bounced downhill—its tire iron off and ringing as it banged against the rocks. The wagon bed seemed to explode on the rocks and the pieces not tangled in the canvas cover tumbled down the slope.

The Enchanted Journal

Captain tied off his rope at the tree even though it held a single piece of the wagon. Hand over hand on the rope, he hopped down the rocky slope to Frank's crushed and bloody, lifeless body. There was no need for Mrs. Richardson's nursing.

"I'm sorry, Frank. You were a good cook and helper. Thank you. God bless you."

Michael and Fred joined Captain. "It happened so quickly," said Fred as he stared at Frank's crushed chest and bloody body. "I tried to pull my rope tighter but couldn't."

"Needed more ropes," said Captain.

"Just Frank's time, I suppose," said Michael. "Poor man. Nothing we could have done."

"There's nothing we can do now," said Captain. "Let's make a travois and get his body down to Ash Hollow." Captain turned to the gathering onlookers, "Search and see what parts and supplies you can salvage. Take whatever you find down to the bottom of the hill. Be careful."

Supplies from Captain's and other wagons were already piling up at the bottom of Windlass Hill.

"Let's get Frank buried, then we must get back to work," said Captain to Michael. "We can't stay overnight with some things at the top of the hill and some at the bottom."

"Thought ya said ya knowed what yer doin'," George Cromwell cackled.

"I thought so, too. We'll reorganize and make a safer plan even if it's slower."

*****

AFTER BURYING FRANK, Captain Bridgewater addressed the group of mourners. "I'm at fault here. I should've used more ropes and had pullers on each side of the wagon. That's what we'll do with the next wagon. George, you ready?"

"Ain't using my wagon," said George. "Not yet anyway. Git somebody else ta test yer new idee."

"My Schuttler wagon is new and stout," said Angus. "I will unload it more, then we can try it."

Captain drew Angus aside. "Angus, we'll never be able to get Nancy's piano down Windlass Hill. I'm sorry, but it must be left. We'll miss Nancy's music, but we must offload the piano."

"I was afraid of that as soon as I saw the hill. Some of my merchandise can be left as well. Let me break the bad news to Nancy." Angus trudged to Nancy. Captain soon heard her sobbing.

After they offloaded the piano, Nancy sat down for one last concert. Her tears dribbled onto the keys as she moved her hands across them, playing her favorite *Goldberg Variations* by Bach.

With more ropes behind Angus's wagon and ropes on each side to stabilize it, it reached the bottom of Windlass Hill intact. A shout of accomplishment accompanied the success. Nancy continued her concert.

After a long day of applying their sliding technique, all wagons reached the bottom of Windlass Hill. They reloaded, drove the few miles into Ash Hollow, and encamped.

Ash Hollow, a canyon four miles long, was a favored resting place on the North Platte River. It was a pretty place and especially appreciated after the emigrants' day long struggle and Frank's death. The Bridgewater caravan needed time to recuperate and peaceful scenery to comfort them. A spring provided clean water and green grass was abundant. Cedar trees mixed with the shady ash trees that gave the hollow its name. Just what they needed.

*****

"THANK YOU FOR SUPPER, Mrs. Roberts," said Captain from the log he used as a stool.

"You're welcome, Captain. Feel free to join us anytime."

"I noticed you doubled the guards," said Michael.

"Yes, this is a good place to camp and hunt. Bandits and Indians use it too. Be careful."

Captain took a big bite of stew. "I don't think 'Beans' would be upset if I said you were the better cook, Mrs. Roberts."

"Poor man," replied Alice. "He was such a nice man as well."

"He played a good harmonica," praised Abigail.

"And he danced well," said Nancy.

The Enchanted Journal

"What will you do for a wagon?" asked Angus.

"I'll buy another one at Fort Laramie," said Captain Bridgewater. "Until then, I've asked others to carry what food and supplies we could salvage from my wagon."

"We distributed your supplies," said Michael. "All the wagons had room now that we've eaten some of the food. Everyone appreciates swapping and spelling the oxen."

"George Cromwell did not take on any of my stuff," said Captain, "said he did not want to overload his oxen. Too late, he realized it would be *my* oxen pulling *his* wagon while his oxen rested. He didn't like it but would not back down." Captain chortled. "Stubborn man."

"Not a Christian thought," said Michael. "But I don't care for George or his son. Mrs. Cromwell seems all right, though."

"I'm afraid of Jeff Cromwell," said Abigail. "I stay away from him. He is a shady character."

"Me too," said Nancy.

"I don't want to cook," said Captain. "I'll just have to beg for my meals."

Alice laughed. "You're welcome here, Captain. Besides, we are eating your food now!"

1843

Windlass Hill was horrible. I have been frightened all day watching the wagons slide down that steep slope. We lost one wagon and most of its supplies when an axle broke. Not much of the wagon could be salvaged. Our train was not the only one to leave broken wagons on the hill. Pieces of wagons were scattered everywhere. We collected the wood for repairs and fires.

> Some people had heavy items in their wagons and simply left them at the top of Windlass Hill alongside items previously discarded by others. One could have their choice of cast iron cookware, bedframes, anvils, and plows, but no one was taking—everyone was leaving.
> Naomi is a hard worker, especially if she is near William.
> William fell on the hill and my heart leaped in my throat. He slid far before scrambling to his feet. His youth, strength, and God saved him! Thank you Lord God!

"How did your friend fare on Windlass Hill?" asked Captain.

Abigail looked up from the journal. "Milli hated it but made it down safely. She remarked on the items that people unloaded at the top of the hill and never reloaded."

"I noticed that stuff too," added Michael. "Looked like someone left a blacksmith shop there. I wanted those tools but had to leave them at the top of the hill. I swapped a few of my worn tools for better ones, though."

"They even discarded food," said Alice, "but it was old and spoiled."

"I already miss Nancy's music," said Abigail.

"Me too," said Alice, "but I hated to see those sewing machines left behind."

"Well, I'm glad Milli survived Windlass Hill," said Captain. "I don't understand how it works, but Milli and her notes have been a blessing to us."

"I think Milli is getting a sweetheart," giggled Abigail. "She mentions William in every entry."

"Perhaps you will too, Abigail," teased her mother.

"I doubt it. I have no prospects."

Chapter 12: May 17 - Ash Hollow

THE SMALL GROCERY STORE in Ash Hollow had a few supplies and collected mail for delivery. Captain checked, but there was no mail for anyone in his caravan. "These little mail stations and stores are popping up along the trail. I'm not surprised there is no mail," Captain explained to Fred Wells as he chewed a blade of Timothy grass. "Of course, mail from Independence will not catch up to us, but a train might leave a message—especially if there are problems. And sometimes, there are travelers going east."

Michael and several other men went hunting and returned with deer, which were shared by everyone. Abigail, Nancy, and Sue picked gooseberries. Fresh venison provided a welcome change from salt pork and Alice's gooseberry pie was delicious. After supper, music resonated from Nancy's covered wagon. Angus smiled proudly. "Her four string dulcimer. Nancy prefers piano but plays the dulcimer and guitar as well. We did not pack her guitar and I couldn't leave her dulcimer behind. I left some of my merchandise instead."

*****

FOR THE ASH HOLLOW LAY-BY, Terrill Johnson convened another session of school.

"This place is Ash Hollow," Terrill began. "Anyone guess why?"

"The ash trees, of course," sniffed Ollie. "Anyone could tell that."

"Captain says that the creek here is fed by a spring and is the best water around. Be sure to use it and fill your barrels. Anyone know what's ahead?"

Mr. Johnson obviously wanted to talk about Ash Hollow and the trail ahead. Henry prepared to take notes.

"In the next few days, you will see three amazing rock formations. Take careful note of them. You'll remember them all your life: Courthouse Rock, Jail Rock, and Chimney Rock. These are famous. You'll want to tell people all about them.

"You'll be able to see these rock formations sticking up from the flat desert from miles away. First is Courthouse Rock but some people think it looks more like a castle. Jailhouse Rock is near Courthouse Rock. They are about 400 feet high.

"Chimney Rock is separate and next. It looks, well, like a 300 foot high chimney. At Chimney Rock, we'll be about one third finished with the trail."

Mr. Johnson unfolded his map. "After Chimney Rock, we'll have about 85 miles to go before Fort Laramie. We'll be traveling along the North Platte River. It flows faster and colder than the South Platte." He refolded his map. "Now for spelling lessons." His students moaned.

1843

We camped in a beautiful place called Ash Hollow. The sweet perfume of wildflowers fills the air. We quickly found a feast of grapevines, wild cherries, plums, wild currants, and gooseberries.

We could use some supplies but will have to wait until Fort William.

The Enchanted Journal

I helped Mama make a wild cherry pie, and William loved it! He says that I am a good cook, and I did not tell him that I just helped Mama.

Captain says that almost no wood is ahead, so everyone laid in extra firewood. William helped me gather wood from broken wagons at Windlass Hill, but I noticed he also brought wood to Naomi's wagon. He lends his helping hands to everyone.

As we were leaving, an Indian chief with about two dozen armed men in war paint approached our caravan and demanded a tribute. As Captain Shaw was negotiating with them, another group of Indians attempted to steal our cattle. Papa fired his pistol over the heads of the thieves and they galloped away with nothing. Captain Shaw gave the chief a cow anyway.

*****

"YOU SEEN CAPTAIN BRIDGEWATER went straight to the Roberts' camp after his man was killed," said Gladys.

James picked at his teeth. "His wagon was destroyed, and he needed supper. Captain and Michael are close friends."

"Captain Bridgewater could come to our camp for supper, but he never has. He just wants to be around that tomboy."

"Poppycock, Gladys. Captain enjoys Michael's company and Alice's cooking. Without his own cook, he'll move from wagon to wagon for meals. What would you cook for him?"

"Not beans. He's had enough beans. Maybe salt pork, onions, and corn bread. We're running out of spuds. Be sure to get some at Fort Laramie. Meanwhile, invite Captain Bridgewater to sup with us."

*****

CAPTAIN BRIDGEWATER was about to blow his horn to begin the next section of their journey when Abigail approached him.

"Good morning, Abigail. Something on your mind?"

"Yes, sir. Milli's caravan had an incident with the Indians. You should read this." Abigail handed Captain Milli's diary opened to the Ash Hollow page.

Captain read Milli's entry. "Michael, you, Fred, and Angus guard the cattle. Fire a warning shot if there's a problem."

"Injuns!" George Cromwell declared as he pointed down the canyon. George and Jeff drew their revolvers.

"No shooting!" ordered Captain. "That's Little Thunder. I know him. Stay here."

Abigail eased away from the Cromwells, deposited Milli's diary in their wagon and retrieved Michael's double-barreled shotgun. She checked its load, removed two percussion caps from the cap box in the stock, and put a cap on each nipple. Abigail slung the powder horn and bag of shot over her shoulder. "Mama, stay low in the wagon." She patted her hidden patch knife, took cover on the opposite side of the wagon, and crouched low. She prepared powder and shot for reloading.

"Whoa, little lady!" Jeff Cromwell rode up. "Best leave the fightin' to the menfolk. Put that blunderbuss down and hide in the wagon. I'll protect you. You can reward me later," he grinned.

Captain reached Little Thunder and smiled a greeting, but Little Thunder's face remained emotionless. Captain used a combination of sign language with mixed Indian and English words to communicate. A gunshot cracked from the end of the train and George and Jeff dashed off to meet it. More shots followed. Half of Little Thunder's men raced to the end of the wagon train, waving bows and spears. The remaining braves closed in on Captain. Abigail cocked her shotgun and crouched even lower.

Captain emerged from the huddle of Indian braves and returned to the caravan. He smiled at Abigail behind the wagon with her shotgun. She uncocked the gun, removed the caps, and returned his smile.

"Welcome back, Captain," Abigail said.

George and Jeff galloped up, waving their revolvers. "We ain't killed any Injuns," George said. "But we scared 'em off, and they didn't git any cattle."

"Good," said Captain. "Now go back there and get an old cow to give them."

"I risk my life, and ya give 'em a cow, anyway?" George jerked his horse around and rode back to the cattle.

"There were about a dozen Indians trying to steal some of our cattle," explained Michael. "They'd a done it, too, except they got greedy and couldn't manage the whole herd. I fired over their heads like you said, then George and Jeff galloped up shooting."

"I'm glad they missed," said Captain. "We'd really have a problem if they had killed someone."

"Angus," said Captain. "Do you have some trinkets and blankets we can give the Indians?"

"Yes, sir. I'll get them."

Captain gave three short squawks on his horn to gather everyone.

"This is Chief Little Thunder. He claims this land has belonged to his tribe for generations. He demands we pay a toll to use it, and it is easier to pay the toll than fight. Angus, spread a blanket on the ground. Every family put something on the blanket. No guns, ammunition, or alcohol. It is important that Little Thunder sees every family put something on the blanket."

Michael made a point of going to his wagon, getting a plug of tobacco, and dropping it on the blanket.

Little Thunder looked inquisitively at Abigail and her shotgun until Michael walked over to her, put his arms around her, and glared at him. Little Thunder looked away and motioned for his braves to take the cow and blanket of plunder away.

Captain addressed his emigrants. "Thank you for cooperating. Despite what you've heard, there are few fights with the Indians. Let's keep it that way. Now, check your water and get extra firewood. Take a few more minutes and load up."

The cushioned green grass of Ash Hollow soon turned into a dirt trail of sand and finely ground rocks scarcely larger than sand. Animals and wagon wheels raised clouds of powdery gray dust that deposited onto every surface. Everyone put a damp kerchief over their nose and mouth and trudged along.

The Enchanted Journal

Chapter 13: May 21 – Courthouse and Jail Rocks

"WE'LL TAKE a little detour here," said Captain Bridgewater to Abigail and Mike. "There're two formations you must see. If you don't see them now, you may never have the chance again."

"But you've seen them several times, haven't you?" said Mike.

"Yes, I have, Mike," replied Captain. "But I'm still amazed every time." He moved the train closer and instructed everyone to make camp.

Maggie set up her easel and sketch pad so she faced Courthouse Rock. She removed charcoal pencils from her leather case and went to work using quick, deft strokes on the pad. Her head bobbed up and down between the scene and the easel.

George Cromwell rushed to Captain. "We stoppin' to look at rocks? There be plenty rocks on the trail."

"Yes, we're stopping for our nooner. Park your wagon and come listen to Mr. Johnson's lessons. You might learn something."

"Bagh!" Cromwell spit. "We need to git movin', not lookin' at rocks."

*****

TERRILL JOHNSON STOOD in front of his students and proudly noticed the adults behind them waiting for his geology lessons. He pointed toward Courthouse and Jail Rocks. "These two huge rock formations are among the most prominent landmarks in Nebraska Territory. They are about 400 feet high. Anyone know what these landmarks are called?"

"Courthouse and Jail Rocks," squeaked Henry Wells, looking at his notebook. He penciled in more notes.

"Correct, Henry. These two features are known as escarpments, meaning that the elevation changes abruptly. This may seem hard to believe, but thousands of years of erosion caused these features. The larger rock is sometimes called Castle Rock. These rock formations are made of clay, sandstone, and volcanic ash."

"What rock formation will we see next?"

"Chimney Rock," Henry squawked.

"Correct again, Henry."

Mr. Johnson continued, "Chimney Rock may be even more famous than Courthouse and Jail Rocks. It's a few miles west of here, and rises about 500 feet above the North Platte River.

"Early fur trappers called Chimney Rock 'Nose Mountain' but the Indians called it 'The Teepee.'

"Like Courthouse and Jail rocks, Chimney Rock is made of clay, sandstone, and volcanic ash. It also was formed by erosion."

Henry was writing furiously in his notebook.

Arithmetic was the next subject, and the parents slipped away.

The Enchanted Journal

1843

We are having trouble finding grass for our animals. Then, today, we crossed a foul alkali swamp, and the oxen and cattle wanted to drink from it. We had to push and prod them through the swamp, but they resisted us all the way. How I wished I could explain to the dumb brutes that the water was bad for them!

Good water and grass were within sight of the famous "Courthouse" and "Jail" rocks. We won't get any closer to them. William and I were examining the cracks and crevices using our spyglass when Naomi joined us. I can hardly get any time with William without Naomi coming along. I think Courthouse Rock looks like a castle, but William prefers Courthouse, and, of course, Naomi agrees with William.

How I wish I could make a drawing of these famous rock formations!

*****

"Look, Mama," said Abigail. "That must be Chimney Rock! Maggie will want to draw it. I hope Captain will stop for a few minutes."

"I hope so too, but your eyes are better than mine. I can't quite make out the details."

A few miles later, Captain blew his horn, signaled to make camp, and the schooners circled.

"Cain't believe yer stoppin' agin," fumed George Cromwell. "What's ya reason this time?"

"This is a famous site, George. Enjoy it."

Maggie got out her sketch pad and pencils, and began to draw Chimney Rock.

"Ya jest want thet little gurl to draw it."

"The light is right for sketching and Maggie is a fine artist."

Maggie overheard their argument. She smiled at Captain and said, "Thank you, Captain."

"Someday, George, you'll be bragging about how you saw Chimney Rock and watched Maggie sketch it. Maybe her sketch will become famous and bring back memories."

"Bah, I kin 'member that rock."

We traveled slowly over sand bluffs again. I was walking with William in the dust when, of *course, Naomi dropped back to join us. She is obviously taking a fancy to William, but he does not realize it. I must face the fact that I am jealous! Lord, have mercy on me.*

We took a break to examine "Chimney Rock" with our spyglass at noon. It is quite an unusual rock formation, and we camped opposite it near the river. There is no wood for fuel, and even buffalo chips are scarce, but our animals have grass.

Today we passed right through an Indian village that had dozens of dogs making a terrific racket. William said they eat the dogs. I got a good look inside an Indian teepee as we drove past it. How forlorn! There was nothing inside except for rolled up animal skins and an occasional blanket. The squaws and papooses sat outside the tent and watched as we passed.

*****

"THANK YOU FOR INVITING ME to supper," said Captain to Mr. and Mrs. Jones. "I easily tire of my own cooking."

"Glad to have you," said Gladys. "We would have invited you sooner, but you had a cook and also the Roberts to feed you."

"Yes, the Roberts packed most of my supplies after my wagon was destroyed, so I'll be taking many meals with them. Here, I brought you potatoes."

"Thank you, Captain Bridgewater. Can that girl cook potatoes?"

"You mean Abigail? Oh, Abigail is a fine cook; indeed, she can do anything. And Nancy is learning; she'll be a good cook by the time we reach the end of the trail."

"I was thinking of the shorter girl that wears those pretty dresses, not the tomboy. Which one is older?"

"Nancy is the one in the dress. She is older and married to Angus Campbell. You've heard her playing piano at night."

"They tell me you like piano music."

Gladys caught the brief sad expression on Captain's face.

"Yes, I do," said Captain.

"I hope you're not tired of salt port, onions, and cornbread." Gladys handed Captain a bowl. "We're running low on meat."

"Sounds wonderful, thank you. I plan a hunting party soon."

"Please tell us more about yourself, Captain Bridgewater. How did you come to be on the trail?"

Captain told Gladys the abbreviated, non-personal, story of his life. After supper, he thanked them again and returned to his own camp.

"He's got secrets," said Gladys. "And I'm going to learn them. You mark my words." She held her index finger up for emphasis.

Chapter 14: May 23 – Scotts Bluff

SCOTTS BLUFF WAS A MASSIVE CLIFF 800 feet above the North Platte River. Terrill Johnson looked up from his guidebook to his makeshift school students. "Here is your history and geography lesson for today. We are at Scotts Bluff, which some call Capitol Hill. They named it after a trapper, Hiram Scott, who died here in 1828. Folklore is that his companions deserted him, but others say that he forced them to leave him. Years later, someone found his skeleton."

"How'd they identify it?" asked Henry.

"I don't know. The guide book just says, 'certain features.'"

"We're about a third of the way to Oregon," Terrill Johnson continued. "That mountain in the distance is Laramie Peak. Captain Bridgewater tells me we'll take Mitchell Pass to Fort Laramie."

"Are any of you keeping a diary?"

Maggie shyly raised her hand. Mr. Johnson said, "Wonderful. You will treasure your drawings and diary in the years to come."

Henry squeaked out, "Mine's more of a notebook than a diary. I might need it someday in the newspaper business. Or maybe I'll write a book."

"If you ever need any help with locations, distances, or history, please tell me."

Mrs. Johnson arrived carrying a few chalkboards. Mr. Johnson said, "You older students may leave. Time for numbers for you youngsters."

Maggie moved off to one side and began drawing the bluff while Abigail and Henry admired her skill and quick strokes.

Captain Bridgewater and Michael were behind Terrill's students. "We should be able to kill some buffalo here," said Captain. "Let's get up a hunting party and make meat."

*****

AFTER A TASTY SUPPER of buffalo hump, Abigail picked up Milli's journal.

Wonder what Maggie writes about? Probably boys. To her surprise, Maggie unexpectedly appeared and interrupted Abigail's thoughts.

"Can you hear it?" Maggie bubbled. "There's music over that way. See the fires? We have company. I want to visit them. Come with me."

"Would be something different," Abigail admitted. Maggie wore a frilly party dress and her long curly hair brushed out. "I'm tempted, but I'm not changing clothes. Is that perfume?"

"I made it from the wildflowers back in Ash Hollow," Maggie bragged.

"Abigail, you may not go without an adult," said her mother. "Maggie, you should not either."

"My father and mother are going with us," said Maggie. "Pa has already met some of the other train members."

"I will go with them," volunteered Angus. "We can dance a bit." He winked at Nancy.

Others joined their group. Abigail hoped Jeff Cromwell wasn't there.

*****

AS THEY APPROACHED THE VISITORS' CAMPSITE Abigail couldn't help but think of them as visitors, even though she was visiting their encampment. Captain Bridgewater stood opposite them talking earnestly to a bearded man even taller than him. Both were chewing on a stalk of grass. *Captain knows everyone.*

It did not surprise Abigail to find Ralph Richardson in the visitor's camp. Ralph had a wide grin on his face and his fiddle in his hands. He hastened up to an ensemble comprising a fiddle, banjo, and harmonica and joined in.

"Oh, no," Maggie warned. "There's Jeff."

On the dance floor, Jeff Cromwell held a girl tightly against him. The girl frowned and pushed away but Jeff pulled her even closer. After their dance, Jeff walked with her to join her friends, but she ignored him. A few moments later, Jeff moved to another group of girls, but they, too, ignored him.

Maggie's eyes skipped around the crowd as she searched for boys. "Abigail, look at Captain," she whispered.

Captain Bridgewater and his tall friend were ambling towards Abigail and Maggie, followed by two tall boys. On reaching the girls, Captain said, "Abigail and Maggie, allow me to present my friend, Daniel Murray. Daniel is captain of this train that is entertaining us."

Daniel said, "Pleased to meet such pretty girls." He stepped aside and said, "These are my two sons." He pointed to the taller one and said, "This is David." Then, nodding at the younger son, "and Glenn."

Maggie blushed, giggled, and raised on her tiptoes but Glenn towered over her.

David stood in front of Abigail. He was nice looking with dark brown hair about the same length as hers. He smiled his welcome through slightly open lips.

Abigail tipped her trail hat backwards so it fell against her back and exposed her hair. *Why didn't I brush my hair?* She returned David's smile. "Pleased to meet you, David and Glenn."

Maggie giggled again. "Pleased to meet you, Glenn and David." Maggie's voice changed to become sweet and breathy—almost sensuous.

The band struck up "Turkey in the Straw." David said, "Abigail, would you like to dance?"

"Thank you," replied Abigail. David was a good dancer, and they began a lively two step. Abigail caught glimpses of Maggie and Glenn dancing as well. Maggie wore a big smile and her eyes were bright and wide. The dance ended, and they returned to Captain Bridgewater and Captain Murray.

In the crowd, Gladys Jones nudged her husband and motioned toward the young dancer with her head.

Captain Bridgewater explained to Patrick Alexander. "Whenever two trains meet, the captains always share information. You know, trail conditions, water, Indians, and such. Daniel and I have known each other for many years. He's moving on in the morning, but we'll stay another night." He scoffed, "I'll give your trail dust time to settle, Daniel."

Jeff Cromwell approached the group. "Dance with me, little lady," he instructed Abigail.

"No."

"Aw, c'mon, little lady. Give me a dance."

"No!"

Jeff grabbed Abigail's arm and tugged. David stepped between them.

"She said no." David was taller than Jeff, although not as heavy. Still, he faced Jeff, perhaps bravely, perhaps foolishly, his face grim and determined.

Jeff released Abigail and turned to confront David, but noticed Captain Bridgewater's scowl and backed away.

Jeff turned to Maggie but she shouted, "No!" Nancy shook her head at the same time.

Jeff left them, cursing under his breath.

David looked at Abigail, his question obvious but unspoken.

"We don't like him," Abigail said.

"Well," said David, "would you dance with me again?"

"I'd like that, thank you."

Abigail learned that the Murray wagon train was on its way to California and would be near the Bridgewater train for about another month. In California, Daniel Murray planned to set up a dry goods store for prospectors.

"Everyone talks about the gold," Daniel explained, "but the prospectors need supplies. That's where the money is. This is my last trip. I'll settle in Sacramento, open my store, and get my boys another year or two of education. Maybe even remarry."

"My last trip too," said Captain Bridgewater. "I'll stay in Oregon, though, and be a farmer."

"I don't see you as a farmer, Thomas."

"You might be surprised, Daniel. Just like I don't see you behind a counter. Talk to Angus Campbell from my train. He's young but grew up as a shopkeeper. He plans to open his own dry goods store in Oregon City."

"Good idea. I'll do that."

"Let me introduce you to more of my train," said Captain. They moved on and worked their way through the crowd. David and Glenn remained with the girls.

117

Abigail and David were talking and laughing when a pretty girl with dirty-blonde hair came up to them. She looped her arm in David's and said, "Please introduce me to your new friend, David."

David turned red as a beet. "Abigail, this is Trisha."

Trisha moved closer to David. "Nice to meet you, Abigail. At first, I thought you were a boy, though."

I just bet you did. "Well, I'm not."

"Come, David," ordered Trisha. "Let's visit my friends."

As they left, Trisha turned around to Abigail, pouted, and mouthed, "He's *my* sweetheart."

"Sorry about that," said Glenn. "Trisha is very jealous."

After a few more dances, Captain Murray called for an end to the party. "We have miles to make tomorrow."

On the way back to their campsite, Maggie stepped beside Abigail and whispered. "I think Glenn wanted to kiss me!"

"Maggie!" Abigail scolded. "You just met him,"

"I could tell that he was nice and liked me, though. I hope I see him again. What about David?"

"Trisha has her hooks in David. He just doesn't realize it yet."

"Well, at least I have something to write about in my diary besides rocks."

"It's getting late and I need to hie me off to sleep."

*****

BACK IN THEIR TENT after the dance, Gladys waved her crooked little twig of a finger and scowled at James, "As I suspected, not only did that tomboy and her flirty friend dance, but they danced with strangers. A waltz, yet! Definitely not Baptist!"

"If it upset you, why did you go?"

"Fellowship, James. Fellowship. And I like music. I just don't approve of dancing for unmarried people. The girls put ideas into the minds of the young men. Ain't proper. You mark my words." She finished her harangue with a flourish and her finger pointed straight up.

*****

"We'll take Mitchel Pass," explained Captain to his group leaders. "Until a few years ago, wagon trains used Robidoux Pass, named for Joseph Robidoux, a fur trader. St. Joseph, Missouri, is named for him as well. But the new Mitchell Pass is a shorter trail and caravans are changing to it. I've been on both and prefer Mitchell."

"At last, we take a shortcut and there's no toll," commented George Cromwell.

"There's even a trading post now," said Captain. "The traffic left Robidoux Pass and the Robidoux family moved their trading post to Mitchell Pass. We'll take our nooner there before moving on towards Fort Laramie."

"Hope they have a doggery. I'm 'bout out of whiskey."

"Yes, but whiskey is expensive. Was four dollars a pint last time I checked."

"Four dollars? It was less than four bits in Independence."

"You should've bought more, packed it all the way here and you could've sold it."

"Hmmph!" George spat and wiped his mouth on his sleeve.

Michael grinned. His investment in whiskey was about to pay off.

We are south of Scotts Bluff and heading for Robidoux Pass to get through the Wildcat Hills.

Somehow, many teams of oxen escaped, and we wasted a day finding them and getting them back to camp.

We see graves all along the trail. Many have been disturbed, and skeletal remains are visible. Most graves are unmarked, but occasionally a

name is scratched onto a rock. Have not recognized any names yet.

    Naomi told William and me that Mormons want to know the names of their ancestors who died without learning about the Mormon Gospel. Those ancestors can be baptized by proxy in the Mormon temple, but I do not believe baptism works that way.

Chapter 15: May 27 – Fort Laramie

THEY CONTINUED TO TRAVEL on the south side of the North Platte River through grassy meadows. The view to the south was bleak with wavy sand hills. Fortunately, they found clear springs and did not need the muddy water of the Platte.

Captain Bridgewater pointed to a low rise and cloud of smoke in the distance. "Fort Laramie, Michael," he explained. "We will resupply here. Prices are much higher than in Independence, though. Think about what we've had to do to get here. The supply wagons must do the same."

"Ugh," said Michael. "I was afraid of that. Well, we're limited to what we can carry."

"For the next few weeks, we'll double our guard and be on the lookout for Indians and bandits. Some people are worried about the Mormons, but I doubt they will bother us. The Mormons tend to stay on the north side of the Platte; we'll be on the south side but we'll be using their ferry in a few days. Bandits will look for easy pickings and are unlikely to bother us as long as we stay together. Indians might be a problem, though.

"I thought there was a treaty with the Indians," said Michael.

"There is. The Fort Laramie Treaty of 1851 sets territorial claims of the tribes. The Indians think the claims are their traditional lands, but the treaty actually limits their claims. Both Indians and whites almost immediately broke the treaty. The gold rush made everything worse. The federal government does not enforce the treaty to keep out the immigrants.

"We'll lay-by for a few days at Fort Laramie to rest and do repairs."

Captain found a good camping place with grass and water on the other side of the Laramie River from the fort. Fortunately, the river was low and easy to cross. They would not need to use the toll bridge to get to the fort.

"Look, Mama," said Abigail. "Chokecherries. Sue and I can pick a pot full of them."

"I'll make a pie. But don't stray far from camp, Abigail. We don't know these people."

*****

THAT EVENING, Terrill Johnson convened his students. "Let me give you a brief history lesson."

"We're at Fort Laramie," interrupted Ollie. "Let's visit it instead of talk about it."

"Indeed, this is Fort Laramie, and these are the Laramie and Platte rivers. Fort Laramie began as a fur trading post in the 1830s and was called Fort William, but it then became known as Fort John. The United States military bought it in 1849 to supply wagon trains on the Oregon Trail and renamed it Fort Laramie. Captain will explain to you about Indian treaties here."

Captain Bridgewater reviewed the history, treaties, and policies toward the Indians. "I'll close with: Be careful. None of you should have dealings with the Indians without an adult nearby."

Mr. Johnson continued, "Thank you, Captain. From here, we head towards the South Pass to cross the Continental Divide into Oregon territory." Mr. Johnson unfolded his map. "Who knows what the Continental Divide is?" No one spoke up.

"The Continental Divide separates the watersheds that drain into the Pacific Ocean from those that drain into the Atlantic. Think of it this way: so far, rainwater and rivers drain toward us as we travel west. Those waters end up in the Atlantic Ocean. After we cross the Continental Divide, rainwater and rivers will drain away from us and end up in the Pacific Ocean."

The parents in attendance nodded their heads.

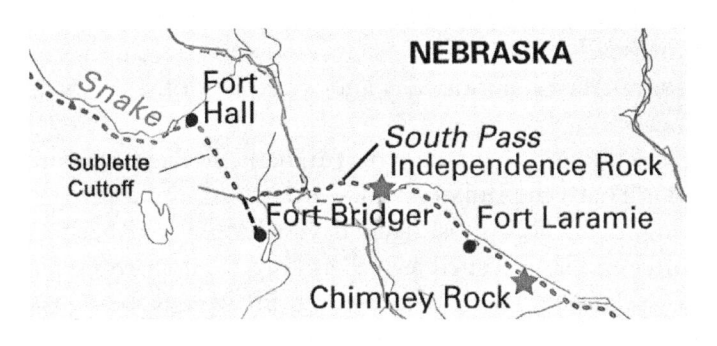

NEBRASKA

Snake — Fort Hall
Sublette Cuttoff
South Pass
Independence Rock
Fort Bridger
Fort Laramie
Chimney Rock

"Now, your arithmetic lesson." His students groaned.

*****

CAPTAIN BRIDGEWATER left Mr. Johnson's school lessons and went to Fort Laramie with Michael Roberts. "Let me give you a quick tour," said Captain. "Then I must have supper with the commander, Colonel Carrington, and his wife, Margaret."

"You seem to know everyone, Captain."

Captain chuckled. "I've been travelling these trails for quite a while. It's always a good idea to share information with the commanders of these forts and captains of other trains. Besides, I'll get a good meal for my congeniality and Margaret is easy to look at."

Gladys Jones walked past and smiled at Captain Bridgewater.

Wagons and tents surrounded the thick adobe walls that rose some fifteen feet in front of them. People were coming and going through the stockade gates.

Fort Laramie was a significant trading post and drew Indians, trappers, and traders as well as the pioneers who typically stayed there for several days. Besides re-supplying their provisions, the pioneers could get wagons repaired and mail letters. Vendors and traders had their stalls both inside and outside the fort.

"The laundresses are over there," Captain showed two tents in the distance. "The laundresses are for the soldiers but can clean migrants' clothes as well. As a matter of fact, they'll be washing my clothes. They have a garden and you can buy fresh vegetables from the laundresses."

"I'll save Alice a laundry day and send our clothes to the laundresses."

Captain pointed past a crowd of Indians, soldiers, and other emigrants. "That's the Bullock and Ward dry goods store. You'll be resupplying there. They most likely have whatever you need—rice, sugar, coffee, flour, and such as well as knives, gunpowder, and shot. Browse around inside before you bring Mrs. Roberts. I've got to buy a wagon before I can resupply myself."

*****

Even though she stayed near her mother inside the Bullock and Ward dry goods store, Abigail was bumped and jostled frequently.

"Excuse me, Gladys," said Mrs. Roberts. "Crowded, isn't it?"

"Yes, indeed. Have you found potatoes?"

"Captain said to check with the laundresses for vegetables."

"Oh, Captain Bridgewater knows the laundresses?"

"He seems to know everyone."

"I heard him talking about Margaret. A sweetheart?"

"The commander's wife and an old friend."

"I see."

"Excuse me, Abigail," said a familiar voice. She glanced up to see David near and smiling.

"Hello, David," Abigail replied, her voice tinged with ice.

"Let me explain..." David began.

"No need."

"Abigail," said Mrs. Roberts, as Gladys looked on with God's judgment in her eyes, "introduce me to your friend."

"Mama, this is David Murray. His train held a dance party at Scotts Bluff."

"How nice. You must visit us, David. Perhaps supper?"

The Enchanted Journal

"Thank you, I'd like that." David smiled at Abigail. "But we are leaving as soon as our oxen are shod. Papa wants to get a few miles down the trail today. We're going to California."

"Oregon for us," explained Mrs. Roberts. "But perhaps our paths will cross again. My pleasure to meet you."

"I hope so. Now I must find Papa before he leaves me! Then I'd have to switch to your train and Oregon." David grinned at Abigail as he turned and left the store.

"He seems nice," said Mrs. Roberts to Abigail. "And very handsome."

"I suppose," said Abigail. "Let's get our supplies." *Having David in our train would change everything.*

*****

1843

We are stopping at a fur traders' post near the meeting of the North Platte and Laramie rivers. The Laramie River is beautiful and teems with fish. William made a joke that the fish were all his because the fort is named Fort William. He has a good sense of humor! Naomi laughed and laughed at William's joke—a bit overdone, if you ask me.

'Fort' William does not look like much. Like Fort Kearney, Fort William is made of adobe, and the area around the fort is nearly a wasteland. The fort is similar to a small town with several businesses, including a blacksmith shop and a wheelwright, which was much appreciated by all.

> We hope to buy or trade for additional supplies here, but Papa says the post does not have much to offer.
>
> We camped about a mile from the fort and planned to stay here a few days. After making camp, everyone visited the fort and its stores. We were careful to keep close to Papa. I do not like how the trappers look at me, and I always stay close to Papa. The trappers are a filthy, smelly lot and usually are drunk.
>
> Naomi went into the dry goods store and enjoyed admiring glances from the soldiers. William was nowhere to be seen.
>
> Tonight, even a mile away, I heard the shouts, cursing and fighting from the fort and was glad to be safely in my tent.

So, Millie knew it as Fort William. Abigail decided to dash off another letter to Lydia in Tennessee. This would probably be her last letter until arriving in Oregon.

Chapter 16: May 29 – Register Cliff

EVEN THOUGH THE TRAIL was between two rivers, it became narrow and dry between the sandstone cliffs known as "Register Cliff" where many travelers carved their names and the date into the soft sandstone.

"Captain Bridgewater says this is Register Cliff and proves we are on the right trail to South Pass. Let's carve our names," said Maggie. She picked up a sharp rock and went to work. After her name, she carved "(Oregon)" and said, "That's in case someone wants to find me."

Abigail giggled. "Oh, Maggie, you'd carve your address if you thought it would bring boys to see you."

"I think my address will be Oregon City, but I'm not sure."

Maggie studied Abigail's carved name. "My full name is Margaret, but I prefer Maggie—sounds more friendly, don't you agree? But you insist on Abigail. Why not Abby?—would be easier to carve."

"I'm named after my great-grandmother and Abigail sounds more feminine than Abby."

"But if you wanted to show you are a girl, you would wear a dress instead of those trousers."

"The trousers are better for the trail. You should try some."

"I disagree. I want to be sure the boys know I'm a girl."

"Maggie," chuckled Abigail, "everyone knows you're a girl."

1843

William carved our initials at Register Cliffs! He made a ladder and reached as high as he could stretch near the western end.

Indians visited us and offered buffalo meat to trade. We can hunt our own buffalo, but the hunting, skinning, and butchering slow down the train. The Indians are curious about white women. They have not seen many white women before— perhaps never. What an odd feeling it is to be in their gaze. The Indians are especially taken by Naomi. She is taller than most of them, and, of course, her long blonde hair fascinates them. I get the feeling that Naomi is enjoying the admiration. She did not even spend as much time around William as usual.

*****

"CAPTAIN," ASKED ABIGAIL after supper, "are your initials on Register Cliff?"

"Indeed, they are. Would you like to see them?"

"Yes, I would." *And I don't want to go past the Cromwells' wagon by myself.*

"C'mon, I'll show you. Alice, Michael, c'mon and scratch your initials in the cliff to prove you were here."

"I carved 'em as high up as I could reach," Captain said as he pointed to "TB-45." "Still enough space around 'em for you and Alice, Michael."

"Is 'DM' for Daniel Murray?" asked Abigail.

"Excellent memory, Abigail. That was a tough year for us and our first trail together."

The Enchanted Journal

Abigail ambled towards the western end of the cliff and searched for Milli and William's initials while her father and mother scratched their own. *So many names and initials...there!*

WA + MM had been carved over 1843 and encircled by a heart. Abigail's throat tightened, and she teared up.

"Mama, Papa, Captain! Come see!" Abigail pointed to Milli and William's initials. "I found her just like she wrote in her diary."

That night, lying in her tent, Abigail gazed at Laramie Peak, its top white with snow and reflecting moonlight in the mountain range to the southwest. *I found you, Milli! You are more than words magically appearing in a journal. I'll find you again in Oregon. Maybe even meet William, too.*

*****

Captain called for a halt and nooner in the bottom of a stunning red-rock canyon. He dismounted, blew his horn to gather his leaders, and broke off a stalk of tall grass to chew.

"This is Natural Bridge--a legendary place. The Indians say that a young brave was struck by lightning and killed while hunting here. They say his spirit lives below the bridge."

"Good," said George Cromwell. "No Injuns here then. I'm goin' huntin'."

"Good idea, George," said Fred Wells. "Me, too." George was notorious for not sharing his kills.

"I'll come along, too," added Michael. "We need the meat."

1843
What a scorching day this was! William, Naomi, and I walked up Horsetail Creek and discovered a natural bridge carved by water

flowing through red rock. What a beautiful sight! The reddest rock I have ever seen.

We took off our shoes and soaked our feet in the cool water. I tried to get Naomi to talk about her upcoming wedding, but she changed the subject every time.

*****

The North Platte River narrowed and turned south near brick red sandstone buttes that served as a landmark and gave the area its name: Red Buttes. The emigrants had to cross the Platte yet again. The river ranged from 300 to 600 feet wide and was 10 feet deep in early June. It would become wider and deeper in late June and more narrow and shallow in late July.

"It's imposing, isn't it?" noted Captain to Michael. "Even though we've arrived at a good time, we'll not try to ford it on our own. Too many people have died here." He pointed to a group of nearby graves. "The Mormons built rafts and a ferry here in the late 1840s for themselves and then realized it was a good business opportunity so they've kept it in operation. They charge three dollars per wagon. There are others in front of us and we'll have to wait a while."

Captain called his group leaders together and explained the situation.

"Three dollars!" George Cromwell, though no longer a group leader, always came to the group leader meetings.

"Yes, and we'll have to wait for our turn tomorrow to cross."

"Well, I'm not payin' or waitin'. Be makin' my own raft."

"Didn't learn your lesson on the Kansas River?" said Captain.

"They's plenty cottonwoods to make a raft. Maybe I'll jest stay here and run my own ferry. Three dollars a wagon! I'll git rich. No need to git to Oregon."

"By the time you build a raft, anchor posts in both banks, rig your ropes and pulleys—you do have pulleys, don't you?—we'll be far ahead of you."

Cromwell was silent for a moment. "I'm going huntin'."

The Enchanted Journal

"That's Daniel Murray's train ahead of us," said Captain. "Make camp behind him. We'll cross the Platte tomorrow."

*****

Abigail opened Milli's journal, feeling that something new had been added. *How could this happen?* Although the appearance of new pages was spooky, Abigail was more curious than frightened.

1843

My uncle accidentally shot and killed himself. I am confident it was not suicide—he loved my aunt and would never have left her alone in this situation. Our captain says that accidental shootings are common because many men are not experienced with guns. They think they need a gun and are correct, but they do not take the time to learn to use it. My uncle fell into that category. Now he is gone, and my aunt is left alone with two small children. She wants to return to Tennessee, but we are too far along. Her alternative is to return to Fort Laramie. My father told her that she would be welcome at Fort Laramie, but for all the wrong reasons. We will try to support her along the trail. William has volunteered to help her as well; he is very kind. Naomi was concerned about Uncle's baptism; she did not accept the Methodist sprinkling.

Abigail closed Milli's journal and resolved to suggest that Captain Bridgewater teach gun safety to the emigrants. *Thank you, Milli, for the idea.*

*****

MAGGIE RUSHED INTO THE ROBERTS' CAMP just as Ralph Richardson began playing his fiddle.

"I'm so glad we have Mr. Richardson with us," Maggie said.

"Me too," replied Abigail. "I love listening to him play—whether religious or popular music."

"That's Mr. Murray's caravan ahead of us. When his musicians hear Mr. Richardson playing, they'll come join him. Before you know it, we'll have a dance. That means Glenn will be here soon. Better change to a dress because David will come too."

"Maggie, is that all you think of?"

"I just want to have fun and this is a good chance. Otherwise, all we do is walk and work. Come on, Abigail, put on a dress."

"Oh, all right."

"I'll brush out your hair but don't put that ratty old hat back on."

"OK, but I'm not wearing a bonnet."

"Me either." Maggie shook out her long curly hair and practiced her best smile and breathy voice. "Do you want some perfume?"

"As long as it does not smell like sage."

"I made it from spruce, pine, and wild flowers. Put some in your hair."

Abigail sniffed Maggie's latest concoction. "Oh, all right. Just a smidge."

*****

MAGGIE WAS RIGHT, thought Abigail as David and Glenn sauntered from the Murray train to theirs. *She's fourteen. How does she know these things? She's just like Lydia.*

Glenn strode to Maggie, hesitated, and took her hand. "H-Hello, Maggie," he stammered. "My, you're pretty. I'm glad to see you again."

Maggie blushed. She released Glenn's hand and pointed to the Murray train. "Oh, is that your wagon train? How nice of you to come visit us."

"Hello again, Abigail," said David cheerfully. "I'm pleased our paths have crossed once more."

"Where's Trisha?" replied Abigail, immediately sorry she asked.

David turned bright red. "She didn't want to come with us."

"Oh? Why not?"

"Well, if you must know, Trisha and I are not sweethearts anymore."

"So you came to visit me instead?" *Why am I acting this way?*

"A new family joined our train and Trisha latched on to their son. He is two years older than me."

At least David was frank and open in his explanation. Don't say anything, Abigail thought.

There was an awkward silence.

Mr. Richardson and his ensemble saved the conversation with a waltz.

"Would you dance with me?" asked David.

Abigail was about to decline, but Jeff Cromwell was striding their way purposefully with a grim look on his face. Her father, Captain Bridgewater, and Mr. Murray were on the opposite side of the dance area.

"Yes, let's." As they danced, Abigail steered their way toward her father and farther away from Jeff Cromwell. *No point in tempting fate.*

*****

AS THE LAST MURRAY WAGON crossed the Platte, Captain turned to his group leaders, "Our turn now."

George Cromwell haggled with the Mormon toll taker about the value of the partially butchered elk strung on a pole between George and Jeff. The exasperated toll taker finally motioned them to board the raft. George grinned at Captain from the raft.

The Mormon ferry boats were made of three long dugout canoes fastened together with planks. The boats could carry one wagon at a time but they had three boats and used a rope and pulley system. The Mormons could move 150 wagons a day across the Platte. The Bridgewater caravan crossed in less than six hours and continued to Emigrant Gap.

1843

We encamped near beautiful red hills where we must cross the North Platte River. The river is too high, too wide, and too swift for our normal fording or even floating methods of crossing. Fortunately, many cottonwood trees line the river bank. The men cut down enough trees to make a raft wide enough for the wagon wheels. It took one day to build the raft and another full day to cross the river. With a combination of animals swimming, men poling, and rope, the raft crossed the river many times. I lost count of how many times William crossed the river. He seemed to be always crossing and became drenching wet. I fixed William hot coffee and he drank several cups. When my family and wagon crossed, William was right there on the raft propelling it with his pole. He did the same for Naomi's family but she didn't fix coffee for him because Mormons don't drink coffee.

As we finished crossing, another train arrived and bought our raft.

*****

NOW ON THE NORTH SIDE OF THE PLATTE, the trail turned dry as they left the river. Sagebrush was the primary vegetation and its pungent smell dominated the air. No matter

The Enchanted Journal

which direction Michael turned, buttes, ravines, gulches, and flats filled the scene. These would be their surroundings for the next week or so as they began their ascent into the Rocky Mountains.

"Fill up your water barrels," instructed Captain to his group leaders. "We've got a hard day with no water."

"Where's the next water?" asked Michael.

"We'll find water at Willow Springs," said Captain. "But first, we must get through ten miles of sand."

Michael trudged through the sand near the lead ox. Abigail was in the wagon seat with Sue behind her, and Alice rode beside Michael on their mule. Mike brought up the rear behind the wagon.

As he trudged along, Micheal thought, *What have I gotten us into? Two months on the trail and, sure, we've seen some fantastic rock formations and rivers and deserts like I've never imagined. But it's been hard.*

They weren't even in the mountains, and already everyone dreaded the mountains having heard the tales of steep ascents, descents, cold, snow, and hunger.

Poor Alice, she did not want to come on the trail, but, no, I had to have my adventure, so here she is. I'll make all this up to her in Oregon.

Abigail thinks she must be a man and help us survive the trail. I haven't intentionally been hard on her—she wants to do her part, but she thinks everything is her part. I wanted a son, but what a daughter!

Mike loves the adventure. He will remember the trail, embellish it, and brag about it all his life. Sue is simply too young and should not be here, but what were we to do with her?

Still walking in the choking dust, Michael's thoughts turned to Captain Bridgewater. *A fine leader and a fine man. Thomas will get us to Oregon. Maybe in Oregon he will marry and raise a family. He needs a good woman like my Alice and a good family like I have.*

We've come too far to turn back now, and I'm really not sure I want to. But this trail is hard. So damn hard.

135

1843

We finally left the Platte River for Willow Springs and I was glad for a change of scenery. But the scenery soon became worse. The arid plain contained only sage, grease-wood, and piles of rocks. Some of the rock piles are graves. A dry day today and probably another one tomorrow. Wish it would rain. We need the water, and the rain would also keep the dust down.

There is no water except for alkali ponds unfit to drink. The ponds are encrusted with saleratus. The animals do not understand and we must pull them away after only a few sips of the alkali water.

I am so ashamed and mad at myself. Today, as I walked alone in the dust, I was thinking about William when Naomi asked to walk with me. I told her I wanted some time alone. Naomi was surprised, but quickly found William and walked with him. They seemed to be having a serious discussion—probably about me.

Chapter 17: June 4 – Cholera Strikes

MICHAEL BENT LOW, scooped up a handful of water from the oozing stream, drank it, and wiped his mouth on his sleeve.

"I wish you wouldn't do that," Alice scolded.

"Wipe my mouth on my sleeve?" Michael chuckled.

"You know what I mean. You shouldn't drink from that slimy stream. You're setting a bad example for the children."

"I've been drinking creek water all my life."

"It was different back home. Our little creek came from a nearby spring and you protected it. You don't know where this spring comes from or what's been in it."

"I didn't want to walk back to camp for your boiled water."

"I know, but you should have.

"The Handbook says to boil stagnant water. This water is flowing. Not the best water I've ever drunk, but it's wet."

They had had this argument several times. Alice handed Michael a bucket. "Well, at least help me carry this water back to camp."

Alice put the water on the fire to boil as soon as they returned to camp.

*****

AS USUAL, ALICE ROSE before dawn and revived the previous night's fire from its ashes. She roasted green coffee beans, ground them, and brewed coffee. Today, they would have cornmeal mush and biscuits baked in their Dutch oven. Baked beans and salt pork rounded out their filling breakfast.

Michael walked slowly to the breakfast area. "Not much for me. Just coffee. Stomach's upset. I've left the animals with Abigail and Angus."

"You do look a little pale. How about tea instead of coffee?"

Michael plopped down on his barrel, and Alice handed him a cup of tea, but he took only a few sips.

An hour into the day's journey, Michael begged to be excused, saying he would catch up in a few minutes. Alice heard him vomiting behind a bush, stopped the wagon, and waited. Michael emerged from the bushes spitting and shaking his head. "Can't keep anything down."

Mid-morning, without saying anything, Michael staggered away from his normal position by the oxen towards a patch of sage brush. Alice stopped the wagon, got out, and found him squatting with his pants down around his ankles.

"I'll be all right in a few minutes. Just need to purge myself."

"Has this happened more than once today?"

"Yes, several times."

"Let me help you. You're burning with fever and turning blue. You should ride in the wagon for a while."

"I'll have to; I can't stand."

With Michael's arms around Alice, they staggered to the wagon. Abigail came running, and they managed to stretch him inside.

Alice could drive the wagon, although it was tiring, and she did not enjoy it—she preferred to walk alongside the oxen. Abigail took Michael's usual place near the lead ox.

Under the hooped canvas, Michael tossed and turned as he alternated between moans and dry heaves. Alice handed him a canteen. "Try to sip this water." He took a swallow but then dropped the canteen, spilling its contents. Alice mopped the spilled water with a towel and put the damp towel on Michael's forehead. "You're burning up!"

"Abigail," called Alice. "Get me more water and a towel so I can bathe his face while I drive. His eyes are glassy and we need to catch up to the others."

"Hup!" Abigail prodded the lead ox to get them on their way.

Captain Bridgewater signaled a stop for the nooner just as the Roberts' wagon caught up to the caravan. Michael was no longer moaning.

Alice climbed into the wagon as soon as the wheels stopped turning. Michael was not breathing. "Michael! Michael!" Alice splashed water on his face but he did not respond. She gave his cheeks light slaps to no avail. Alice grabbed Michael's shoulders and shook him. "Michael! Michael! Don't you leave me!"

Abigail, Mike, and Sue came running at their mother's scream.

"Abigail, get Mrs. Richardson. Hurry."

"Mike, get Captain Bridgewater. Run."

Alice lifted Michael's eyelids and gazed into his lifeless eyes. "Michael, I love you and I need you. Please don't leave me alone on this trail. Please come back to me."

Abigail returned with Mrs. Richardson to find Alice sobbing in the wagon, her head on Michael's chest. "Oh, Michael! Please Michael! Please don't go!"

Mrs. Richardson checked for a pulse and breathing. "I'm so sorry, Alice. There's nothing we can do."

"No! No! He can't be dead! He was walking just a few hours ago. He can't die! I need him. Give him some tea!"

Captain Bridgewater arrived and they advised him of the situation. He and Mrs. Richardson removed Alice from the wagon. His voice stuffy, Captain said, "I'm sorry, ma'am. Michael was a good man—one of my best—and I'll miss him, but we must bury him quickly. Mike, go get Parson Field."

"I think it was cholera," Mrs. Richardson said. "Hope no one catches it."

Michael's funeral was brief but not hurried; his grave was directly on the trail. Captain Bridgewater explained, "I know putting a grave on the trail seems strange, even disrespectful, but the trail is the best location. Wagons rolling over the grave actually keep the wild animals away from it."

Abigail scratched "Michael Roberts 1859" on one of the flatter rocks, knowing that her scratches, like her father, would soon disappear. "Papa, I promise I'll get us to Oregon just like you wanted. Promise."

"Abigail," said Captain, his voice softly trembling, "we must go now." He took her hand and she staggered away from her father's grave, sobbing.

*****

ALICE WAS ABOUT TO PREPARE supper when Mary and Fred Wells came to the Roberts' camp carrying pots of food. Henry and Ollie accompanied their parents.

"No need to cook," said Mary. "We have enough food for all of us."

Alice hugged Mary and sobbed.

Abigail was holding Marcy's handbook and crying into the fire. "Damn you," she murmured.

"Abigail!" scolded her mother. "Don't you curse and certainly do not curse your father."

"I'm not cursing Papa. I'm cursing Randolph Marcy for writing the damn book that lured Papa to the trail that killed him." She threw the book at the fire, but it landed on one of the stones ringing the flames.

Alice retrieved Marcy's handbook. "This trail was Michael's grand adventure. He would not blame Mr. Marcy and he would not approve of your language. We will keep the book to remember the trail and Michael." She put the handbook away with the few other books they had.

"What next, Alice?" asked Mary.

"I don't know. I just don't know. What would Michael do? What would he want us to do?"

"Papa would want us to go to Oregon," replied Abigail, "and I promised him I would get us there."

Still crying, Abigail picked up Milli's journal. *Milli, why didn't you tell me about Papa?*

The Enchanted Journal

This trail is unbelievably difficult and dangerous. Today, a rattlesnake bit a man and he died. Other people passed by that same rattlesnake but were not attacked. Why?

Even the water that we must drink to survive can kill us. Some say that boiling can purify the water, but most people do not boil their water. Certainly, the animals do not boil water.

I wish I had told that man to be careful of rattlesnakes. But would he have listened to a girl?

Will we ever get to Oregon?

*****

CAPTAIN BRIDGEWATER'S RUGGED FACE showed concern as he approached the Roberts' tent. Mrs. Roberts was red-eyed and sobbed as she removed the coffee pot from the fire.

"Good morning, Mrs. Roberts. I again extend my most sincere condolences. Perhaps I can help you prepare for our continued journey?"

"Thank you, Captain. I can't help but believe I am deserting Michael. I feel so empty and alone."

"I understand, ma'am. I wish I could do more, but I can at least hook up your oxen."

"Excuse me, Captain. I should have offered you coffee. Where are my manners?"

"Thank you, ma'am. Don't mind if I do." He unhooked a tin cup from his belt and sat on the stump they used as a stool and chopping block.

Alice Roberts filled Captain's cup with hot coffee. "Captain, I want to go home."

"I'm sure you do, ma'am. That's one reason I came to you this morning. I must be frank—leaving this train is a bad idea, and I can't simply reverse us and return to Independence—not for you or anyone. I promised over a hundred people that I would lead them to Oregon. No, the best course of action is for you to continue at least to Fort Hall and probably beyond."

"The trail was Michael's dream and adventure, not mine. I want to go home," she sobbed.

"Yes, ma'am. But if you leave by yourself, Indians or bandits will certainly attack you. Consider your children, if not yourself. Fort Hall is our next major trading post. Furs are collected there and shipped out by caravan. You might join an east bound caravan there, but I recommend you continue to Oregon City and build a new life."

Captain finished his coffee. "Now to get your oxen hitched. Abigail, Mike, come help me."

Both Abigail and Mike were accustomed to helping their father hitch the oxen, and Captain Bridgewater nodded his approval of their efforts. "Good, that's one less thing to worry about."

Captain turned to Mike. " Mike, you are young, but now you are forced to grow up quickly."

"Yes, sir. I will try my best."

Abigail had tears streaming down her face, but the most resolute look Captain had ever seen.

"I will get us to Oregon," Abigail choked out between sobs. "I promised Papa. Please do not leave us behind, Captain. Treat me as you would Papa. I can do it. I've studied Marcy's handbook. Teach me about the trail and how to survive it."

"Abigail, you are a strong girl, but you don't have the strength of a man. Don't hurt yourself trying to do a man's job. You can't replace your father; you need help. Angus and I can help you.'"

"I will get us to Oregon."

Captain thought a moment. "Michael was one of my group leaders. Please take his place as group leader. Whenever I call for a group leader's meeting, be sure to attend. Your main job is to pass along information to and from me. Abigail, I will see that you get to Oregon. Promise."

The Enchanted Journal

"Thank you for trusting me. I will get us to Oregon, I promised Papa."

"One more thing, Abigail—without your father around to protect you, boys and young men may trouble you. If that happens, tell me immediately."

"Yes, sir. I understand."

They returned to the fire where Alice was cleaning and packing dishes between sobs.

"Mrs. Roberts," said Captain. "I've been on the Oregon Trail several times and on other trails as well. Things happen, and situations change. It is not unusual for people to die on the trail; about one in ten never reach Oregon. I will do my best to see you and your family safely there."

"Thank you, Captain. I'm sad and scared, but I'm glad you're guiding us."

*****

JEFF CROMWELL OGLED Abigail as she repacked the wagon. He boldly entered the Roberts' camp. "Sorry about your Pa. If there's anything I can do to help you, just let me know." Jeff winked and showed a cunning smile.

Oh, no! I will not let this happen. I will not trade myself for his help. Oh, Papa! Please give me strength.

"Thank you, Jeff, but I don't need your help." *Best to be polite.*

"You will need me someday," Jeff leered. "All you have to do is ask, and I'll be glad to help you with anything. *Anything.* We can work something out."

I will get my family to Oregon, but I will not prostitute myself. We'll just have to die on the trail and join Papa.

Jeff stepped toward Abigail, but she backed up and dropped her hand to her hidden patch knife.

"Remember my offer." Jeff grinned ear to ear as he sauntered out of the camp.

Abigail reached for Milli's journal hoping for comfort.

1843
I'm sick with watery bowels and can hardly walk. Mama is giving me broth made from portable soup and rice.

1843
I can't walk and am riding in the wagon. William walks alongside the wagon and sings and talks to me. I feel feverish. Mama insists I drink a lot of broth.

1843
I LOVE YOU, WILLIAM.

Oh, no! Milli is dying! Abigail sobbed. *This damn trail!* She half expected Milli's journal to disappear from her hands, but wiped her eyes and turned the page with trembling fingers.

1843
My fever has broken now, but I'm still riding in the wagon. William sings to me and describes the scenery.

1843
I'm weak but can walk a short distance. William walks with me.

Abigail exhaled a sigh of relief. *I can't take much more of this.*

The Enchanted Journal

*****

ABIGAIL BLUBBERED AND BLURTED, "Captain, what causes cholera?"

Captain Bridgewater chewed his blade of grass thoughtfully before answering. "Many people believe cholera is passed from one person to another. That's one reason for a quick burial. I disagree."

"What causes it?"

"Foul water. It's that simple. Animals and sick people foul the water. Consider all the people and animals who are ahead of us on this trail."

"That's what Mama says as well."

"I agree with your mother. She is a smart woman—in case you were not already aware." Captain smiled.

"Do animals get cholera?"

"I've seen animals get sick and wondered if they had cholera but that is unusual. I really don't know."

"How do we prevent cholera?"

"Boil your water. Wash your hands—especially if you are giving aid to someone who might have cholera."

"What is the best treatment for someone who has cholera?"

"I've discussed treatment with doctors and with Mrs. Richardson. Best thing to do is drink lots of water—boiled water—or broth. Mrs. Richardson favors a rice broth."

"So, in addition to everything else, we must fight cholera all the way to Oregon?"

"Yes, that's true; however, in my experience, the risk of cholera decreases once we get to the Sweetwater River although it can still happen. Don't drink from ponds or slow flowing streams. Boil your water. Wash your hands."

"Thank you, Captain. I'll be careful. I promised Papa we'd get to Oregon."

"You will get to Oregon, Abigail. I can sense it."

Chapter 18: June 8 – Independence Rock

AFTER FORT LARAMIE, the terrain became more desert. The pioneers and their animals were wearing out. *It's not just the difficulty, it's the sameness,* thought Captain. *The sameness. They need a break.* As they neared Independence Rock, Captain Bridgewater called for an early stop.

As soon as the wheels stopped turning, Maggie opened her sketch pad and began drawing.

George Cromwell rode up to Captain and complained. "Another short day! We ain't never gonna git to Oregon afore the snows."

"Hold your horses, George. This is a famous landmark; Everyone needs to see it and learn about it. We've made good time and can have a lay-by here. It is something to talk about in your old age. Besides, we need to prepare for the desert. Time for a group leader's meeting."

Captain assembled his group leaders with a single long squawk of his horn. Abigail joined the group and stood by Captain's side. Terrill Johnson stood quietly at the back of the group.

"What's the gurl doin' here?" George snarled.

"I've asked Abigail to replace Michael as group leader."

"Humph, no gurls."

"The main job of a group leader is to pass along information. Abigail can certainly do that, and she wants to learn more about the trail. She can even read and write." *And you can't, George.*

"Humph!"

"You're not a group leader anymore, George."

"How 'bout Jeff replacing me?"

Abigail's head jerked up.

"No, not Jeff," replied Captain. "He wouldn't do."

"So yer takin' Michael's gurl, but not my older son?" George spat. "I see what's goin' on here."

Captain scowled. "I've been acting as temporary group leader for George's group, but I now appoint Terrill Johnson to replace him."

A voice of relief and approval went through the group leaders at the appointment of the well-liked schoolteacher.

"Humph! A gurl and a schoolteacher! See iffen I listen to 'em."

Captain turned to the group leaders. "This is Independence Rock."

"Why is it called Independence Rock?" asked Fred Wells.

"Travelers on the trail should arrive at Independence Rock by July 4," replied Captain. "Or else they are running late and could get caught in snow later on. We've made good time and can take a lay-by here. Independence Rock is a huge chunk of granite that people carve their names into. It has thousands of signatures. I stepped it off once. It is 1,900 feet long, 700 feet wide, and 128 feet high. After we're settled, you can write your name on the rock." He gave George Cromwell a taunting glance.

"Just a big rock."

"Another thing," said Captain, "during our lay-by, "we need to inspect all the wheels. It's been dry and we haven't forded a stream in several days. As the wood dries, it shrinks and the tire iron may get loose. Look at this example." Captain Bridgewater pointed to the rear wheel of his own wagon. A small space showed between the felloe and the tire iron.

"If this gets much worse, the tire iron could come off and the wheel would break. It must be repaired."

"What do we do? We don't have a blacksmith."

Captain produced four thin tapered wooden wedges. "Hammer thin wedges into the gap from both sides. Trim the excess. Remove the wheel and soak it in the river for a few hours. The wood will swell and close the gap. If you see a tiny gap that is too small for a wedge, you can still soak the wheel to close the gap."

"Never hear'd tell of that or had ta do it," interjected George. "Ya needed a better blacksmith back in Laramie."

"You're in the desert now, George," Captain reminded him.

*****

"ABIGAIL IS NOW our group leader," said James to Gladys as he returned to their camp.

"The tomboy?"

"Yes, Abigail will relay information and orders from Captain to our group. I'm sure she will do a good job."

"I tell you, James, there is something strange going on between that tomboy and Captain Bridgewater." Gladys's voice rose in tone and volume. "You mark my words. With her father dead, no telling what will happen. I think you know what I mean…Captain Bridgewater's a lonely man, I bet, going on all these long roads without a woman. Oh, her mother must be too grief-stricken to notice. I should tell her."

"Consarn it, Gladys. Leave it be."
"You watch your language, James. Just 'cause we are away from civilization is no excuse for cussing."

*****

ABIGAIL, MIKE, HENRY, and Ollie were on their way to inspect Independence Rock more closely when Maggie, Nancy and Angus joined them. They passed in front of the Cromwell's tent, and Abigail shuddered as she sensed Jeff's eyes following her.

At the rock, they were amazed to see names everywhere. Some names were carved deep into the rock, but others barely scratched the surface. Some names were painted.

Mike touched one of the painted names with his finger. "Axle grease. I brought some for us."

Henry shook his head. "We need a ladder to reach an empty space."

"We can join hands to lift someone," said Mike. "Or stand on someone's back."

Abigail searched for Milli's or William's name but could not find them among the thousands written there.

Eventually, they found an empty space within arm's reach. Everyone stood on Angus's back and stretched to write their name on the rock using axle grease.

Captain Bridgewater and Alice found them as Henry was climbing off Angus's back. "Let me show you something," said Captain. He led them around to the back of Independence Rock and pointed up. "Thomas Bridgewater 1845" was chiseled into a smooth space. "Not as many names back then, but I still had to stretch even though I was on horseback."

"Your name will remain forever," Alice observed. "I'll use Mike's grease for ours though." She stretched and scrawled "Michael & Alice Roberts 1859" as tears fell from her eyes.

The Enchanted Journal

1843

I am much stronger now. My mother's broth and William's support pulled me through my illness.

We have reached Independence Rock! It is so covered with names that I had difficulty finding a place to write mine, but I managed. William wrote his name with mine! Naomi had to write her name a couple of yards away from mine. Ha! We did not stay at Independence Rock long but continued to Devil's Gate.

Several of us, including William and Naomi, explored Devil's Gate, only a few miles from Independence Rock. The Sweetwater River flows so rapidly through the small gap in the mountains that it makes a roar.

We got a little confused and were gone so long that the wagon train stopped and sent out a search party for us. We had to promise to stay in sight of the wagons in the future.

*****

Lost in thought, Abigail kicked at the dusty trail as she trudged along beside her lead oxen. *Oh, Papa!* A tear rolled down her face and landed on her boot leaving its mark.

"Devil's Gate," announced Captain to Abigail from his horse. "The Sweetwater River runs right between those two perpendicular cliffs."

"I know." Abigail raised her eyes from the trail. *Maggie will love drawing Devil's Gate.* "My friend Milli--well, the journal I found--wrote about Devil's Gate. She explored it and almost got lost."

"You think of her as your friend now?"

"Yes, I like her. She seems nice and makes interesting observations about the trail." Abigail hesitated. "Milli writes a lot about William."

"A budding trail romance? Happens often. Might happen to you," Captain grinned.

"I doubt it and don't want it.

"You never can tell what will happen on the trail."

I know that all too well. Oh, Papa!

The wagons were too wide for Devil's Gate with the river flowing through it, so the Bridgewater caravan had to go around, but returned to the grassy trail alongside the Sweetwater River.

"Well, I'll be blessed," said Captain. "Looks like someone has built a bridge, a store and blacksmith shop here since I last passed through. Won't be too much longer before the trail becomes civilized."

Civilized? It killed Papa and will kill more of us.

"I'd best check it out. The bridge looks handy." Captain turned his horse towards the bridge and its tender.

*****

CAPTAIN BRIDGEWATER RETURNED to his caravan and blew his horn furiously. His group leaders gathered quickly around him.

"Squatters!" Captain fumed. "These people have claimed this section of trail as their own and built that toll bridge. They charge a dollar per wagon. Without a bridge, this was an easy crossing when I came through here last. The squatters built the bridge, and damaged the banks and river above to force travelers to pay a toll. I don't like this at all, but I thought you should at least know the options. There is another crossing about an hour downstream from here. We'd lose an hour getting there, another hour in the crossing, and still another hour to return to the trail. How do you feel about this?"

"Captain," said Abigail, "why not offer them, say, two bits a wagon with no charge for animals and people?"

The other group leaders murmured their approval.

"Well, it's worth a try," Captain rode over the bridge and entered the store.

Captain came back smiling. "They accepted your offer, Abigail. They hope everyone will go through their store and perhaps buy a few things, but I glanced around their store and it doesn't have much to offer."

"Seen whiskey?" asked George Cromwell.

"Yes, they have whiskey, but it is likely to be expensive."

"Well, let's git goin'." George rode toward his wagon, yelling, "Jeff, git out thet elk hind quarter from last week."

*****

"WE'LL HEAD STRAIGHT to that split in the rocks," Captain used his stalk of Timothy grass as a pointer for Abigail.

"Captain," said Abigail, "thank you for teaching me the route and the details of the trail."

"You might need the information one day, but, mostly, I enjoy your company."

"That split reminds me of a rifle sight."

"You like to shoot, don't you?"

"Yes, sir. Papa taught me."

"I bet you're a good shot."

"Yes, sir. I am." Abigail patted the Hawken in its scabbard on Jake.

"Do you like to hunt? We can go hunting someday."

"I'd like that, thank you."

"For now, let's find a place to camp. Remember water, grass, firewood, and enough space to circle."

They moved up farther, found a campsite, and returned to inform the train.

*****

JAMES JONES PULLED his wagon into the circle and prepared to pitch his tent. It would be a rainy night. Gladys was waiting for him and he braced himself.

"You seen what I told you," Gladys shouted. "Captain Bridgewater and his tomboy left the train unchaperoned again."

"Gladys, calm down. They were scouting. Now grab some hardtack and coffee and come in the tent before the rain starts."

"I can't believe her mother lets that tomboy do anything she wants. I know she has a dress 'cause I seen her in one, but she wears men's trousers instead. She prefers that filthy old hat instead of a proper bonnet." Gladys shook her shriveled witch's finger at James. "There'll be trouble someday, you mark my words."

*****

"HERE COMES THE RAIN," Mrs. Roberts announced. "Abigail, Mike, open the rain barrels and spread out all the pots and pans." She climbed into the wagon with Sue. Abigail and Mike soon joined them.

"Hardtack again!" It did not impress Mike.

"It's raining so hard I can't get a fire going," replied Mrs. Roberts. "I'm glad for the pemmican." The Roberts' family huddled together inside their wagon, where Alice passed out hardtack and pemmican.

No one liked hardtack, but the simple flour and water-baked biscuit had to suffice in heavy rain.

"Here," offered Mrs. Roberts. "Dunk your hardtack into the leftover coffee from this morning to soften it and spread some jelly on it."

"Ugh," said Mike. "At least the pemmican is softer."

"Better than nothing." Abigail dunked her hardtack.

"If the rain stops tonight, we can have a full, hot breakfast tomorrow."

Captain Bridgewater stuck his head in the hooped opening, water dripping from his hat. "Everything all right, Mrs. Roberts?"

The Enchanted Journal

"Yes, Captain. Thank you for checking. We're all hunky-dory."
Captain left to visit the other wagons.
"He worries about us," said Mrs. Roberts.
Abigail lit a candle and read Milli's latest entry from inside the wagon. She no longer wondered if or when new pages would appear; she just knew.

1843

Today, William asked what was going on between Naomi and me. I was surprised and tried to deny any problem, but he persisted. Finally, exasperated, I blurted out, "You!" William insisted that he had done nothing wrong and would not get involved in our argument. Oh, William! You naïve and foolish boy!

*****

THE BRIDGEWATER TRAIN CROSSED and recrossed the Sweetwater River many times. Snow-fed, the cold river twisted and turned through winding shallows, and Captain wanted to travel in a straight line. Wood was scarce but the animals enjoyed plenty of grass.

Steep hills close to the river forced three crossings in two miles. In some places, only one wagon at a time could fit between the roaring river and a wall of granite. The wagons inched along.

"The Narrows, Abigail," said Captain. "Reckon why it's called that?"

Abigail laughed. "I can't imagine, Captain, but thank you for the lesson."

"It is also called 'Three Crossings'," noted Captain. "There is a route around it but it is longer and sandy. The oxen would have a tougher time on the sandy trail. If you can find a blank space, write your name on the wall with axle grease,"

Abigail scrambled in search of dark grease. She wondered if Milli Madison's name was scrawled on the granite wall. Would William Anderson's name be beside Milli's? What about Naomi?

1843
Today, we crossed the Sweetwater River many times. This passage is called 'The Narrows' for obvious reasons. In some places, we could squeeze in only one wagon at a time, and it was too narrow to walk beside the wagon.

William and I wrote our names on the walls of the Narrows while Naomi was not around. I wonder how long our names will remain? I hope forever.

*****

Captain walked beside Alice. "This is 'Ice Spring Slough.' It has ice year round."

Everyone filled buckets with ice. The ice and melted water would be welcome in the heat of the afternoon.

"At last, I can teach you something," said Nancy to Alice. "Put some sugar and cream in a cup and put it in the ice. It will freeze and be delicious! We call it 'iced cream.'"

Alice prepared iced cream and dished some into a cup for Captain. "Captain, here's a little treat for you," she smiled as she handed him the cup.

Captain took a spoonful of iced cream. "Oh, my! How tasty! Thank you, Mrs. Roberts."

"Don't eat it too fast," cautioned Nancy. "You'll get a headache."

"Where do we go from here?" said Abigail. She already had a full cup of iced cream.

"One final crossing of the Sweetwater River and then on to South Pass."

*****

SOUTH PASS WAS a valley, twenty miles wide, with a gentle ascent and descent. It marked the Continental Divide.

"I was looking forward to South Pass, but it is just more boring desert," complained Abigail. "The scenery is the same no matter which way I turn. I'd love to see something green."

"There's an area ahead called Pacific Springs," said Captain Bridgewater. "You'll see greenery there. Water from Pacific Springs flows towards the Pacific Ocean. We are now in Oregon Territory."

Unfortunately, there was little wood in the South Pass and cooking fires were fueled by fast-burning sage with its grassy aroma.

Captain motioned for the wagons to circle for the nooner, but George Cromwell rode up to him instead. "I say we keep on agoin'. This is easy trail, let's make up some time. Don't want to be here iffen it snows."

"George, you're always worried about snow. Have you ever seen snow?"

"'Course I seen snow. It snows in Kentuck."

"Then why worry?"

"I heercd tell 'bout the Donnert wagon train havin' a party and eating each other in the snow. Ain't gonna happen to me." George patted his revolver.

"George, where in the world do you hear such stories?"

"Ever body talks 'bout the Donnert Party."

"Donner was foolish and unlucky—a bad combination. He wanted Daniel and me to go with him but we wouldn't. You know he was going to California, right? Not Oregon."

"Jest know he got stuck in the mountins."

"But not these mountains. California mountains. Donner left Independence in mid-May—too late. We left on April 3. They spent July 4th in Fort Laramie; we got there at the end of May. We're way ahead of the Donner Party. We'll take a nooner, and still get to Pacific Springs this afternoon. We'll camp in Pacific Springs tonight."

1843
I'm grateful for South Pass and its boredom. At least we are not fighting mountains for a few days, but I wish we had water and firewood.

Naomi walked with me for a little while. I know she wanted to talk about William, but I resisted and changed the subject whenever she mentioned him.

I am looking forward to Pacific Springs. It sounds wonderful.

Chapter 19: June 17 – Pacific Springs

PACIFIC SPRINGS IS NAMED after the Pacific Ocean," explained Captain to Abigail as they peered down into the lowland. "Rain falling here flows to the Pacific Ocean, not the Atlantic."

"The Continental Divide," Abigail remembered Mr. Johnson's lesson.

"We are roughly halfway to Oregon."

Abigail passed her eyes over the extensive low-lying marshy grass. No trees or flowing water. It was not the springs she expected, but there was a little greenery. The many hooves passing through had trampled the dry areas into uneven layers of brown dirt. All in all, Pacific Springs was gloomy and depressing. *Barely half way?*

"Not exactly flowing springs," admitted Captain. "But it is our first source of water since the Sweetwater River." He hesitated but had to say it. "Be sure to boil your water."

Abigail nodded sadly.

"We'll stay here tonight and continue tomorrow. There isn't much extra grass. Too many trains pass through here."

There were several other wagon trains at Pacific Springs and Abigail wondered if the Murray train was among them. *Maybe she would see David. Did she really want to?*

"Does someone live here?" Abigail pointed to a log cabin. Several graves behind the cabin marked the beginnings of a cemetery.

"That cabin is new to me. I'll find out later."

Captain selected one of the less trampled areas and motioned for his train to circle and settle in.

Nancy arrived and helped Mrs. Roberts prepare supper. Mike pulled their tent from the wagon and Abigail helped him set it up.

Captain and Angus arrived for supper. Angus and Nancy always ate with the Roberts family and Captain increasingly joined them. "Thank you for inviting me, Mrs. Roberts."

"You're always welcome, Captain."

Captain Bridgewater turned to Abigail. "That log cabin is a sort of post office with a few supplies. No mail for us, but you can mail a letter for fifty cents."

"Wonderful!" said Abigail. "I'll write a letter to Lydia."

"I bought a newspaper!" Captain proudly waved a copy of the *New York Ledger*. "It's several months old but is new reading material to us." He glanced through the newspaper.

"War is coming," Captain predicted. "I hate it, but a terrible war is coming over slavery."

"Will the war affect us in Oregon?"

"Who knows? Oregon does not allow slavery, but it also does not allow Africans to live there at all."

"If war comes," asked Alice, "will you fight in it? Your military experience would be coveted by either side."

"Civil war is a good reason to live in Oregon and avoid fighting. Besides, which side would I fight for? My parents owned slaves, and I grew up working alongside them, but I think slavery is wrong."

"Slaves are in the Bible," said Abigail. Her grandparents had owned slaves.

Angus lifted his head at the mention of the Bible. "Even Dr. Buck defended slavery, but I don't think his heart was in his arguments. He wants the government to purchase all slaves and send them back to Africa."

"The Bible also includes murder, multiple wives, and incest," noted Captain. "But that doesn't mean these are acceptable."

"In seminary," said Angus, "we would debate such things but there was never a consensus of opinion. Just because the Bible records something does not mean God endorses it."

Abigail blushed. "How can Mormons say that a man can have more than one wife?"

Angus took a deep breath. "Joseph Smith, the founder of Mormonism, said God revealed to him that a righteous man could help many women go to heaven by being sealed in plural marriage. It seems that he did his part." Angus laughed.

"Don't you even consider another wife," said Nancy as she joined in his laughter.

"The war," said Captain, "will be about slavery and state's rights, not polygamy. I believe that individual states have the right to leave the Union and form their own government."

1843

We have crossed the Continental Divide and are now at Pacific Springs. It is really just a marshy area, but there is water and grass. No wood though. The grassy areas are soft and miry, and our oxen sometimes get stuck.

Naomi invited William and me to sup with her and her family. She will leave our train soon, and I wanted to be polite, so I accepted. I think she really did not want me to come, but was afraid William would not attend without me. All this is a strain on me and, sad to admit, I will be glad when Naomi is no longer with our train.

During supper conversation, I again attempted to get Naomi or her parents to discuss Naomi's upcoming wedding but no one wanted to talk about it. How could she have taken such a fancy to William while planning to marry

some old man in Salt Lake City? Is Naomi being forced into this marriage?

*****

ABIGAIL DECIDED TO VISIT MAGGIE. She walked to Maggie's tent and found her sewing absentmindedly by lantern light. *Wonder what boy she's thinking of?*

"Hi. Mind if I join you?"

"I was hoping you would. I've got to patch this dress."

Abigail sat on a nearby barrel and watched as Maggie expertly stitched a tear in the dress.

Maggie pointed off to her right. "I think that's the Murray wagon train. Captain went over there a while ago."

"Captain visits all the trains".

"I know, but I still think those are the Murrays. I'm sending Glenn mental messages to come visit me."

Abigail laughed. "Maggie, those boys barely remember us, much less receive your thoughts."

"We'll see. If Glenn gets my message, he'll bring David, so stay here a little while." Maggie inspected Abigail. "I wish you'd worn a dress."

"I'm not sure I want to see David again."

"I think you do. Oh, look! Here they come!" Maggie dropped her eyes to her sewing and resumed.

Glenn and David Murray sauntered up to the Alexander's wagon. "Hello, Maggie," greeted Glenn. "David and I guessed this was your train, so we took a chance on it."

Maggie smiled her best smile. "I'm pleased you came, Glenn."

"Hello, Abigail," said David. "I'm glad to see you."

"Our paths cross yet again." Abigail smiled. "We should stop meeting like this."

"I'm sorry to hear about your father.".

Abigail gulped. "Thank you. I miss him every minute."

"We're leaving in the morning. We'll turn off towards California in a few days. I'm sorry you and I didn't become better acquainted."

"Me too," Abigail admitted. She looked around. *Where were Maggie and Glenn?*

A horn sounded in the distance. Not Captain Bridgewater's squawk, but a pure tone.

"My Papa's bugle," explained David. "We must return to our camp."

Maggie and Glenn emerged from behind her wagon. Maggie's eyes were wide, and she glowed, Glenn's hand in hers.

Glenn flushed as he released Maggie's hand and joined his brother. "I'll miss you, Maggie." The two boys left the Bridgewater campsite and disappeared into the dark as they returned to their own.

"I kissed him!" Maggie gushed. "Did you kiss David?"

"Maggie! You barely know Glenn. Of course I did not kiss David."

"Well, you could have and should have. Now you'll always wonder."

*****

CAPTAIN BRIDGEWATER BLEW his horn at four in the morning and his train organized for the journey to Dry Sandy Creek. Knowing the dry route in front of them, Captain allowed Daniel Murray to begin the trail first while he delayed an hour in Pacific Springs to let his oxen graze and Murray's dust settle.

Maggie waved her kerchief goodbye to the Murray train and used it to dab a tear from her eye.

Captain was neither blind nor insensitive and had witnessed many romances during his years on the trail. "Glenn is a good boy. I've watched him grow up and have always liked him."

"I'll write to Glenn from Oregon City," Maggie vowed. "Maybe he will visit me."

"Good. Well, let's get to Oregon City to mail that letter." Captain tooted his horn to get his emigrants moving.

True to its name, Dry Sandy Creek had little water. Few trees lined its banks and there was little grass. At least the trail was smooth and made for easy traveling.

Captain rode his horse up to Alice as she walked. "Mind if I join you?"

"I'll be happy for your company," Alice smiled.

Captain dismounted and stepped beside Alice. "Ah, feels good to stretch and walk. How are you doing, Mrs. Roberts?"

"Sad, tired, sore, and dusty."

"I was afraid of that. You can ride my horse."

"I'd rather have your company," she smiled. "Do you ever get lonely on the trail?"

"Often. That's why I'm giving it up after this trip."

"What's waiting for you in Oregon? Anything—or anyone—special?"

"No one's waiting for me, that's for sure. As to what, I don't know. Farming, I imagine. A gentleman farmer."

"Gentleman farmer? Never heard of that. Farming's hard work. Not as hard as the trail, but hard work."

"I have a little money set aside and hope to avoid the hard labor part. What about you, Mrs. Roberts?"

"I don't know, and that concerns me. I'm frightened, to tell the truth. As a widow, I can't even stake a claim to land, so farming is out. I'm a decent seamstress and might open a business in town. Angus has promised me one of those newfangled sewing machines. Abigail could help me, but I want more for her. Actually, I'm more concerned about Abigail than I am about myself."

"Abigail will latch onto a good-looking young man in Oregon. You can bet on it. Just hope he is enterprising and lucky."

Captain stopped walking and gazed at Alice. "For that matter, Mrs. Roberts, some enterprising man is more than likely to find you appealing. Your situation is better than your fears."

"I can't think of that, Captain. It is too soon."

The Enchanted Journal

1843
We came across an abandoned wagon today. There are so many of these that travelers usually pass them by, but William and I hurried to it and searched it. Naomi did not come with us as she now tries to avoid me. To our surprise, we found some lantern oil and a small axe. William claimed the axe and used it to remove pieces of the wagon for firewood.

Alone and behind the abandoned wagon, William took me in his arms and kissed me! My heart pounded so I thought it would burst!

Abigail smiled. *I knew this was coming! Maggie would love Milli's story. Should I let Maggie read it? Would the story change if Maggie read it? William was with Milli, but Glenn had left Maggie. Would this make Maggie sad? Best to not chance the effect of Maggie on the journal.*

*****

"I SAW CAPTAIN WALKING with Mrs. Roberts for most of the day," James teased Gladys during supper. *What will she say about that?*

"He's probably hoping to get on her good side, but perhaps he can't decide between the mama or the daughter."

James speared an onion from the stewpot. "Sometimes he rides in the wagon with Mrs. Roberts. She's the only one I've seen him ride with." *That ought to get her going.*

Gladys took the bait. "You mark my word, James." Her voice became louder. "There will be a trail marriage before we get to Oregon. Captain Bridgewater, Mrs. Roberts, and Abigail are on the list. I doubt any woman here would have the Cromwell boy. That curly haired flirt who hangs around the tomboy might bring in someone new—a soldier or emigrant from another train.

"You mean Maggie? She's too young."

"So is the tomboy, but this is the trail."

"Besides, Captain is a confirmed bachelor."

"I doubt that. If he doesn't marry on the trail, he'll marry in Oregon. You mark my words." Gladys wagged her finger and narrowed her little yellow eyes. "Mrs. Field will soon be on the available list, and the trail will add others as we go. According to the newspapers I read, there is always at least one trail wedding in every caravan."

"If I die," asked James, "would you remarry?"

"Most likely. Life is too hard alone."

"Picked anyone out?"

"Captain Bridgewater, of course. But he'd never have me. I'm too old for him."

"Jealous!"

"What?"

"I just realized you're jealous of a fifteen-year-old girl."

"Hah! You think I want to be a tomboy?"

"How about you? Would you remarry?"

"No."

*****

CAPTAIN BRIDGEWATER ENTERED the Roberts' campsite at Dry Sandy Creek. "Good morning, Mrs. Roberts, Mike, Sue. Is there anything I can help you with?" It was time for breakfast and too early to travel.

"Good morning, Captain," Alice reached for his coffee cup. "Would you like some coffee and a biscuit with salt pork?"

"Thank you, ma'am. I can make johnnycake but my biscuits are not so good."

"Sue, give Captain a biscuit while I pour his coffee. Captain, you are always welcome to take a meal with us."

The Enchanted Journal

"Thank you, ma'am." Captain flashed his best smile at Alice and seated himself on a convenient rock just as Abigail came in with three rabbits.

Captain Bridgewater smiled. "Abigail, you are amazing. I've never known anyone who could snare more rabbits than you."

"Papa taught me."

"And he taught you well."

"We must eat to get to Oregon."

Captain glanced around the Roberts' camp taking a quick inventory. "Mrs. Roberts, do you have enough meat?"

"Scarcely a little salt pork and these rabbits."

"Cromwell has enough meat to share."

Abigail waved the rabbits indignantly. "Mr. Cromwell won't share. He insists on trading. He'd rather let the meat spoil than share it. I won't deal with him or his son."

"I agree," said Alice. "We want nothing to do with them."

"You'll get to Oregon, Abigail. I'll see to it. We'll stay here an extra day and I'll organize a hunting party. Will you join me?"

"Yes, sir!" Abigail jumped up. "I'll get my gun."

"Hmm, Abigail, would you check Milli's journal for a hint about where to hunt?"

"Yes, sir, I'll check right now."

> We left Dry Sandy Creek and followed the trail towards the Big Sandy River, but stopped at Little Sandy Creek, where Captain Shaw discovered deer and antelope. He quickly organized a hunting party that killed several deer.
>
> William killed an antelope! He was extremely proud and bragged that the distance was quite long. Tonight we celebrated by having antelope steaks with the Andersons. I think I prefer

antelope to deer. I love William's family; they treat me as though I am special.

Naomi continues to avoid me, and I am glad.

*****

CAPTAIN BRIDGEWATER SUMMONED his group leaders with a long blast on his horn. As usual, George Cromwell, though no longer a group leader, joined them anyway.

Instead of issuing instructions for traveling, Captain Bridgewater said, "We'll lay-by here today for hunting. Many people need meat. Send your best hunters to join me."

"Don't need ta hunt," objected George. "I have plenty meat ta trade. Let's git movin'."

The group leaders gave George such a nasty look that Captain realized Abigail was correct in her assessment. *How could I have missed this?*

Abigail had her father's rifle and was wearing his revolver. "I'm ready," she announced as she pulled her felted hat snug.

"No gurls in my huntin' party," insisted George.

"It's not your hunting party," Captain reminded George. "It's my hunting party. You may join it, hunt separately, or remain here. Sounds like you don't need meat, anyway."

"I'm with you," said Fred Wells. "Let's make meat."

"Me too," added Patrick Alexander.

Abigail called Captain aside. "Milli's train actually moved a little farther to Little Sandy Creek, where they found deer and antelope."

"Good idea." Captain reconvened the group leaders. "Here's what we'll do. My hunting group will proceed to Little Sandy Creek. It's hardly a few miles ahead. Ralph, organize the wagons, move out to Little Sandy, and make camp there. We'll join you with our kills and celebrate tonight.

"Why didn't we push on to Little Sandy last night?" asked George Cromwell.

"It was time to stop," said Captain. "Now it's time to go. Everyone that hunts, get your guns and mount up."

The Enchanted Journal

"I'll go my own way." Cromwell waved his rifle. "I ain't hunting with no gurls. Game smells 'em."

Captain tilted his head back and sniffed. "Surely the game can smell you as well."

Cromwell glared at Captain. "I ain't got ta be right on top of the game ta kill 'em. Gurls cain't shoot."

Captain reached into his trouser pocket, jerked out a five dollar gold piece, and waved it in George's face. "George, I've got five dollars that says Abigail is a better rifle shot than you."

"You're on Bridgewater," Cromwell chortled. "Gotta shoot standin', no supports. A hundert yards and we shoot 'til the target's hit. A misfire counts as a shot. The gurl gotta load her own rifle."

Captain pulled Abigail aside. "I'm sorry, Abigail. I should have asked you first, but my temper got the better of me. You don't have to do this."

"That's all right, Captain. I can do it," Abigail smirked. "Papa taught me."

Captain found a short piece of log, peeled the dark bark away, and made an 'X' using a burnt stick. He stepped off a hundred yards, found a stump, and placed the target on it.

Word of the contest spread throughout the caravan, and a crowd collected. George Cromwell was unpopular, but no one could imagine him losing a shooting contest. There were few wagers.

Alice joined the crowd. She stood by Captain's side and smiled at Abigail.

"Mrs. Roberts," began Captain. "I apologize for getting Abigail involved in this contest and wager. She assured me she does not hold me at fault, but I'm sorry for pulling her into my problems with Cromwell."

Alice laughed. "I don't approve of gambling, but Michael made a lot of money betting on Abigail in shooting contests. After a while, no one would bet against her."

George Cromwell waved his arms in the air to get everyone's attention. "Practice shot." He taunted Abigail, "This makes ya load yer own gun."

"I loaded it the first time."

George raised his rifle, sighted, and fired at the target. Dirt kicked up where his bullet hit below the stump.

"Thought so," complained George. "More than a hundert yards. Ya stepped it off wrong."

Abigail stepped to the firing line. She hitched up her trousers and adjusted her hat before raising her rifle and cocking it. Abigail pulled the set trigger, drew in a deep breath, exhaled half a breath, aimed carefully, and gently pressed the hair trigger. Her Hawken barked, and the target jumped.

"Sure, after I showed her the range," insisted Cromwell. "But now she gotta reload."

Heehaws and murmurs came from the crowd as wagering resumed.

Mike sprinted to the log target just as he had done back in Tennessee. He held up the two pieces of split log, drew a bull's eye on the larger piece using dirt, placed the new target on the stump, and sprinted back to the firing line.

Abigail swabbed her barrel using a cleaning patch and poured in a precise measure of gunpowder. She inserted a patched bullet, rammed it home, half-cocked the rifle, and placed a cap on the nipple. "I'm ready when you are."

George raised his rifle, aimed, and squeezed its trigger. Click. Nothing happened.

"Bad cap," said Abigail generously. "Not your fault. Try again. Want one of my caps?"

"I got caps," Cromwell fumed. He flipped the misfired cap off and jammed on another one. Cromwell raised his rifle, cocked it, and fired quickly, but the target remained untouched. "Wind!" he explained to the laughing crowd.

Abigail stepped to the firing line, licked her finger, and raised her hand above her head. She hesitated a moment.

"Ya gonna shoot?" heckled Cromwell.

Abigail licked her finger again and repeated her test. She raised her Hawken, cocked it, pulled the set trigger, drew in a deep breath, exhaled half a breath, aimed, and lightly squeezed the hair trigger. Her Hawken boomed fire and smoke, and the target fell over.

Horselaughs swept through the crowd and money changed hands. Even the losers were guffawing.

Captain held out his hand and Cromwell reluctantly put a five-dollar gold piece in it. Captain turned to Abigail and handed her the coin.

Alice shook and laughed until she gasped for breath. Tears ran in rivulets down her cheek.

Abigail grinned and Captain saw her mouth, "Thank you, Papa!"

*****

FOLLOWING THEIR SUCCESSFUL HUNT, Captain Bridgewater joined the Roberts' family for supper. Everyone was laughing about the shooting contest.

"Thank you for inviting me, Mrs. Roberts. You are a wonderful cook."

"We thank you, Captain, for providing us with meat."

"You should thank Abigail, her rifle, and her little book." Captain took a bite of antelope steak.

"I don't understand Milli's journal, but it often gives good advice," said Abigail.

His mouth full of antelope steak, Captain praised, "Abigail, you are a fantastic marksman—or should I say, markswoman. Your shot at this antelope was too distant for most people but your bullet went right to the mark."

Abigail gleamed. "I knew I could hit it. Papa taught me."

Captain chuckled. "I shouldn't feel this way, but it pleased me that George and Jeff did not kill anything. Serves them right. Let them eat from their stores tonight while we eat fresh meat."

Chapter 20: June 19 – Parting of the Ways

"THIS IS the *Parting of the Ways*," said Captain to Abigail, pointing his stalk of grass to one trail and then another. "We'll stay along the Sweetwater River. Some people prefer the original trail, but we'll take a shortcut called the Sublette Cutoff and save about 70 miles. It used to be called the Greenwood Cutoff. We'll have to cross a high desert without water or grass for 45 miles—about three days if we're lucky before we rejoin the original trail."

"Why 'Parting of the Ways'?"

"Some people may insist on taking the original trail and will leave us at that point. I can't force them to stay with us. Other trains, like Daniel Murray's train, will take the southern trail to Fort Bridger and Salt Lake City and continue to California.

"Actually," Captain continued, "that looks like Daniel's train just ahead of us, turned off towards Fort Bridger."

Captain Bridgewater's train continued toward the junction, but Daniel's train had stopped. Three men on horseback rode from Daniel's train toward Captain Bridgewater and Abigail.

"Thought I'd say goodbye one last time," said Daniel, "and my boys wanted to come for some reason." He guffawed and stuck out his hand to Captain Bridgewater. "Come visit me in Sacramento, Thomas. Specially if you need prospecting supplies."

"I hope to see you again someday, Daniel, but I seriously doubt I'll be prospecting."

Maggie waltzed to Abigail and stood by her side, wide eyed and smiling. Alice watched from the wagon seat, laughing silently. Mike stared from behind the wagon, curiously.

David and Glenn shook Captain Bridgewater's hand before dismounting. They hesitated a moment, and sauntered over to the girls.

Glenn went straight to Maggie. "I'm pleased to have met you, Maggie. I hope to see you again someday."

Maggie held out her hand. "Me too."

Glenn squeezed Maggie's hand gently and held on for a moment before releasing it.

David found Abigail's eyes. "Wish I had more time to know you, Abigail. Good luck in your travels."

"Thank you, David. I wish we'd had more time as well. My best wishes follow you."

Maggie reached into her sketchbook. "I have something for you," She gave Glenn a sketch of herself and gave David a sketch of Abigail. "Don't forget us," Maggie admonished.

David looked from the sketch to Abigail and back to the sketch. "This is amazing. No way I could forget you, Abigail."

"Thank you, Maggie," Glenn added. "I'll always remember you, even without the sketch."

The boys remounted, gave a last wave, and rode away behind their father.

"When did you make those sketches? I didn't pose, but your sketch is a wonderful likeness."

"I can draw from memory. Don't ask me how. Here, take this." Maggie handed Abigail a sketch of David. "He's quite handsome, you know."

"I suppose so."

"Like I said, you should have kissed him."

1843

Today was awkward and yet relieving. I am glad it's over. We came to the 'Parting of the Ways' where some wagons take the southern trail to Salt Lake City or California. We took the northern trail to Oregon.

Naomi Christensen, her family, and the other Mormons turned toward Salt Lake City. William and I walked to her wagon to tell her goodbye. In all honesty, I was glad to see Naomi leave. She was crying and gave me a quick hug. Naomi then wrapped both arms around William and gave him a long, lingering kiss on his lips! She stepped away from William but held on to his hand until distance forced release. Naomi then ran to catch up to her wagon and never looked back.

I was shocked, but not as shocked as William. Poor William! He had no idea of Naomi's feelings toward him. William did not say a word as we returned to my wagon.

Mama and Papa did not see Naomi kiss William, but they could tell something was wrong. Papa was about to inquire and attempt to resolve the issue, but Mama put her hand on his arm and restrained him.

I said, "William, you may not leave wearing Naomi's kiss. Excuse me a moment." I returned with a washbasin, washcloth, and soap and handed them to William. He understood and scrubbed his face and lips. After William put down the washbasin, I stepped as close to him as possible, put my arms around his neck, and kissed his lips! I could taste the lye soap! William put his arms around me and held me close for a few moments.

After William released me, I glanced at my parents. Papa was shaking his head, stunned by his wanton daughter, I imagine. Mama was beaming.

"You may wear my kiss instead, William."

William walked away—in a daze; I suppose.

William is mine and mine alone!

That Naomi! She's got her nerve! Good for you, Milli! Wait, what am I thinking? Would Milli approve of Maggie? Should I have kissed David? What does this mean?

*****

THE NEXT NIGHT, around the campfire, Captain said, "Let me tell you the story of Fort Bridger. We're not going that way but earlier wagon trains did."

"Jim Bridger and his partner Louis Vasquez made a trading post and named it after Bridger. It was a simple high wall of logs with the ends buried in the ground. Bridger lived there for many years. He was called 'Old Gabe'."

"Is he still alive?" asked Mike.

"I think so but he's not at the fort anymore. William Carter runs the fort now. He is also the sutler and postmaster.

"Getting back to Bridger, he was a mountain man, trapper, Army scout, and wilderness guide. I knew him fairly well. Anyone who stopped at Fort Bridger wanted his advice. They also loved to hear his tales and Old Gabe loved to tell them."

"What kinds of tales?" asked Mike.

"Well, I heard him tell this story. One time a hundred Cheyenne warriors were chasing him. After several miles, they trapped him at the end of a box canyon. He shot all his ammunition, but the Indians kept coming. Bridger then stopped his story and became silent. One of the listeners asked, 'What happened next, Mr. Bridger?' Bridger replied, 'They killed me.'"

Abigail and Mike laughed at themselves. The Bridger story had taken them in.

1843

The day after I kissed William, he caught up to me as I walked beside our wagon. He stammered, "A-A-About last night…" but couldn't continue. I just smiled at him, touched his hand, and remained silent. William is extraordinarily smart and will eventually figure this out—he's just a naïve young man.

*****

THEY CAMPED ALONG THE BIG SANDY to prepare for the long dry trip across the cutoff. Water filled every possible container.

Animals grazed as though they were aware of the upcoming lack of grass. The emigrants feasted while there was wood to cook on and the aroma of roasting meat filled the air. Extra wood was jampacked into the wagon beds.

Abigail sipped her evening coffee, now taken black and bitter to save sugar. *The trail, chores, tiredness, Papa, Mama, Milli, William, David. Why David? I'll never see him again, but he seemed interesting. Now, I'll never know.*

"Mind if I join you?" Captain poured himself a cup of coffee and sat down on a log near Abigail.

Captain Bridgewater took more and more of his meals with the Roberts and almost always had his morning coffee with them.

"I'm glad for the company. Besides, I have a question. How did you meet Mr. Murray?"

Captain smiled sadly. This was not about Daniel Murray, but he continued as though it were. "Daniel and I met many years ago. His sister, Isabella, was my sweetheart. Daniel's wife Liz was my sister, so Daniel and I were almost double brothers-in-law."

"Almost?"

"Isabella was too young to marry, so I left to seek an adventure. She died of smallpox while I was away. I've never forgiven myself for leaving her." Captain gasped on a suppressed sob.

"But you couldn't have done anything to save her."

"I know. I'm sorry to upset you, Abigail. I don't understand why I'm telling you all this. I haven't told this much about my past to anyone other than Daniel."

"I can listen."

"Liz died giving birth to Glenn. Daniel and I were young and could not handle the double tragedies. We hit the trails seeking adventure…escape, really… while his parents raised Glenn and David. Somehow—I'm never quite certain how—Daniel and I survived our youth. We served together in the Mexican War and did some trapping before getting into this wagon train business. Daniel is a fine man—the finest I know."

"His sons seem to be good boys."

The Enchanted Journal

Captain's smile broadened. "David and Glenn have grown up on the trail. They are trail tough and strong. You can depend on them. Their formal education might be irregular, but they are intelligent. If I had to choose a team to match a difficult situation, I'd choose Daniel, your father, David, and Glenn. Frankly, I'd include you as well."

As always, Abigail's throat tightened, and her heart pounded at the mention of Michael. *Papa would have liked David.* "Thank you, Captain. I'd be pleased to serve with you."

Captain's grin stretched from ear to ear. "Women tell me that David and Glenn are quite handsome. Would you agree?"

Abigail blushed. "I suppose so."

Captain chuckled and added, "Thanks for listening to my story."

"Thank you for sharing it with me, but I won't be sharing it with others." Abigail bussed Captain's cheek just as Gladys Jones walked past the Roberts' camp, and Glady's head snapped toward Abigail.

"Now I have a question for you," said Captain. "How did Milli get to Fort Hall? Did her train take one of the shortcuts?"

"I don't know. Let's see."

1843

We turned onto the Greenwood Cutoff, which is supposed to be a shortcut. This shortcut proved incredibly difficult. It was so dusty and windy that I could scarcely see the length of our ox team. We had neither wood nor water for the entire cutoff, and we traveled at night. Two nights. There were many dead cattle along the way. We finally arrived at Green River and will remain there for two days to recover.

"I like the idea of travelling at night. The sky is clear and the moon will be bright tonight. We can push hard and get through this desert quickly. I'll talk to the other group leaders." He finished his coffee and stood. "Thank you, Abigail. And Milli."

Abigail opened Milli's journal to double-check. She flipped to the end and found a new entry. *Already? Where do they come from?* The unexplained appearance of new entries was spooky and this one doubly so because it appeared so quickly.

Another terrible and sad day. A little boy, perhaps four years old, was playing near the wheels of a moving wagon and he slipped and fell under the wheel. He was instantly crushed to death. That's the second time a wagon wheel has killed a child. They cannot resist the temptation to play with the wheels.

Abigail dropped Milli's journal. "Sue, Sue. Where are you?" Her eyes surveyed the surrounding area. There was Sue, playing under the wagon. Abigail ran to Sue, grabbed her shoulders, and pulled her from underneath the wagon.

"Don't you ever play under the wagon again!" Abigail shouted.

"Not move."

"I don't care. The wagons are dangerous for someone small like you. Do not play under the wagon. Promise me?"

"Promise."

Abigail hugged Sue and cried. *Thank you, Milli.*

*****

GLADYS CAUGHT JAMES outside their tent and shouted, "I knew it! I seen them kissing!"

"Seen who?"

Gladys lowered her voice to an excited whisper. "Captain Bridgewater and that tomboy. I've a good mind to go tell her mother right now."

"Gladys, calm down. Captain is our leader, and Abigail is not our child or responsibility."

"If we had children, I'd want someone to advise me of such wanton behavior—especially with an older man."

"There's probably a good explanation, Gladys. At least learn more before you go blabbering it all over the trail."

"I've just told a few women. And there's another thing. You think I'm a gossip, but I tell you, I seen them kissing with my own two eyes."

Gladys noticed Abigail approaching and became silent.

"Good evening, Mrs. Jones," said Abigail. "Mr. Jones, instead of staying the night here, we'll treat this as a nooner and travel at night when it's cooler. Excuse me, I must tell the others."

"You seen how she lords it over us now that she's a group leader?"

"She's just passing along Captain's orders."

Chapter 21: June 25 – Green River

THE GREEN RIVER FLOWED SWIFTLY and really was green. Its banks were lush with grass and trees. After forty-five miles without water, the animals stampeded toward Green River with their remaining strength as soon as they smelled it. Other prairie schooners crowded the banks in their camping circles.

Captain Bridgewater gathered his leaders. "This water is deep and swift and dangerous. There is a ferry here, but it costs five dollars per wagon, and we'll have to wait until our turn tomorrow." Meanwhile, these waters hold plenty of trout. Might as well go fishing."

Captain found Mike, Frank, and Ollie playing together. "Let's go fishing, boys." He rigged lines and cut poles while the boys found worms and grubs. Soon their lines were in the river and they were pulling in trout nearly as fast as they could bait their hooks.

Mike ran to their tent where Angus and Nancy were helping Alice with supper preparations. "Look what Captain and I caught," he announced. He held up several massive trout and grinned. "Supper!"

"Angus," said Captain, "do you know how to clean fish?"

"No, sir.".

"Time you learned. Come with me."

"Captain seems to know everything," said Nancy. "I'm so glad he's taken Angus under his wing."

Alice had both hands in a bowl of flour. "Captain has been very good to us. I don't know what we'd do without him." She dusted off her hands and put a pot of water on the fire.

The men returned with trout filets. Alice said, "Put the bones and scraps in that boiling water. I'll add potatoes and onions to make a chowder."

Alice showed Nancy how to bread and fry fish while Abigail mixed cornmeal for hushpuppies.

"Hushpuppies?" said Nancy.

"Yes," replied Alice. It's just cornmeal, goat's milk, onion, and eggs. We'll fry them after the fish are done. They're called hushpuppies because they were given to the dogs instead of fish. Now we make them fancy and eat them ourselves."

They settled around the campfire on various logs, rocks, and barrels, and Captain asked the blessing.

Captain speared a piece of fried trout and held it up. "This sure is a welcome change from antelope. You are a fine cook, Mrs. Roberts."

"Thank you, Captain. Try a little sprinkle of vinegar on your fish."

"You're right. Brings out the taste."

"Abigail, you and Mike, go get us some water."

As usual, Mike grouched but picked up his bucket.

*****

JEFF CROMWELL WATCHED as Abigail and Mike walked past the Cromwell camp. He took a drink from his whiskey flask and followed them at a distance until they reached the river. Jeff stopped and searched for Mike, but he had disappeared.

Good, the kid has wandered off. Maybe she'll be friendlier by herself. Taking care to be quiet, Jeff inched up to Abigail.

Abigail scooped up a bucket of water and turned around.

"Surprise!" said Jeff with a grin. He licked his decayed eyetooth.

The Enchanted Journal

Abigail dropped her bucket and water spilled over her boots. "Mike! Mike, where are you?"

Jeff stepped close to Abigail and picked up her bucket. "Let me help you with that, little lady."

"Get away from me!" Abigail backed up.

Jeff refilled Abigail's bucket and put the bucket down at her feet. He stepped still closer. Abigail stepped back again, but a tree blocked her retreat. Jeff continued toward her, his smirk broadening.

"Now, how do you say thank you, little lady?" Jeff pinned Abigail against the tree, wrapped his dirty hands around her waist, and bent his head to kiss her.

Abigail slapped Jeff and dug her nails into his face, but he just laughed and did not release her.

"You're a feisty one! Let's try that again." Jeff leaned his body into Abigail and moved his hands to her breasts. "I can't believe I first thought you were a boy. You're a fine young woman."

Abigail took a deep breath, but Jeff covered her open mouth before she could scream. He poked a dirty finger inside her lips, forced her teeth apart, and rubbed her tongue. Abigail chomped down on his finger and Jeff yanked it out, but kept her mouth covered. He smeared blood from his finger on her face.

"So, you got a good taste of ol' Jeff, now. There's more acomin'."

Abigail attempted to knee Jeff in the groin, but he blocked her kick. "Careful now. You'll be there soon enough."

Outraged, Abigail jerked her head from side to side and up and down, but her attempts to shout were muffled by Jeff's rough hand.

"It won't do you any good to scream," Jeff crowed. "Just relax and enjoy it." He dropped his free hand down to Abigail's leg. "Wish you weren't wearing these confounded trousers." He fumbled at her belt..

"Leave her alone!" Henry's loud squeaky voice surprised Abigail and interrupted Jeff's one-handed attempts to pull down her trousers. Henry rushed up to Jeff with his fists upraised.

Jeff sniggered at Henry and pushed him away so hard that Henry fell and his eyeglasses popped off. Jeff roared even harder. "Go away, you pipsqueak, unless you're waiting for your turn."

With Jeff's attention diverted, Abigail retrieved her patch knife from her trousers and rotated the sharp edge up. She thrust upward towards Jeff's belly, but he stepped back and deflected her stab. Instead of entering his belly, Abigail's knife cut a deep gash across his chest. She waved her bloody knife at him.

Jeff wiped his hand across his bleeding chest. "Bitch! Now you'll really get it." He lunged for Abigail's knife arm, but she dodged his moves.

Henry regained his footing and again moved toward Jeff, but more cautiously. Jeff turned slightly to fend off Henry and did not see Mike coming at him, holding a big stick.

Both hands gripping his stick, Mike put all his twelve-year-old power into clubbing Jeff on the side of his head. Jeff went down like a poleaxed cow, twitched, and lay still.

Abigail screamed in horror.

"I think he's dead!" exclaimed Mike, but he held his club ready to deliver another blow.

"I hope so," sobbed Abigail.

Henry said, "Let's get out of here." He retrieved his eyeglasses, and they sprinted toward the Roberts' camp.

*****

CAPTAIN AND ALICE JUMPED TO THEIR FEET at Abigail's scream.

Captain pulled his Colt Navy revolver from its holster and ran toward the scream. Alice picked up the iron fire prod and ran after Captain.

They met Abigail, Henry, and Mike sprinting from the edge of the woods leading to the river. Henry had his eyeglasses in his hand, Mike's club bounced on his shoulder. Abigail, her face, and trousers bloody, held tightly to her knife.

"What happened?" asked Captain.

The Enchanted Journal

"J-J-Jeff Cromwell tried to rape me," sobbed Abigail. She was shaking but still held her knife. "Henry and Mike stopped him. He might be dead. I hope he is dead."

"Oh, Abigail. You poor baby."

Captain held out his hand. "Let me have the knife, Abigail."

Abigail handed the bloody knife to Captain and fell into her mother's arms, quivering.

"Did you stab him?" asked Captain as he examined the knife.

"I cut him. Mike hit him with a club. He fell like he was dead. I hope he is."

Captain detected motion, and turned towards the woods. Jeff staggered out shaking a bleeding finger. His shirt and face were painted with blood, his cheek had a purple bruise, and one eye was turning black.

Captain raised his revolver. "Stop right there, Jeff, or I'll shoot."

Jeff stopped. "Why're you threatening me? I ain't done nothin'."

"Your face, bloody shirt and black eye confirm Abigail's accusation. Mike and Henry were witnesses. I ought to shoot you right now. Hell, I want to shoot you, but I'll take you to your father instead.

"The bitch lured me into the woods, and then these two kids attacked me."

Captain cocked his pistol. "You should thank God that Michael is not alive because if he was, you'd be dead now. Get moving to your camp. Don't give me an excuse to shoot you. It won't take much."

*****

"WHAT HAVE YOU DONE to my son?" George Cromwell was indignant as Jeff staggered into camp closely followed by Captain and his revolver.

"Jeff attempted to rape Abigail Roberts."

George frowned at Jeff's bloody shirt, scratched bloody face, and purple bruise above his cheek. "That gurl did this?"

"Abigail cut him. There are witnesses."

"Jeff, is this true?" asked his mother.

"No, ma'am. The bitch lured me into the woods, and her brother and Henry Wells jumped me. One of the little bastards clubbed me."

"Watch your language, Jeff," Ester warned.

"Who made ya sheriff, judge and jury, Bridgewater?"

"You did, Cromwell."

"I don't believe ya, but what ya gonna do?"

"I ought to shoot him, but I won't."

"If ya shoot, I shoot, too." Cromwell patted the revolver on his belt.

"In most trains," Captain said. "Jeff would be given thirty-nine lashes or forced out of the train."

"Ya ain't gonna whip my son."

"In that case, you must leave the train," said Captain. "Mrs. Cromwell, you may stay if you can find someone to take you in."

Ester shook her head. "They're foolish, but I'll stay with my men. They're all I've got."

"Very well. Move your wagon out of the circle, Cromwell," said Captain.

"I'll git out in the mornin'. We're set for tonight."

"Move out of the circle now."

"I seen you hangin' around the Roberts' camp," jeered Jeff. "You want the mother and her daughter, too."

Captain kept his cocked revolver pointed at Jeff. "Don't push me, Jeff."

"If ya force me out, ya got to gimme my money back," George said.

"No. I read the contract to you, and you made your mark on it. Your wife and son read the contract and signed as witnesses. No refunds. Stay away from my train."

"It's a free trail. Ya can't force me offen it."

"Stay away from my train. You can go ahead of us or behind us. Stay far away. You'll get no assistance from us. I'm warning you."

"Ya can bet I'll be ahead of ya. Yer slow as molasses."

The Enchanted Journal

"Jeff, make no mistake. If I ever see you anywhere near Abigail, I will shoot you." Captain uncocked his pistol, returned it to the holster, and returned to the Roberts' camp.

*****

"YOU DID IT, DIDN'T YOU?" Ester was furious. This was just the kind of trouble that forced them out of Kentucky.

Jeff blotted his bloody finger on his torn shirt. "She wanted it."

"I don't believe you. You've been lusting after that girl ever since you saw her. Let me look at that finger."

Jeff dutifully extended his finger.

"Bitten to the bone. You're lucky she didn't bite it off." Ester poured whiskey on the bite and wrapped it. "How'd your finger get in her mouth in the first place?"

"She tempted me."

"Take off that shirt and let me dress your cut."

"She tried to kill me," said Jeff as he removed his bloody shirt.

"No wonder. You deserved to be killed. Now be thankful to be alive and pray for forgiveness."

Ester found a clean cloth for a bandage and poured whiskey on it. She wiped the scratches on Jeff's face and poured whiskey on the open chest wound. "This cut needs stitches."

Jeff flinched as his mother's needle and thread went in and over his wound. "Give me some of that." He reached for the bottle.

"No, you've had too much already. Look at the trouble your whiskey has caused us."

George pulled his revolver from its holster and idly inspected it while turning the cylinder. "Thought I was gonna have to use this again, but we'll be all right. Beat Bridgewater to Oregon too."

"Michael would have killed you, Jeff. Now you've killed all of us. I doubt we'll ever see Oregon."

*****

IN THE ROBERTS' CAMP, Alice was consoling Abigail. Mike and Henry stood guard nearby.

"This is not your fault, Abigail. Jeff Cromwell is an evil man."

"I know. He's been after me since the first day. I could feel his lust and tried to avoid him. The other girls fear him as well."

"Thank goodness Mike and Henry were around to save you. They were especially brave to take on such a big man," praised Alice. "Thank you."

"Yes, thank you, Mike, and Henry. I owe you a great debt. I could never have defended myself alone."

At Abigail's praise, Mike and Henry swelled their chests and drew up their shoulders.

"I saw Jeff following Abigail, and I followed him," bragged Henry. "I knew he was up to no good. I tried to fight him, but he was too big and strong for me."

"I clubbed him," said Mike, "but Papa would have shot him."

"More likely, strangled him to death with his bare hands," admitted Alice.

"I'm so glad Papa bought me that patch knife," said Abigail. "He told me to always keep it on me. He didn't even know Jeff, but he must have expected such problems."

"I'm afraid the Oregon Trail is nearly lawless in addition to being rough," said Alice. "We must be prepared for anything."

"I might need to carry Papa's revolver," said Mike. "I know how to shoot it."

Alice shook her head. "No, Mike, but I'll keep Michael's revolver handy."

"I wish Jeff were dead, Mama. I know this makes me a terrible sinner, but I wish he were dead. I'll never rest easy until Jeff Cromwell is dead."

Captain entered the Roberts' camp in time to hear Abigail's wish.

"I have expelled the Cromwells from the train," Captain explained. "They are leaving immediately. Jeff will not be around to bother you again, Abigail."

"What if he sneaks back? I won't be able to sleep at night."

"I don't think you'll ever see Jeff Cromwell again. I will guard you tonight. I'll get my bedroll and be right back."

The Enchanted Journal

1843

Five young men left our company at Green River because they were in a hurry and did not like our Sunday stops. They were jolly and entertained us with their fiddles and guitars in the evenings. They were talented singers as well although not as good as William.

Naomi has been gone nearly a week now and I must admit that I would miss her except for her throwing herself at William. William never mentions Naomi and, if I do, he changes the subject. I wonder if she is married now? I almost hope so because then she would not be available.

I still cannot believe that I so brazenly kissed William, but I know I did not force myself on him, whereas Naomi did. William did not respond to Naomi, but he definitely responded to me. I will never forget our first kiss behind the abandoned wagon and now my 'lye soap' kiss! Oh, my! I am already looking forward to more! Our relationship has changed. What is to come?

*****

CAPTAIN BRIDGEWATER HAD ALREADY PLANNED a lay-by at Green River before moving on, and he was glad he had. Their lay-by allowed the Cromwells to get farther ahead, and George would push hard.

The morning after Jeff's assault on Abigail, Captain gave three short toots on his horn to assemble everyone.

Maggie rushed to Abigail's side and hugged her. "Are you hurt?"

"No, but I'm still shaking."

Nancy joined them. "That evil man chased after every woman in the train. I wouldn't go near him. He always wanted to dance with me, but I told him no every time. He would even ask me to dance if Angus was with me."

"Me too," said Maggie. "I'm glad they are out of our train."

The Roberts family gathered around Captain with Alice and Abigail at his sides. Mike and Henry stood near Abigail, proud of their role as protectors. Captain raised his hand for silence.

"I'm sure you've heard the news that I've expelled the Cromwells from our train. Let me explain my reasons."

A low murmur through the crowd showed everyone had already heard the news.

"Jeff Cromwell attempted to rape Abigail Roberts, but she, Mike and Henry fended him off. Jeff was injured but will heal. However, the Cromwells are not welcome in this train. They've moved on ahead of us, and I expect we will never see them again. If we meet them, I will not visit or assist them in any way.

"The trail is not lawless. There are common standards of decency that everyone knows and should abide by. The Ten Commandments provide guidelines for everyone. After I expelled him, George accused me of being the sheriff, judge, and jury. That is correct. In fact, when you signed up with me, you agreed to those terms. If anyone disagrees with my governance, please leave the train now."

No one moved or spoke for a few moments as they glanced at their neighbors. A worried voice said, "George was our best hunter, and now we each need to hunt more."

"I'll hunt more," said Fred Wells. "And I'll be more generous than George."

Everyone guffawed.

*****

Instead of his usual sound sleep, Thomas Bridgewater tossed and turned. *Why? Because of Jeff Cromwell? Abigail? Michael?*

Thomas wanted to kill Jeff Cromwell—an urge he had not experienced in many years, but that was not the reason for his insomnia.

Alice. Thoughts of Alice Roberts kept Thomas awake. *I haven't had this feeling in decades. I'm tired of living alone. If I proposed, would she accept? I will discuss marriage with her tomorrow. We can work this out.*

Decision made, Thomas turned on his side, gathered his quilt around him, and fell asleep.

*****

AFTER LEAVING Green River, Judy Field rushed to Captain Bridgewater as soon as the caravan stopped for its nooner.

"Captain, Charles is not doing well at all. I'm afraid he is dying."

Captain Bridgewater was not surprised. Charles Field could hardly breathe and had been coughing continuously for weeks. He no longer walked the trail and barely moved around in camp.

"Mrs. Richardson is with him now. She thinks he has the grippe on top of his consumption. His breath is bloody and foaming."

Captain called his group leaders and explained the situation. "We'll be staying here, at least for tonight." He left the group leaders and hurried to the Field's wagon.

Inside the wagon, Charles lay on an improvised bed of blankets. He gasped for breath as Judy wiped his blood-stained mouth and nose. He looked up at Captain and gasped, "I tried."

Captain touched Charles' shoulder. "Everyone appreciated you bringing us closer to God."

Angus Campbell leaned in and sniffed, "I especially appreciated your words of wisdom, Charles. Thank you for helping me understand and accept God and His Will."

Charles smiled, closed his eyes and turned his head aside.

Judy sobbed, and Mrs. Richardson tried to console her.

"Angus," said Captain, "organize a burial party."

*****

WITH EVERYONE GATHERED around the pile of rocks that protected the grave of Charles Field, Angus Campbell, his Bible in hand, said, "I will deliver the eulogy for Charles." He spoke of Charles' love of God and the love and comfort he gave to the emigrants.

Angus read from Matthew 5:4: "Blessed are those who mourn, for they will be comforted." Angus paused, "But the reality is that we will grieve forever for Charles and the others who have died on this trail. We must learn to live with their deaths as we were blessed by their lives."

Nancy sang *Amazing Grace* a cappella.

Angus spoke to Captain Bridgewater as they left the grave, "A word, sir, if I may."

Captain stopped.

"In seminary, I was taught to never defer the performance of a duty. Captain, I will take on the task of lay minister. Same as Charles, I am a Methodist. I attended seminary for two years but was not ordained. My beliefs are sometimes confused; however, I will not confuse others. Please accept me as a lay minister, but do not call me reverend."

"Welcome, Angus and thanks."

*****

AFTER THE FUNERAL for Charles Field, Judy and Captain joined the Roberts' family in their campsite, along with Nancy and Angus.

"Thank you all so much for your help and consolation today," Judy sniffed and dabbed her eyes. "Angus, Charles was so proud of you. You will make a wonderful lay minister. And thank you, Alice, for this meal. I wasn't up to preparing a meal."

"I know all too well, Judy."

Angus asked the blessing, and they settled down to their meal.

"Captain," said Judy. "You seem so solemn. Are you all right?"

"Much on my mind, Mrs. Field."

"You've scarcely touched your supper, Captain," said Alice.

"Could I have a word with you, Mrs. Roberts? In private?"

"Of course. Abigail and Nancy, please clean up and pack for tomorrow."

"I will help," said Angus.

*****

"A ROUGH WEEK," noted Captain as they moved away from the camp.

"What's on your mind, Captain? You've been wonderful to my family and me. I'll do anything I can to return your favors."

"M-Mrs. Roberts, w-would y-you m-marry me?"

"Excuse me! Captain, did you just ask me to marry you?"

"Y-Yes, ma'am."

They took a few steps before Alice said, "Captain, I enjoy your company and appreciate your help. Truth is, I rely on your help. Can't we continue as we are?"

Captain regained control of his voice. "Mrs. Roberts, I apologize. I did not intend to blurt out a proposal. I thought we could discuss marriage as rational adults."

"Are you saying you're in love with me, Captain?"

"Well, maybe. I don't know. It's been a long time." He hesitated. "You should know that I had a sweetheart. Her name was Isabella and I loved her very much. Abigail knows about Belle. She died of smallpox nearly twenty years ago." His voice trembled. "I can never forget Belle."

"And you know that my sweetheart and husband died only a month ago. I will always love Michael." Alice choked on her words and wiped her eyes.

"So you want a trail marriage of convenience. We almost have that arrangement now. Some people say that we do. Is that all you want?

Captain's face was bright red. "Well, more."

"Do you want to bed me as well?"

"I, uh… Y-Yes, ma'am, I do. You're always on my mind."

Alice laughed. "This is the strangest proposal I've ever heard of. Captain, I like you, and I must admit I've wondered about a trail marriage. I'll consider your proposal—Alice laughed again—and pray about it tonight. I'll give you an answer tomorrow night at supper, but come to supper late so I can explain to my family."

She's going to say yes!

The Enchanted Journal

Chapter 22: June 30 - Proposal

MIKE GLARED AT THE PILE of beans on his plate. "Beans again? I want meat."

"There is potato pudding and bacon," Abigail pointed out. "I cooked it myself."

"We always have bacon. I want buffalo or deer." Mike stabbed a piece of bacon with his whittling knife.

"Serve your plates," said Alice. "Nancy and Angus are taking care of themselves, and Captain will be late. I need to discuss something serious and personal with all of you."

Abigail's eyes and ears snapped to attention. Mama had never opened such a conversation before. *With Papa dead, would they be returning to Tennessee? Is that what I want? I promised Papa I'd get us to Oregon.*

"I'll get right to the point. Captain Bridgewater has proposed marriage to me."

"Mama!" blurted Abigail. "Papa has been dead for less than a month. How can you even consider a trail marriage? I can't believe it! I don't want to believe it! Please don't do this."

"I know, Abigail, I know. I think about your father every day—sometimes every minute. I still cannot accept that he is gone, but he is. I must provide for all of you and myself as well."

"But Mama…"

"Captain Bridgewater is a good man, and he needs a woman. I need a man." Abigail's head popped up, and Alice noted the shocked look on her face. "No, Abigail, not for that. I—you, all of us—need the protection and the strength of a man. Without the support of a man, we probably could not continue, and we almost certainly could not return safely to Tennessee or even Independence. We would be doomed. I cannot allow that to happen."

"I'll get us to Oregon," Abigail vowed. "I promise Oregon to Papa every night in my prayers. I'll get us there."

Alice sniffed and broke down. "Abigail, you're working impossibly hard, but we can't make it alone. We need help."

"But you loved Papa."

"Indeed I did. We met when I was a little older than you. I couldn't believe that handsome, older boy was interested in me, but we fell in love, got married, and here you are." Alice smiled at Abigail. "I will always love your papa."

Through her tears, Abigail vowed, "I'll marry only for love. You said this was a discussion, but you've already made up your mind, haven't you?"

"It is practical and necessary. I think your papa would understand and approve. He liked and respected Captain Bridgewater."

"But you don't love Captain Bridgewater."

"I like him. Life can be strange. I might even come to love Thomas."

"Is that his name? What will we call Captain Bridgewater?" asked Mike. "I don't want to call him Papa."

"He suggested you call him Captain, and your surname will still be Roberts."

"When is the wedding?" asked Abigail.

"As soon as we get to the next trading post and find a preacher. I've insisted on a preacher."

"Mama, I'm so embarrassed. How can I tell my friends? What will they say?" *Should I have accepted Jeff's offer that day? I didn't think about Mama sacrificing herself, but I should have considered it.*

199

"Mama, you don't have to marry Captain Bridgewater. He will continue to help us. Other people have offered to help."

"Abigail, this is a long and dangerous trip. Stranger and even more dramatic events may occur. We must all adapt."

Captain walked into camp just in time to hear Alice say, "I will marry Thomas Bridgewater."

Captain's smile lit up his face and he flashed it at Alice.

Abigail sobbed and ran crying into her tent.

1843

Strange events occur on the trail. Only three months on the trail and several unexpected things have happened on our train.

A family of five children was orphaned when their parents died from cholera. A man and wife who had no children took them in.

A man's wife died, leaving him with their baby. A husband died, leaving his wife pregnant. The pregnant widow soon married the widower.

A happy wedding between two young single people (16-year-old girl to 18-year-old boy)! They are determined to take on the trail together.

Two wagons left our train to travel on their own because they were impatient with our rate of travel. Three days later, we discovered them murdered, and their wagons ransacked.

My own unexpected event was meeting William Anderson! How wonderful!

Before the trail, I could never have believed or accepted such events. Most likely more to come...

The Enchanted Journal

Part 3

A New Father

The Enchanted Journal

Chapter 23: July 1 – Smith's Trading Post

CAPTAIN BLEW HIS HORN to assemble his group leaders. Abigail was the first to arrive.

"Good morning, Abigail. I'm pleased to see you."

"I do my job, Captain Bridgewater."

Well, that tells me something.

The other group leaders arrived ready for the instructions of the day.

Captain spit out his stalk of grass. "We'll be moving on to Smith's Trading Post. It's a few days away. Pegleg Smith is quite a character. He amputated his own leg many years ago. Pegleg has operated his trading post for about ten years. Don't expect much. Smith's Trading Post has a few cabins and Indian lodges. Pegleg rarely has many supplies, although he may surprise me. His prices are high, but you may need to purchase them anyway. We will not force a fast pace but will not lay-by until we get to Smith's. Pegleg is a bit of a blowhard and loves to tell tall tales, so be careful, or he will trap you and talk your ears off!"

"And now, a more important announcement."

Abigail's face turned bright red.

"I proposed to Alice Roberts, and she accepted. We'll be married at Smith's Trading Post if a preacher is there."

"Congratulations, Captain!" Terrill Johnson was the first to extend his hand. "And to you as well, Abigail. You have a fine new father."

Abigail sobbed and ran from the group.

"I'm sorry, Captain," said Terrill. "Not the best choice of words."

*****

CAPTAIN ENTERED THE JONES' CAMP. "Good morning, James, Gladys; we'll be moving on to Smith's Trading Post and should be there in a few days. Also, I have an announcement. Alice Roberts and I will get married at the post. Excuse me, please, I have others to notify."

"See, I told you," Gladys radiated confidence, "he chose the mama."

James laughed. "No, you predicted the daughter."

"And you said that Captain Bridgewater would not get married. Shows how much you're worth. Now let me go see what everyone is sayin'."

*****

"WELL, I'LL BE BLEST if it ain't Tom Bridgewater! Had the notion ya was done with the trail."

"Good afternoon, Pegleg. This is my last trip. I'm staying in Oregon this time."

"If that's so, we'd better have a drink one last time."

"Later, Pegleg. Business now. We'll be here two nights."

"Pegleg, allow me to introduce you to my fiancé, Alice Roberts. We're getting married as soon as we can find a preacher. You wouldn't happen to have a preacher around, would you?"

"Married? Ya gittin' married?"

Captain grinned. "Yes, indeed."

"Pleased to meet ya, ma'am. Good luck with this feller!"

Alice chuckled. "Thank you, Mr. Smith."

"Ha," snorted Pegleg. "No one calls me Mr. Smith. Call me Pegleg—'specially since yer marryin' Bridgewater here.

"Tom, I ain't got a Bible-beater. Had one, but he left a month ago—gave up on me! I can loan ya a broomstick to jump." Pegleg snickered.

"No broomstick. Alice insists on a preacher. Please ask around, maybe one of the other trains has a preacher."

"Say, Tom, one of yer emigrants passed through day before yesterday. Big man with a big son and small wife. Said he left yer train 'cause ya travel too slow. Traded his oxes for mules. I tried to talk him out of the trade but he insisted. Barely stayed a few hours. Was in a hurry. Said he wanted to beat ya to Oregon."

"That would've been George Cromwell. I kicked him out after his son assaulted a woman."

"Not surprised. His son was on the hunt while he was here, but even the squaws wouldn't have nothin' to do with him after the old man insulted them. The old man bought a few supplies, ammo, and whiskey. Doubt ya'll catch him 'til the mules give out."

"Don't want to catch up to George and don't care if he gets to Oregon before me. He'll be even farther ahead after our lay-by."

Captain inspected the store. To his pleasant surprise, Smith's Trading Post was well stocked.

Pegleg explained, "Jest got a big shipment."

"Pegleg, you treat my people right."

The emigrants bought salt pork, flour, corn meal, rice, potatoes, salt, sugar, and complained about the prices. Pegleg was shrewd in his dealings, and he knew that Fort Hall was a hundred miles away and had comparable prices.

With the help of two Indians, Pegleg served his customers, but he was eager to tell the children of his adventures. "Gather 'round, young'uns and listen to ol' Pegleg's story."

Mike, Henry, Ollie, and Cathy sat on the floor to listen. A few younger boys plopped down as well. Maggie shyly joined the group. Abigail and Nancy could not resist. Captain Bridgewater grinned at Pegleg's audience.

"I'm a mountain man, trapper, prospector, and horse thief," Pegleg began. "I had the biggest, baddest bunch o' horse thieves

The Enchanted Journal

around. Wonder I didn't get hung. I knew and worked with Jim Bridger, Kit Carson, and Jed Smith. Heard tell of 'em?"

Mike and Henry nodded. Henry said, "I've read about them."

Pegleg grinned, "Can't read but knowed 'em well.

"I was borned in Kentuc' but went to Missouri on my own. I joined Antoine Robidoux on a trappin' trip and we was goned two years trappin' and tradin' with Injuns. Antoine set up a tradin' post on Robidoux Pass and showed me how to do it. I been all over—even Mexico and New Mexico. I'd get me a big batch o' furs to sell and hav'ta dodge the Mex army and the Apaches.

"Ya must be wonderin' how I lost my leg. I had me a big bunch o' furs and was takin' 'em to Fort Bent but Injuns attacked. I was shot in the leg. Sure 'nuff, it turned color and stunk. I knew it had to come off. I cut it off myself. I used a red-hot bullet mold to stop the bleedin'. Some Ute Injuns chewed roots and berries and spit it on my stump. I spent that winter in an Injun teepee whittlin' this wooden leg. Did a good job of it, don't ya think?" He pulled his trousers up and waved his peg around.

"I prospected for a while in California. I even found gold! Let me tell ya how I found gold. One day I was in the desert and a sand storm came up. I must admit I got lost in the sand storm. After it blowed over, I clumbed a hill to get located. I picked up me some speckled black rocks but forgot about 'em for a few weeks. Next time I was in a town with an assayer, I had 'em assayed. They was gold! Problem was I could not 'member where my hill was. Still can't 'member; I've searched all over and can't find it.

"I ended up here about ten years ago. Before I set up, anyone on the trail had to go to Fort Hall for provisions. I also trade good and rested horses, mules, cattle, and oxen for worn-out ones. The worn-out animals recover on my good grass and water. You seen my store, now go taste some of my chow.

*****

"ALICE," SAID CAPTAIN. "I want to save you from preparing supper. Get Abigail, Mike and Sue and follow your nose." He led them to a small cabin near the dry goods store and entered.

"What's for supper, Cookie?"

At Captain's voice, a rotund Indian woman turned around and cackled. "Captain Bridgewater! No one calls me Cookie but you." She gave Captain an enormous hug.

"Cookie, allow me to introduce my fiancé, Alice Roberts. These are her children, Abigail, Mike, and Sue."

Cookie grinned at Alice. "Does fiancé mean what I think it does?"

"I 'spect so. We are to be married as soon as we can find a preacher."

"Well, sit yourself down to a bowl of my bean soup with ham and barley. I made fresh bread, and we have butter. You kids can drink milk."

"Look, Mama," said Abigail. "There are Angus and Nancy!" She stepped to their table to greet them.

"I'm not surprised," said Captain to Alice. "This is much more their lifestyle than the wagon train, and Angus has money to spend. I bet Angus is already planning something similar for Oregon City."

Angus came to Captain's chair and shook his hand. "Captain, I can conduct your wedding ceremony. I have never officiated a wedding but was trained and licensed in Ohio as part of my seminary requirements. My license is valid out here. I will be honored to solemnize your wedding."

"And I will sing," chimed in Nancy.

Alice smiled, and tears came to her eyes.

"Thank you, Angus," said Captain. "I'm in your debt."

"I am the one in debt, Captain. Thank you for all you have done for us. I can never repay you, but I can do this small favor."

"Will their marriage be legal?" questioned Abigail. "Official before God and Man? Recorded?"

"I will use the blank documents from Charles Field's books. I'll record the marriage in his journal and report it in Oregon. Yes, Abigail, it will be official and binding—a legal contract."

Cookie returned with bowls of soup and placed them on the table.

Alice studied her soup. "Is that carrots mixed with the onions and corn? I haven't seen a carrot in a long time."

"Yes'm. My little garden is out back."

"I did not see any carrots in the store, or else I would have bought some."

Cookie disappeared but soon returned with a small burlap bag. "Carrots and onions for you, Alice. My wedding present."

Alice sniffed. "My first gift! Thank you so much, Cookie! That is, may I call you Cookie?"

"Certainly! 'Specially since you are marrying Captain Bridgewater."

"I hope you are cooking tomorrow, Cookie," said Captain.

"Of course I am!"

"We'll be here for breakfast, dinner, and supper."

"I knew that as soon as you came in," smiled Cookie.

1843

We are encamped near Bear River in a beautiful area with good grass and wood. We would like to lay-by for an extra day or two but are low on food, and Fort Hall is a hundred miles away.

Matt, Sam, and I picked berries, and Ma made them into a pie. The pie was excellent but tart since we are out of sugar.

William caught many trout and shared them with us, so we had a good and different supper. He is quite a good provider and says he will get more fish tomorrow.

*****

ON LAY-BY MORNINGS, Captain Bridgewater did not blow his horn to wake everyone, but he woke up at four in the morning, anyway. Not only was this a lay-by day, but it was also Sunday. On top of that, he was getting married! Captain allowed himself an extra half hour of sleep before splashing a little water on his face and dressing for worship services. He stepped to his banked fire, intending to restart it and make fresh coffee. Instead, he glanced towards the Roberts' camp and, seeing Alice building a fire, approached her.

"Good morning, Mrs. Roberts. Mind if I join you?"

"Time you called me Alice. That is, if you still want to marry me today."

"Indeed, I do—if you'll still have me, Alice."

"Of course, I'll still have you. I'm even getting fond of you, Thomas. How about some coffee?" Alice removed the coffee pot from the fire and poured two cups.

"Remember, there is no need for you to cook today. We'll eat in Cookie's cabin.

"Her soup was delicious."

"Wait until you taste breakfast."

"You're spoiling me and making me jealous all at the same time. I can cook, you know," Alice waved her hand around the campfire. "And I can cook even better in a proper kitchen."

"I'll see that you have a house with a proper kitchen as soon as we get to Oregon. Ours will not be limited to a trail wedding; I promise you."

"I believe you," Alice beamed. "I just hope we make it to Oregon." She took a deep drink of coffee. "Let me wake up the children."

"I wish Abigail liked me."

"Oh, Abigail likes you fine—she just doesn't realize it. She is missing Michael. They were unusually close. Abigail is trying to adjust to us being together. Don't worry, she will accept you as my husband, although it may take some time."

"Not too long, I hope."

*****

The Enchanted Journal

Inside their tent and snuggled in her blankets, Abigail stretched at her mother's soothing voice outside. *Another day on the trail. No, wait. They were having a lay-by.* She glanced towards the fire and a man sitting there drinking coffee. Her father! She was about to yell "Papa!" when she realized the man was Captain Bridgewater. *Had he been there all night? Where did he sleep?*

Abigail relaxed as she remembered her mother sleeping by her side in their tent. This was awkward and difficult to handle. Captain Bridgewater was a nice man and certainly helpful to her family but he was not Papa and never would be. Abigail watched as Captain Bridgewater drank a last sip of coffee, stood, and walked away. Time to get up and get dressed. She put on her Sunday dress.

"Sue, wake up." Abigail's little sister was a sleepyhead. She did not have chores like Abigail and Mike. "C'mon. I'll help you get dressed." She pulled Sue's wannis over her head and brushed her hair. "Now let's go to breakfast." They walked to the fire. *Where was Mama?*

Abigail poured herself a cup of coffee and added a splash of milk. She poured Sue a cup of milk and added a splash of coffee and a lump of sugar. *Oh, I've got to milk the goats and cows. Where are the buckets?*

Captain came to the tent with the milk buckets in his hands. "I've milked the goats and cows." He grinned. "Are you ready for breakfast?"

Confused, Abigail stared at the empty pots and pans.

"We're having breakfast at Cookie's cabin," reminded Captain. "Dinner and supper too. No cooking for you and Alice today."

Captain called Mama 'Alice'. Something has changed.

Alice emerged from the wagon wearing a dress Abigail had not seen, and Captain rushed to help her. "You are especially beautiful today, Alice."

"Thank you, Thomas." He continued holding her hand.

Mike rolled out from under the wagon, a twelve-year-old boy who had slept in his clothes. Alice glared at him, then shrugged. "At least brush your hair, Mike."

"Let's have breakfast." Captain kept Alice's hand and led them to Cookie's cabin and its delicious breakfast aromas.

They entered Cookie's cabin just behind Angus and Nancy Campbell.

*****

CAPTAIN BRIDGEWATER WAS SURPRISED to see Pegleg Smith in the congregation. *Has Pegleg gotten religion?* There were other unknown faces in the crowd as well. *Worship services must be irregular.*

Angus looked more nervous than Captain, but he opened services with a prayer and Judy Field led the congregation in singing accompanied by Nancy on her dulcimer. After a brief message and closing prayer, Angus smiled at the assembly. "And now, it gives me great pleasure to solemnize the wedding of Thomas Bridgewater and Alice Roberts."

In the congregation, Gladys Jones nudged her husband.

With Abigail, Mike, and Sue standing nearby, the wedding ceremony took scarcely a few minutes. Alice and Thomas signed their names in Charles Field's journal as Abigail sobbed.

Captain's emigrants lined up to congratulate Alice and him.

Pegleg grinned as he shook Captain's hand. "I had a cabin prepared for you. It has a proper bed."

Captain turned bright red. "Thank you, Pegleg."

The new family, plus Pegleg and others, made their way to Alice's wagon where their friends had prepared dinner. Cookie stood with them and flashed a smile behind her delicious spread.

Angus asked the blessing and Captain Bridgewater addressed the small group. "Thank you for coming and thank you for your support. Tomorrow, we'll continue our travels after a leisurely and late start for a brief celebration of Independence Day. I hope you forgive my indulgence."

Everyone sniggered. Alice blushed but joined them in eating.

After their meal, Abigail pulled her mother aside. "Mama, where will you sleep tonight?"

Alice blushed. "Pegleg has prepared a cabin for us for tonight. With two wagons on the trail, we need to rearrange our things. I'll move my things to Thomas's wagon, and you'll have more room in the wagon and tent. On the trail, I'll be sleeping in Thomas's tent. You might even stretch out in your tent now." At five feet eight inches, Abigail was taller than her mother.

"Oh, Mama," sobbed Abigail. "This is so hard. I don't know what to do."

"You don't need to do anything, sweetie; I'm the one who must adapt and I'll be fine."

*****

"WELL, NOW THAT CAPTAIN AND ALICE are married," said James. Who will you gossip about now?"

"Hmmph! Married? Might as well have jumped over the broomstick as to have been married by the shopkeeper. He's probably not married to that highfalutin piano player either."

"Angus is now our lay minister. He says he is authorized to solemnize marriages. Who will be next?"

"I don't approve of people living in sin—trail or no trail. No good will come of this. You mark my words." She wagged her finger.

1843

We have already had three trail marriages. Today's wedding united a new widow and a long-time bachelor. Captain Shaw says that trail marriages are not unusual. He told me of two occasions when a woman married twice on the trail! How happy and yet, how tragic. I wonder how trail marriages work out after completing the trail? My guess is the trail is so challenging that it can be the 'tie that binds' thereafter.

I also wonder how many young people meet on the trail and marry once they come of age?

*****

CAPTAIN BRIDGEWATER WOKE at his customary four in the morning on Independence Day but stayed in bed an extra hour as he reviewed his plans and the status of his caravan. The emigrants and their animals were well rested and fed. Some emigrants traded worn or injured oxen for fresh ones. They were thirty-three miles from Soda Springs and would stop about halfway there.

Captain smiled. *I'm a married man. Who'd a thunk it?*

Captain dressed in his freshly washed and repaired trail clothes, thankful for the services offered by the Indians at Smith's Trading Post. His smile broadened at Alice sleeping late in their wedding cabin. She would meet him for breakfast in Cookie's cabin.

Captain walked to his wagon and deposited his church clothes. After 'Beans' Allen was killed, Captain alternated drivers for his own wagon. Today, Ollie Wells would drive for him.

Captain headed for Cookie's cabin and a cup of coffee.

Cookie smirked as she welcomed Captain and gave him a cup of coffee. "How's the old married man?"

"Wonderful, Cookie. I'm blessed."

"Ham, eggs, and pancakes?"

"Of course, but I'll wait for my family," replied Captain as he sipped his coffee. *My family.*

Soon, Alice, Abigail, Mike, and Sue joined Captain. Alice was glowing. "Good morning, Thomas. You are spoiling me."

"You look radiant, Alice." Captain bussed her cheek.

"I'm pleased you bought fresh clothes for the trail, thank you."

Abigail was wearing fresh trail clothes as well and flushed bright red as she sat at the table. "Good morning, Captain Bridgewater," leaving no doubt as to her relationship with Thomas. "Thank you for breakfast. And for my clothes," she added.

"I'm starving," added Mike as Cookie brought their breakfast to the table. "Let's eat."

The Enchanted Journal

As they left Cookie's cabin, Captain gave her a hug. Cookie hugged Alice. "Now, you take care of Captain Bridgewater." She handed Alice a sack, "Dinner."

*****

FOLLOWING BREAKFAST, Terrill Johnson acted as Master of Ceremony for the Independence Day celebration. After a brief introduction and reminder of the day's significance, Terrill read the first few paragraphs of the Declaration of Independence. Mrs. Field led everyone singing patriotic songs. Mike, Henry, and Ollie whistled *Yankee Doodle*. Pegleg had a small cannon which he fired with great gusto. Ralph Richardson played a rollicking dance song and several people danced—to the great amusement of the Indian spectators. Finally, Angus closed with a prayer for the safety of the wagon train and its people.

Thomas extended his hand, "Pegleg, thank you for your hospitality. I'll never forget it and certainly never forget you."

Alice agreed. "I've made a new friend in you, Pegleg."

For once, Pegleg was bashful. "My pleasure, Tom and Mrs. Bridgewater. Ya've give ever'one somethin' new to talk about. Now git yer people to Oregon."

*****

ABIGAIL NOTICED Captain sitting beside her mother and driving the wagon instead of his usual horseback circulation among the wagons. Alice and Captain were talking and laughing, occasionally touching each other.

Despite their shortened day, the Bridgewater train made the halfway point to Soda Springs, circled, and prepared for the night. Abigail and her mother cooked supper as Captain and Mike pitched two tents.

"Well, Abigail," said Alice. "The lay-by was wonderful, but now it's back to normal."

"This isn't exactly normal, Mama," replied Abigail. *What did she mean by saying the lay-by was wonderful?*

Captain entered the supper area, and Alice bussed his cheek. Abigail blushed.

Alice handed a laden bowl to Thomas. "Not exactly the same as Cookie's stew, but it has potatoes and carrots. The bread is from Cookie." She smiled and sat down by Captain, their legs touching.

Mama!.

As Abigail was tucking Sue into bed that night, Sue said, "Where Mama?"

I was afraid of this. What do I say?

- "Sue, remember the ceremony and blessing Angus did for Mama and Captain? They are married now. Mama will sleep with Captain Bridgewater. You and I have much more room in the tent now. On rainy nights, Mike can sleep in the tent."

"Want Papa."

"Oh, baby!" Abigail sniffed. "So do I, but he's gone to be with God now." She hugged Sue for a long time, then realized Sue was asleep and laid her down.

> Independence Day! What a fantastic time to be alive and celebrate our independence! We will arrive in Oregon in a few months and hope to bring it into the United States.
>
> Tonight we listened to speeches in honor of the men and women who first declared their independence and then fought to get it. Just think, many of those brave souls are still alive! My grandfather was a revolutionary soldier and once met George Washington. He told me he would follow George Washington anywhere.
>
> We celebrated with food and music. William is a fine dancer. We even danced a waltz! I loved being in his arms.

Abigail hoped she could find Milli in Oregon. She'd bet Milli and William married.

*****

THEY REACHED SODA SPRINGS in the middle of the following afternoon and stopped to enjoy the attraction.

Terrill Johnson quickly organized his classroom. "Just a quick lesson here and then you can enjoy Soda Springs. No arithmetic or spelling today." His students applauded.

"We're on our way to Fort Hall, and this is Soda Springs. Sometimes it's called Beer Springs. Volcanic action created Soda Springs hundreds of years ago. The water is naturally carbonated with sodium carbonate. It is alkali water and will make you and the animals sick if you drink very much of it.

"The Indians discovered Soda Springs long ago, and fur traders learned it about from them. Some people think it is medicinal and bathe in it. I'm not sure of its medicinal value but plan to bathe in it myself."

Chapter 24: July 13 – Fort Hall

ENCAMPED OUTSIDE of Fort Hall, Terrill Johnson assembled his students for their geography and history lessons.

"We are at Fort Hall in Oregon Territory," he told the class. "This river is the Snake River. It is buried deep in a canyon and there are few places where crossing is possible. One of those places is here at Fort Hall.

"A businessman from Boston, Massachusetts, Nathaniel Jarvis Wyeth, founded Fort Hall in 1834 as a fur trading post. After a few years, Wyeth sold Fort Hall to the Hudson's Bay Company. Fort Hall is now one of the largest trading posts on the Oregon Trail.

Captain tells me we will stay here for two nights to rest and resupply.

"There is a tragic story associated with the early settling of this area and somewhat related to Fort Hall. In 1836, the missionary Dr. Marcus Whitman and his wife Narcissa came west on the Oregon Trail."

Captain Bridgewater eased away from Mr. Johnson's lesson, but Alice remained.

"Narcissa Whitman and Eliza Spalding were the first white women to take the trail. They continued west and then north from here and built a comfortable mission near Walla Walla with a large house and a blacksmith shop. By 1847, sixty-six people lived there. Their mission was well received by the Indians at first, but a measles epidemic broke out in 1847 and the Indians blamed the Whitmans. The Indians killed the Whitmans and 13 missionaries. They also took 53 people hostage."

"Ugh!" said Abigail. "Are the Indians still a problem?"

"Not usually," answered Mr. Johnson. "We'll follow the trail created by Dr. Whitman's wagons, but we won't be going to their mission."

Mike cut a notch in his whittle stick. "To avoid the Indians?"

"No, to save time. Captain says we'll have enough supplies after resupplying in Fort Hall. We don't need to go to the old mission."

*****

FORT HALL WAS NOT AS NICE as Fort Laramie, but its dry goods store was full of emigrants from the Bridgewater and other trains. Abigail, Captain, and Alice replenished their supplies, and Maggie came with them. Flour, rice, coffee, and sugar were popular purchases.

Maggie was in a corner pretending to look at ribbons. Abigail stepped over to her, knowing her actual interest.

"I miss Glenn," Maggie whispered to Abigail, "but there are some cute soldiers here." She searched the room with her eyes, not moving her head.

"Maggie," Abigail scolded, "you didn't even know Glenn and you should stay away from the soldiers. You're just asking for trouble with them."

"Well, I'm glad to see some fresh faces anyway, and they seem happy to see me."

"Of course, the soldiers are happy to see you. There are few girls here, and you are pretty. They'll be talking about you for days after we leave; that is, until the next wagon train gives them someone new to talk about."

Maggie giggled. "They will talk about you, too."

"They all look at me the way Jeff did," said Abigail, "and I don't like it." She pulled her hat down on her head and patted her patch knife for assurance.

Alice interrupted their conversation. "Girls, let's get out of here and take our supplies back to camp. Thomas and I are having supper tonight with the fort commander and his wife."

*****

"COMMANDER!" CAPTAIN SALUTED. "Good to see you again. This is my wife, Alice."

"Married? *You?*"

"Yes, sir. We were married two weeks ago at Pegleg's place."

The commander's wife came into their dining room. "Anne, you remember my friend, Captain Bridgewater? Well, surprise! He is now a married man. This is his wife, Alice."

"So some lucky woman finally trapped you, Thomas. My congratulations, Alice, although I'll say Thomas got the better deal."

"Wish I had been able to be at your wedding, Thomas. Has Pegleg dreamed up any new stories?"

Thomas chuckled. "No, he just keeps embellishing his old ones."

"This calls for a celebration, Thomas. Will you have a glass of wine?"

The commander poured a glass of wine for everyone. "This calls for a toast: To the newlyweds!"

Alice took a tiny sip. The wine was sweet. She took another sip.

"One of your emigrants came through here a couple of days ago, Thomas. A big man. Raised quite a ruckus. His son was chasing after a squaw—beg pardon, ma'am. Anyway, the old man beat him—likely got away with the beating because the boy was drunk, but I suspect that's the last time the old man will beat him."

"That would be the Cromwells. I kicked them out of my train for the same reason."

"I threw them out of the fort as well. Be careful, Thomas. They're about two days ahead of you and pushing hard. I expect his mules will give out soon. If so, you'll catch them."

"Don't want to catch 'em."

"I'm glad you're camped outside the fort. There's a sickness goin' round. The grippe, our doctor calls it. Lots of coughin' and fever. Best to minimize your time in the fort."

"Thanks, I'll warn everyone."

"Now tell me about the trail, Thomas."

1843

Fort Hall is made of logs and is not as large as Fort William or as well finished. Its buildings are without windows and made of logs with mud-brick fireplaces and chimneys.

We dined with the Commander of the Fort and sat at a real table on comfortable chairs bottomed with buffalo skin. The table and chairs were the best part of the meal. Of course, we had buffalo to eat, and I am tired of buffalo now. But we also had turnips, onions, and mountain bread. Mountain bread is simply flour and water mixed together and fried in buffalo grease. We did have tea, though and stewed service berries for dessert.

William and I studied the Snake River from a tower on Fort Hall. We will follow it for many days. The river indeed looks like its namesake and we must cross it many times.

*****

"Caldron Linn? What an odd name," said Abigail, as she marveled at the turbulent falls stirring the river below. "It's beautiful, but I'm glad we're travelling on land and not by river."

"A Scottish trapper named these falls," explained Captain. "It reminded him of a waterfall in Scotland. Some people call it the 'Star Falls'. Notice how narrow the river gets at the falls. We'd never make it through the falls if we were traveling by river. Have to portage around it."

"My ancestors came from Scotland," said Alice. "the MacDonalds, just before the revolution."

"Mine too," said Angus. "The Campbells came after the Battle of Culloden in 1746. The English soundly defeated them and exiled them to the New World. Pity they lost, but maybe it was for the better that we ended up here."

Nancy smiled at Angus. "My ancestors were English," she teased.

"As were mine," said Captain.

"Mama," asked Abigail, " where are the Roberts from?"

"Michael's grandfather told him they were Welsh. Wish Grandpa Roberts had written something down. At least I have the Roberts' family Bible."

"I haven't looked at that old Bible in years. Could I see it tonight?"

"Of course.

*****

The Enchanted Journal

1843

Tonight we dined on elk! Our hunters killed two of the great beasts. William was on the hunt but did not make the kill and was disappointed. He is eager to kill an elk. I was glad to eat something other than dried buffalo meat. However, our hunters say that there is little opportunity for hunting in the days ahead.

Captain Shaw says that we will eat fresh salmon in a few days!

*****

WHAT A TREASURE! thought Abigail, as her mother handed her the worn Bible. Her great-grandfather's name, Matthew Michael Roberts, was written boldly on the first page. Never having met him, she knew him only by his name and stories told by her father. She turned the Bible slightly to better illuminate the pages by the campfire.

Turning to the page of births, she found Michael Andrew Roberts along with her aunts and uncles. Abigail smiled. Theirs was a prolific family. *How many children would she have?* She found her own name and birthday mixed in with her cousins, as well as Mike and Sue.

On the page of marriages, she touched her father's name as though she were touching his hand. Michael Andrew Roberts married Susan Alice MacDonald and their anniversary date. The last entry on the marriage page was Susan MacDonald Roberts married Thomas Edward Bridgewater, July 3, 1859, written in her mother's handwriting. *This makes their marriage official.*

Abigail turned one more page, dreading the list of deaths. At the bottom of the page was Michael Andrew Roberts died June 4,

1859, on Oregon Trail. Her mother remarried a month later. She touched his name. *Oh, Papa!*

Abigail was about to return the Bible to her mother but checked the marriages page again. She did some mental arithmetic. *I didn't realize I was born prematurely. Mama always said I was a strong, healthy baby.* She double-checked her math by counting on her fingers and turned bright red. *Mama! Papa! Shame on you!*

The Enchanted Journal

Chapter 25: July 25 – Upper Salmon Falls

JEFF CROMWELL STUDIED THE RAPID FLOW of the Snake River. "I don't know, Pa—looks dangerous to me."

"Pshaw Jeff, you're gitting as slow and careful as Bridgewater. Look, they be tracks leadin' right into the water."

"I wish we had a map. Those tracks look old."

"Don't need no map, just follow the tracks."

"I don't like it, George," said Ester. "Let's find another place to cross."

"No! We cross here."

"Maybe we should let the mules rest first," Jeff suggested.

"No, let's go. They can rest on the other side." George snapped his whip over the lead mule's head but it refused to move. He snapped it again, and the mule reared up but still didn't budge forward. The other mules adopted the same attitude, stomped their hooves and brayed.

"Pa, the mules don't think this crossing is safe."

"The damn mules ain't boss o' me! I be boss!" George flogged the mules until they entered the river, still stomping, lurching side-to-side, and braying. The prairie schooner jerked forward and heaved sideways with every beat of George's whip as Ester sat idly in the driver's seat, slack reins in her hands.

Not even halfway across, the mules had to swim. Jeff shouted, "It's too deep! Float downstream." He glanced back at his mother. The wagon was floating skewed to the current as the mules fought the current, George's whip and each other. Ester had no control of the wagon or the mules. She dropped the slippery reins and grasped the wet driver's seat with her small hands.

"I can't hold on!" Ester yelled. "I'm coming to you, Jeff!"

"No! No, Ma! Don't jump!"

Ester stood, took a deep breath, and leaped feet first into the icy water upstream of the floating wagon box. Her dress billowed in the breeze, then floated momentarily as she sank. The swift current grabbed her bulky dress and banged Ester against and then under the floating wagon. She did not emerge on the other side.

The wagon, thoroughly caulked, bobbed like a cork but took on more water with each bob. Boxes and barrels from the wagon bed were slung out, caught in the rapid current, and disappeared downstream. The wagon tongue broke and the mules were freed. Still in harness, the mules disappeared down river.

George Cromwell, downstream of the mules, released his grip on the lead. He tried to swim his horse at an angle to the opposite bank but the speeding, waterlogged wagon bed crashed into him and knocked him off his horse. A loud clunk as George's head smashed into a boulder resounded in Jeff's ears. George only jerked once. Bright red blood around his neck diluted and disappeared in the swift current. Swirling water washed George's body from the rock and downstream. The wagon, mules, his father's horse, and his father's body disappeared down the raging river.

Jeff angled his swimming horse toward the bank and the exhausted animal staggered ashore. He dismounted, collapsed on the bank, and yelled, "Papa! Mama!"

*****

CAPTAIN BRIDGEWATER WAS STUDYING the trail when Patrick Alexander came up to him.

"What are you studying so intently, Captain?"

"This is an old turnoff that usually is not used, but someone has taken it recently. I think the river is too high and rapid to cross here. We're yet a few miles upstream of Salmon Falls and will stop there. We'll cross the Snake at the Three Islands location."

"Patrick," said Captain. "I think the wagon that turned off here might be George Cromwell. He changed from oxen to mules at Smith's and his horses were big. Those are mule tracks. I did not want to catch up to him."

*****

ABIGAIL STARED AT SALMON FALLS and Thousand Springs in amazement. The falls were more of a cascade, whereas the springs emerged from the bluffs and fell nearly vertically into the Snake River. Indians were spearing salmon in the cascades of the falls. They traded fresh and dried salmon with the emigrants.

"The salmon come from the ocean," Captain explained. "Every year, mature salmon fight their way upstream to lay their eggs in freshwater. They die after laying their eggs. The eggs hatch in freshwater and the little salmon gradually make their way back to the ocean.

"This will make us an excellent campsite. We've got water, wood, lots of grass and plenty of salmon."

The Enchanted Journal

After making camp and pitching the tents, Captain said, "Abigail, grab a basket and come with me. Let's trade for some salmon. Nancy can help your mother prepare for cooking fish."

As they were leaving, Captain stopped, leaned into Alice, and gave her a buss on the cheek. Alice's eyes were wide and bright. Abigail blushed.

Captain and Abigail walked to the cascades that made up the falls. Indians were everywhere. Some speared fish, some cut and dried fish, and some traded fish. Captain found an Indian he approved of and began negotiating for salmon. They reached an agreement and the Indian handed Captain fresh salmon. Captain placed the fish in Abigail's basket. However, negotiations continued until the Indian finally shook his head and walked away.

"What was that all about?" asked Abigail.

"You." Captain grinned.

"Me?"

"Yes, he said he could tell that you were a girl, and he wanted to buy you. He offered three horses—quite a high price, I might add."

"What? He wanted to *buy* me? What did you tell him?"

"I asked for five horses, but he said that was too much."

"What? How could you…?"

Captain laughed uncontrollably, Abigail laughed anxiously, then cracked up herself. They merrily returned to camp and told their story to Alice and Nancy.

Nancy burst out laughing. "I may start calling you 'Five Horse Abigail!'"

Nancy made hushpuppies in between laughs while Alice fried salmon. Captain split a piece of cedar into boards, tacked a salmon filet onto each board, and roasted the filets close to the fire.

"This is absolutely delicious!" Alice said, wiping a bit of salmon grease on her dress. "I learn something from you every day, Thomas."

"As I do from you, Alice."

Oh, please don't kiss, Abigail thought. But they did. Nancy giggled.

Full of salmon and snuggled in her tent, Abigail read Milli's entry from Salmon Falls.

1843

We caught salmon for supper! The Indians use spears to catch the salmon. Of course, William had to try spearing salmon, and he finally got one! He was so proud!

The salmon were delicious and a welcome change. We had fried cakes—dough rolled into thin strips and fried with the salmon.

William supped with us. He loves salmon—especially the one he speared himself!

We traded for dried salmon to eat on the trail. It is much easier and saves time to trade for salmon than catching and drying them ourselves.

Captain Bridgewater could teach you a trick about roasting salmon, Abigail thought.

*****

AFTER A BREAKFAST OF FRIED SALMON and johnnycakes, Captain excused himself to visit the other trains and discuss the trail. He came across a lone tent near two freshly dug graves where a large man sat silently on a log, his head hanging down. It was Jeff Cromwell. Captain's hand dropped to his revolver but he did not remove it from its holster.

"Jeff, what's happened?"

Jeff barely glanced up. "Ma and Pa are dead. Died crossing the river upstream of the falls. Their bodies floated here and the Injuns pulled them out. Said their bodies would mess up the fishing."

"I'm sorry."

"I doubt it. You killed them when you kicked us out of the train. You hoped we would die.

Captain kept his hand on his revolver. "I did no such thing, Jeff. Your fate was in your own hands. George's hurry to beat me to Oregon caused his death. I had nothing to do with it."

Jeff was silent. Captain glanced around his camp. Jeff had nothing but a horse, a bedroll, his rifle, and revolver.

"What will you do now, Jeff?"

"Oregon was Pa's dream, not mine. I don't want to be a farmer in Oregon. I'm going to California. Maybe prospect a bit. I don't know, but I'll find something more exciting than farming."

"We're going on to Oregon. Don't think you can rejoin us. Nothing has changed in that regard."

"Don't want anything to do with you. Heard you married the mama, though, and not the girl." Jeff grinned.

"I meant what I said about Abigail. If I ever see you near her, I'll shoot you. Should have shot you after you assaulted her."

"If you had, you'd be dead now. Ma and Pa would still be alive. Pa would be captain of the train."

"Don't mislead yourself about that." Captain Bridgewater turned and left to find other trains.

*****

ABIGAIL DID NOT TAKE THE NEWS about Jeff well. "I thought he was far ahead of us," she fretted.

"George probably wore out his mules and was forced to take lay-bys. He didn't have a map and made a poor decision to cross the Snake River upstream of here. He's not the first to make that mistake—was following old tracks."

"Mrs. Cromwell seemed a decent Christian woman," said Alice. "Not exactly warm and friendly, though. Her life with Mr. Cromwell and Jeff must not have been pleasant."

"Abigail, I doubt Jeff will bother you, but stay close to camp and never be alone. Keep your pa's revolver near you and use it if Jeff comes near. I reminded him I will shoot him on sight if he comes near you."

"Don't worry, Captain Bridgewater. I'll be careful." *I hope Jeff doesn't join David Murray's wagon train, but Captain Bridgewater probably warned Mr. Murray about Jeff.*

> I hold my breath every time we cross water. William usually crosses the water at least twice: once with me and again with his parents and wagon. I definitely feel safer when William is with me, but I do not like him crossing twice. William says he can swim well and his horse is a strong swimmer as well.

*****

Captain Bridgewater's horn woke Abigail from a deep sleep. She fumbled for the revolver and found it. Relieved and now awake, Abigail returned to the routine of the trail. She found Sue near her and remembered that her mother was in Captain's tent. *Oh, Mama!*

Abigail put on her new trail clothes and helped Sue with her wannis. She peered cautiously out of her tent. Her mother was relighting the banked fire, and Nancy was already there. It was time to milk the goats.

Fried salmon was tasty, but they had eaten nothing else since Salmon Falls. *A bit of buffalo would be bodacious.*

Captain explained his plans at breakfast. "We're on our way to Three Island Crossing. Don't be intimidated when you see the crossing. The Snake is wide but is shallow now. The north side of the Snake has better water and grass than the south. There are three islands, and we'll ford from one to the next.

As the train moved slowly toward Three Island Crossing, Abigail noticed the many relics of wagons and discarded implements along the trail. In particular, heavy iron items lined the trail. The many crossings of the Snake River were taking their toll on wagons and heavy loads.

"Angus," said Captain. "Take Abigail and Nancy shopping."

"Sir?"

"Look over all those discarded items, tools, wagon parts and whatever. See if there's anything useful or in better condition than what we have. We can't add much weight, but maybe we can trade up. Be sure to get wood for repairs and the fire."

When the trio returned, Captain asked, "Find anything interesting?"

Abigail waved pieces of harness. "It was rather picked over, but these pieces of harness might repair ours."

Nancy held up a partial bolt of cloth. "Enough cloth for two bonnets!"

"Lessons to be learned out there," said Angus. "Henry Wells was making a list of things people threw away. These are things I should stock in my store, so I asked him for a copy. He has quite a notebook of the trail. I found some decent boards and collected firewood."

Sandlin

Handwritten margin notes (partially legible): "Why is there so much affection & demonstration of this? Man is the woman's previous husband, whom she loved!"

Chapter 26: Fort Boise

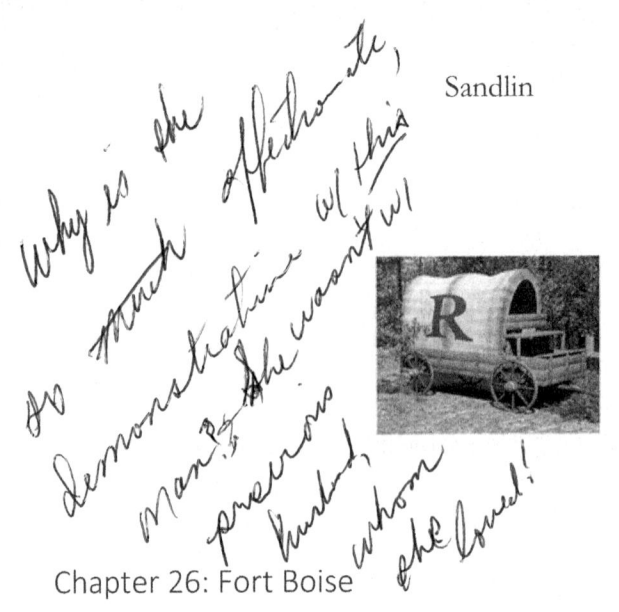

"FORT BOISE WAS OVER THERE," Captain pointed to log cabin ruins. "It was a Hudson's Bay Company fur trading post that competed with Fort Hall. It flooded a few years ago and they abandoned it. There is no point going there now. But this is a good place for us tonight with water, wood, and grass. We'll stop early." He helped Alice from the wagon and held her close for a moment.

Abigail blushed and interrupted, "I'll help you with supper."

Alice bussed Thomas' cheek and stepped to the rear of the wagon to unload her kitchen equipment.

"Guess what we're having for supper?" Alice teased. "Dried salmon, but that's the last of it."

1843
We have arrived at Fort Boise after 130 miles of trail from Three Island Crossing. The Boise River Valley was a welcome relief.

Fort Boise is a series of low adobe buildings and is smaller than Fort Hall, but it seemed cleaner. We have good water and good grazing for our animals.

The Enchanted Journal

> We need supplies, as we are almost out of meat, sugar, and flour. Even our dried salmon is almost gone. Papa says prices are high. He bought cornmeal and sugar from the store and a plant called camas from the Indians. He said the beef prices were too high. Instead of buying beef, he and William went hunting and, fortunately, killed a buffalo. They call this 'making meat!'

*****

ABIGAIL CLOSED MILLI'S JOURNAL and retrieved her father's Hawken rifle from the wagon. She was tired of salmon and there would be light for several more hours.

Captain had finished erecting his tent and spotted Abigail. "Going hunting?" he asked.

"I think there are buffalo nearby," Abigail answered.

"Mind if I join you?" Captain removed his Hawken from his wagon. "Hold off on that salmon, Alice, while Abigail and I hunt."

"Been reading that journal again, Abigail?"

"Yes, sir, Captain Bridgewater." Abigail saddled Jake, and they rode away from camp.

After a couple of miles, Captain pointed. "Over there."

A few large dark shapes moved slowly in the tall grass.

"We'll ride a little closer, then dismount and crawl. I know you're an excellent shot. Shoot just behind the front leg—same as a deer. We'll each kill one buffalo. Ready?"

"Yes, sir." Abigail knew well that Captain Bridgewater was playing up to her and wanted her to like him. *I do like you, Captain Bridgewater. I just miss Papa.*

They crawled to about a hundred yards from the small herd of a dozen buffalo. Captain indicated he would take down a young cow. Abigail selected a similar one towards the rear of the herd.

"You shoot first, whenever you are ready," whispered Captain.

Abigail pulled the set trigger, took a deep breath, aimed, and pulled the hair trigger. The Hawken roared, belched its flame, smoke, and deadly lead, and kicked Abigail's shoulder. Captain's

235

shot followed immediately. Two young buffalo lay on the ground. The other buffalo moved along slowly. *Never!*

"Congratulations, Abigail! You can hunt with me anytime."
Papa would be so proud.

*****

"HOT SPRINGS," ANNOUNCED CAPTAIN to his group leaders. "Don't drink the water. Just cook, bathe, and wash in it. The minerals will make you sick if you drink it."

Back in his own camp, Captain warned Alice. "That water really is hot. You can cook in it. No need to build a fire."

"I can see the steam. Think I'll wash clothes." *In chemical water?*

"I'll get buckets of hot water." Captain unloaded the heavy wash pot, and filled it with hot water bucket by bucket. "Tell me what to do and I'll help you." *Never.*

"You can tell newlyweds when the man helps wash clothes!"

Captain looked to the next wagon and saw Angus helping Nancy wash clothes. "I suppose so," he chuckled.

> At Hot Springs, we did not need a fire! The water is so hot that food can be cooked in it! We just put a bit of salmon and camas plant in a pot of fresh water and placed the pot in the hot springs.
>
> William ate supper with us. He likes the camas plant and ate several with his salmon.
>
> We found many hawthorn berries. They are the size of a cherry with the flavor of an apple. Mama made a berry cobbler in our Dutch oven but William saw her so I could not claim to have cooked it!

The Enchanted Journal

*****

"SAY GOODBYE TO THE SNAKE RIVER, Alice," said Captain. This is *Farewell Bend* where we turn northwest from the Snake and go up Burnt River to the Grande Ronde Valley. Burnt River will be a tough, rocky ascent, but the Grande Ronde Valley is beautiful.

"Burnt River?"

"Burnt River flows in a canyon that has reddish black walls. Looks burnt. Sometimes we'll be driving in the riverbed. Good grass and wood."

A few miles later, Alice said, "The colors are beautiful, Thomas, but your memory is truly amazing. You rarely look at a map or notes, but you always know where we are."

"Oh, I have maps and notes, all right. Wouldn't want to get lost out here. We'll be at the Grande Ronde Valley soon. You'll love it."

1843

We enhanced our diet with wild duck! Papa and William killed several with their shotguns. I found clams and boiled them. We roasted camas mixed with berries. Our fancy meal was a welcome change from dried salmon and dried buffalo and cheered everyone.

Chapter 27: Aug 20 – Grande Ronde Valley

ABIGAIL WAS IMPRESSED by the Grande Ronde Valley, particularly after fighting their way through the Burnt River Canyon. The Grande Ronde Valley was a nearly circular plain covering perhaps 20 miles in every direction and surrounded by mountains. Two beautiful rivers ran through it, and timber lined its banks. But first, they descended a steep hill using ropes and locked wagon wheels.

Captain selected a pleasant campsite near the Grande Ronde River. "There are geese by the river. I'll try to get a couple for supper. Abigail, are you with me?" He scooped up a stalk of grass.

"Yes, Captain Bridgewater. Let me get my shotgun."

Captain and Abigail followed the river. Captain paused a moment and removed the grass from his lips. "Abigail, I truly love your mother. Our marriage is not merely a convenience."

Abigail blubbered, her throat closing up. "Yes, Captain. I'm coming to realize that."

"Look!" A flock of geese appeared on their left. Both automatically cocked their shotguns, raised them, and fired both barrels. Three geese fell. Captain waded into the shallow water and retrieved them. "One of my shots missed," admitted Captain with a chuckle. "But we'll eat well tonight."

The Enchanted Journal

Back at camp, Captain cleaned the geese and made spits to roast them. Alice had traded cloth with the Indians for potatoes and corn. Nancy, Angus, and Mike had picked many berries. They would have a fine supper.

Captain speared a potato with his Arkansas toothpick. "The Whitmans taught the Cayuse to farm, especially potatoes. Before the Whitmans, the Cayuse were ignorant nomads."

Alice cleared her throat. "Thomas and I have an announcement."

What could this mean? Oh, no, don't tell me…

Alice took Thomas' hand, her eyes bright. "I am pregnant! Thomas and I are having a baby."

"Mama!" Abigail blurted.

"Don't be surprised, Abigail. I'm not too old to have a baby—just as you are not too young.

"Mama!"

Nancy moved to Alice's side and hugged her. Congratulations!"

Angus joined Nancy and she took his hand. "I'm pregnant as well," she announced with a smile.

Thomas and Angus shook hands, both grinning.

How many more are pregnant? I hope we get to Oregon City soon. I helped the midwife deliver Sue when I was twelve but I couldn't do it by myself. I need to discuss this with Mrs. Richardson. Silly, neither Mama nor Nancy is showing; these babies will be born in Oregon City.

1843

I write from the Grande Ronde, a beautiful round valley filled with horses and Indians. The Indians brought baskets of food, especially corn and camas.

Today, we learned how to harvest and cook the camas that grow wild in the moist meadow of

Sandlin

the Grande Ronde. There are so many camas that the entire meadow is colored with them. Two Indian women showed us how to identify the camas and dig them up with a pointed stick. The camas can be roasted in a pit or boiled. It looks and tastes like a sweet potato or fig.
William prefers the pit-roasted camas.

*****

GLADYS PLACED HER WASHPOT beside Mary Wells' pot and prepared to wash a few clothes.

"Gladys, have you heard the news?" asked Mary.

Gladys promptly forgot about the clothes. "What news?"

"Alice Rogers—well, Bridgewater—is pregnant."

"I'm not surprised," said Gladys. "How far along is she?"

"They were married seven weeks ago, so only a few weeks."

"Of course." *Hah, probably much farther along than that. We'll see.*

"And Nancy Campbell is pregnant too."

Of course she is. I knew that already. "Thank you for telling me. I must give them my best wishes and offer my help."

*****

The Blue Mountains were a formidable obstacle to emigrants on the Oregon Trail and were the last mountain range the pioneers had to cross. The route through the mountains passed over Crawford's Hill.

Abigail caught up to Terrill Johnson as he walked by his oxen. "Mr. Johnson," she asked, "might I have a word with you?"

"Certainly, Abigail. Is this group leader's business?" He laughed. He and Abigail were the latest appointees to the group leaders and the most different.

Terrill removed his wet kerchief mask. "Whew, those dead cattle sure stink, but I don't want to talk through the mask."

"I agree." Abigail removed her own mask.

240

The Enchanted Journal

"What's on your mind, Abigail?"

"Do you still plan to open a school in Oregon City?"

"I do. I'll teach the upper grades and Ellen will teach the lower grades. I'll search for a building as soon as we get to Oregon City."

"Will you have a place for me in your school?"

Terrill laughed. "As a student or as a teacher?"

"Oh, as a student. My education is not enough to teach."

"I disagree. Ellen appreciates your help with her students, and she has often remarked that you are already an excellent teacher."

"But I need more education myself."

"You are already well educated, and I can only extend it slightly, but I will try if you help Ellen with the younger students."

"Thank you, Mr. Johnson."

"Oh, and Abigail, please encourage Maggie and Henry to enroll at my school. Tell Henry that I once worked as a newspaper reporter and can show him methods of reporting." He laughed. "Tell Maggie that boys will be in the classes."

Abigail snickered as she re-tied her mask.

Terrill retied his mask. "Ah, that's better. I enjoyed talking with you Abigail, but the stench is making me sick. We need a breeze."

They got past the aroma of dead beasts and a light breeze removed its last traces. Captain Bridgewater located a suitable site, and they halted for the day.

1843

We are leaving the beautiful Grande Ronde Valley and ascending the Blue Mountains.

Indians appeared soon after we stopped for the day. They brought fresh buffalo! Of course, they wanted to trade and visit. We traded for potatoes—the first we have had in a long time. The potatoes were from the Whitman's Garden.

**Violin and dancing fascinates the Indians.
I love dancing with William! He is the best
dancer in our train, but I don't want to share him.**

*****

At their morning meeting, Captain advised his group leaders, "We'll be taking the traditional Rocky Pass and Emigrant Hill route. Rocky Pass is a steep downhill and we'll have to lock two wheels. Emigrant Hill is the opposite and we'll double the ox teams. I think we can do it without unloading the wagons, but this will be a long and difficult day, so let's get to it."

As they reached the onset of Rocky Pass, Captain went to the wagon Alice was driving. "Alice, best to let me drive. You should walk." He helped her from the wagon, locked the two rear wheels with chains, and climbed back aboard to begin the slide.

Alice, Abigail, Mike, and Sue walked down Rocky Pass remaining up-slope and slightly behind the wagon. Sue held tight to Abigail's and Mike's hands.

A little creek ran clear at the bottom of Rocky Pass. "We'll take our nooner here," announced Captain to the group leaders. "Get buckets of water before the oxen drink. Boil the water."

Captain pointed up Emigrant Hill. "There is the tombstone of four-year-old Elva Ingram who died of cholera in 1852."

Abigail burst into tears for little Elva—only a year older than her little sister, Sue.

"Her train lost ten people to cholera. Must have used some really foul water. Maybe not water from this creek, but let's not take chances."

After the nooner, Captain blew a squawk on his horn to signal the ascent of Emigrant Hill. Two teams of oxen pulled each prairie schooner. The drivers walked alongside the oxen instead of sitting in the wagon.

The Enchanted Journal

1843

Today we were challenged by a steep descent, Rocky Pass, followed by a steep ascent, Emigrant Hill.

In some places, Rocky Pass was almost perpendicular and other places the switchbacks reminded me of winding stairs. We zigged and zagged all the way down with wheels locked. Our animals' hooves suffered from the stony path. Fortunately, there was water at the bottom of Rocky Pass.

To ascend Emigrant Hill, we had to double the ox teams.

After such a long day, we were late making our encampment at Broom Creek.

William ate supper with us. I had scarcely seen him all day. He worked hard to help everyone down Rocky Pass and up Emigrant Hill. He is a strong, hard worker and everyone treats him as a grown man. But tonight William was exhausted and hungry. I prepared him a generous plate of buffalo and camas.

*****

ON THE WAY TO ECHO MEADOWS, Abigail joined Angus beside his oxen.

"Angus, could you become fully ordained?"

"With a little more study, vows, and certification, yes."

"Will you?"

"No, but I will volunteer to be a lay minister in Oregon City and serve more often than I did in the past."

"Why don't you want to be ordained? Are you still confused about some aspects of our religion?"

"There is no answer for many of my questions, so I simply accept Methodist doctrine. But there are two other considerations. Ministers do not get paid for their efforts. Or, if paid, their salary is tiny. No one lives on a minister's salary."

"I forgot about that. In Tennessee, our circuit preacher was a farmer. People often donated provisions to him, but not money. He farmed for a living."

"Yes, it will be that way in Oregon, too. Dr. Buck—remember him?—is trying to get preachers a salary, but is struggling himself."

"What will you do to earn a living in Oregon?"

"Not farming, that's for sure. No, I still plan to be a shopkeeper. I actually like shopkeeping and look forward to the challenge of developing my business. Besides, I want Nancy to have the best of everything—in particular, another piano, and shopkeeping is more profitable than farming."

"But how will you get goods to sell? Didn't you lose most of your merchandise to the trail?"

"I still have some, but Nancy and I have written to our fathers inviting them to become partners in our Oregon store. I feel certain that they will join us. They can ship merchandise from the East Coast and New Orleans down to the Isthmus of Panama, freight it across the Isthmus, and then sail it up to Oregon. Shipping that way is more expensive than the trail, but is faster and will become even quicker and cheaper in the next few years."

Angus was smart, and he had a plan. *I should have known.* He might not be as big or as strong as some of the other men, but he would prosper. Henry Wells was like Angus. Henry would get bigger and would prosper. He was a good young man, smart, and dependable. Whoever Henry married would marry well.

"Then why did you come on the trail?"

"Adventure," Angus grinned.

*****

The Enchanted Journal

ECHO MEADOWS WAS A POPULAR place to stop for a nooner and offered good grazing for the animals.

"Do you remember Mr. Johnson teaching about the Whitman mission?" asked Captain of Abigail. "It was east of us some fifteen miles. There is no mission now and we're in good shape with our supplies, so we will proceed to Fort Walla Walla."

We are at the Whitman Mission! I was so excited to see the Mission and meet Mrs. Whitman. She was the first white woman to cross the Oregon trail and traveled it in 1836 before the trail was improved. We plan to stay here several days before departing for Fort Walla Walla.

The Whitman Mission was built to minister to the Cayuse Indians. It has a large adobe Mission House and a smaller adobe house, a gristmill, a blacksmith shop, and a sawmill. The grounds include an orchard, millpond, irrigation ditch and extensive garden. Everything is green and beautiful—by far the most civilized place since Independence.

The sawmill fascinated William, and he studied it in action for several minutes. I could scarcely pull him away.

I met Dr. Marcus Whitman briefly. He is a fine man, and Mrs. Whitman loves him with all her heart.

Mrs. Whitman had a tea with biscuits for the ladies, and I was honored to attend.

> **I will be sad to leave the Whitman Mission, but it is only seven miles to Fort Walla Walla and the next bit of civilization.**

*****

ABIGAIL CLOSED MILLI'S JOURNAL. "Captain," she asked, "did you know the Whitmans?"

Captain got a strange look in his eyes. "I first met Marcus Whitman in 1843 as he led a wagon train to the Columbia River. He had already been up and down the various trails several times—it wasn't even known as the Oregon Trail in those days. I learned a lot from Marcus. He was a good man, a good leader, a devout Christian, and a good doctor."

Captain chuckled. "Marcus was also a good trader. Don't get me wrong, he ministered to the Indians and any emigrants that came his way, but he profited from selling and trading to the emigrants."

"Narcissa Whitman was beautiful inside and out," Captain said wistfully. "And sing! Oh, my! I was 28 years old when I met Narcissa and still angry at the world for killing my sweetheart with smallpox. Narcissa was 37 and still mourning her drowned daughter. Narcissa adopted seven Sager children who had been orphaned along the trail in 1844. She converted me. I would have done anything for Narcissa.

"Narcissa tried to help the Cayuse Indians, but they killed her, Marcus and eleven others in 1847 right there in the mission where she had helped them. The Indians captured everyone else—53 people, including children—and held them for ransom for a month. The Whitman Massacre led to the Cayuse War, and I'm ashamed to admit that I took part in it. May God forgive me."

"I'm certain God has forgiven you, Captain." Abigail gave him a hug. *No wonder we're not going to the Mission.*

"After the Whitman Massacre, no one goes to the mission anymore. Our trail from here goes due west to the John Day River and Deschutes River, then to the Dalles."

"Dalles?"

"A French word for sluice or gutter or rapids. At the Dalles, people put everything on a raft and floated down the Columbia River. It was dangerous, with multiple rapids and portages. Many rafts, wagons and lives were lost there. Some still choose to raft down the river. I've done it before, but I won't do it again. I'll pay the five-dollar toll and use the Barlow Toll Road. The toll road is longer and still difficult, but much safer."

*****

ALICE SMILED as Abigail read Milli's journal. *I'm so glad she found that journal. It's made a difference. Perhaps Milli has even softened Abigail.*

Captain approached and tipped his hat. "Need any company?"

"Thank you, Thomas. He sat beside her and she kissed him. They watched the young folks stroll to the river to fish.

"They really are fine children, aren't they? And they do seem to be our children—even Angus."

Thomas laughed. "I still can't believe that Nancy and Angus took on the Oregon Trail with so few skills and no experience."

"You've pulled all of us through. Now, what lies ahead?"

"About two weeks of trail to Oregon City."

"Still planning to farm? Won't farming be boring?"

"Alice, my plan is to be with you and raise our child. Our life will not be boring."

Chapter 28: Fort Walla Walla

THEY CAME TO THE COLUMBIA RIVER and remained on its south side but turned west.

"Oh, my," said Alice. "What a beautiful sight. So clear."

"Fort Walla Walla is just ahead where the Walla Walla River meets the Columbia River," Captain pointed ahead. "You can barely make out the fort against the cliffs. This is the third version of it. Originally, it was a fur trading post for the North West Company. Hudson Bay Company bought it and renamed it Fort Walla Walla. When Hudson Bay abandoned it, the army took it over. It has good grass, water, and timber as well as stables, a blacksmith, dry goods stores, and a sawmill. We'll lay-by an extra day."

*****

ON THE TRAIL TO FORT WALLA WALLA, Abigail caught up to Maggie. "We're going to make it, Maggie! Captain says we'll be in Oregon City in three weeks."

"I hope there are some cute soldiers at Fort Walla Walla."

"Maggie," scolded Abigail. "You stay away from them. You're too young and they're unlikely to be gentlemen."

"I'm just going to look. No harm in looking."

"Maggie, what are your plans for Oregon City?"

The Enchanted Journal

"First, I'll help Papa build a house and farm. Then I'll go back to school for a year or two. After that, I'm not sure."

"You could be an artist; well, you already are an artist, but you can earn money with your art."

"I don't want to be a farm girl the rest of my life," said Maggie. "I like the idea of being an artist, but I need to improve my painting with oils. I can probably find work in the city. You know, sewing, cooking, governess, something like that? The same stuff we do on the farm, but in the city where there are more people. Different people. I don't want to marry a farmer. What about you?"

"Same thing as you for now. Captain wants to buy a farm that already has a house. Maybe he can find something. A house with a stove and a bed sounds wonderful. Perhaps I'll go back to school for a while—even become a teacher. I don't want to be a farmer's wife either, but I'll have a small garden."

"I don't want to teach. The kids are too bad."

"Mama says that the sewing machine will change everything. She wants a sewing machine and I'm sure Captain will get her one." Abigail laughed. "He gets Mama anything she wants. She says she might even go into the seamstress business. I could help her, but that's not what I want to do."

"Oregon City may have jobs we've never thought of. We'll soon find out."

"I learned about exciting new ideas in Memphis and St. Louis," said Abigail. "Times are changing. We had a daguerreotype made in Memphis; I could learn to make those likenesses. I watched a telegraph operator in St. Louis. Oregon must need many surveyors. Tinsmith, silversmith, jeweler, or potter might be interesting."

"But all those jobs are for men."

"We did a man's job on the trail, didn't we?"

"Well, you did."

"We all did what we had to do."

"Mama says my most important job is to find a good husband," said Maggie. "I'm going to concentrate on that. Besides, it will be fun."

"Papa called it 'marrying well'. Don't rush yourself, Maggie."

1843

We arrived at Fort Walla Walla and I am a bit disappointed. It is just another fur trading post and not really a true army fort. Even so, I was impressed to see chickens, turkeys, pigeons, goats, and pigs.

We made a delicious meal of pork, cabbage, turnips, bread and butter and real tea. William and his family joined us. I ate a muskmelon for the first time and loved it—so sweet.

The Columbia is a beautifully clear river and flows smoothly at the fort. Once away from the fort, the timber disappears and is replaced by banks of rocks and bluffs.

*****

The Deschutes River is a tributary of the Columbia River. Crossing the Deschutes River could be difficult, and emigrants often stopped to rest and make plans. They floated wagons across the river half empty, so two trips were necessary. It took most of the day to cross, even with the help of the Indians.

"Load up," said Captain to his group leaders. "Let's move up that hill for better grass to reward our animals."

"Indians are spearing salmon in the Columbia," Captain told Alice. "I'll trade for some for supper. We'll be at the Dalles in two days." He bussed her cheek. "I'll be back in a few minutes. Abigail, Nancy, get us a good fire going for grilled salmon."

Angus grabbed a basket and followed Captain. "I will go with you. Reminds me of my shopkeeping days."

"Thank you, Captain, for accepting Nancy and me into your wagon train. You, Michael, Alice, and Abigail have got us this far, despite my lack of skills. I am in your debt."

"You've come a long way, Angus. Frankly, I wondered if you would make it, but you learned a lot, and we're almost done. You'll make it."

"I will buy the fish. Nancy loved the way you grilled them on the cedar plank. Show me once more how to do it."

Part 4

Around the Mountain

The Enchanted Journal

Chapter 29: Sept 4 – Camp Dalles

In 1846, Sam Barlow got official permission from the Provisional Government to build the Mount Hood Toll Road. Barlow hacked out a narrow one-way road for 150 miles through forests, rivers, and marshy meadows from The Dalles to Oregon City. He charged $5 a wagon and 10¢ a head for livestock, which infuriated the pioneers. The first year, 145 wagons and 1600 head of cattle used the toll road. Barlow operated the toll road until 1848, when he turned it over to the state, but the state did not maintain it well. The Barlow Toll Road had been improved since 1846 but was still difficult, especially a steep downhill called Laurel Hill.

"Abigail," said Captain. "How did Milli get down the Columbia River?"

Abigail opened Milli's journal and found the latest entry.

1843
Our float down the Columbia River began with clear water and beautiful scenery. However, at the Chutes, we had to unload and carry our baggage

and the boat for half a mile to avoid huge rocks and rapid current. We hired Indians to help make this portage. Five miles later, another portage and more Indians were waiting to be hired.

At the Dalles, two immense rocks with the river flowing rapidly between them stopped us. Again, we were forced to make a portage. The river current is so swift that whirlpools are everywhere.

I witnessed a terrible crash of two rafts bearing wagons. All was lost because of the reluctance to make the portage, and two emigrants were killed. The emigrants were not of our party but lost everything near the finish after surviving the long trail.

We finally made camp, but the winds blew so fiercely that conversation, even with William, was difficult. I am exhausted and hope I can sleep after this long, hard day.

"Just as I remembered," said Captain. "Milli was lucky. I'm not doing it again."

*****

"When Barlow built his toll road," Captain informed his group leaders, "there already was a trail from the Dalles to this valley, the Tygh Valley. The Tygh Indians lived here. Here's where we pay the first toll."

"First?" asked Abigail. "You mean there will be more?"

"I'm afraid so. But the toll road is still better than the river."

"Captain, some of our people are out of money."

"I know," said Captain. "Angus Campbell has offered to make small loans and remain quiet about them."

"That's generous of Angus," said Fred Wells. "I always thought he had money. What interest rate?"

"No interest, but he expects to be repaid."

"Is Angus planning to be a banker?"

"No, still a shopkeeper. Of course, he hopes you will be customers at his store."

Angus and Nancy were popular, and a murmur of agreement circulated among the group leaders.

"If we're lucky, the trains in front of us have cleared the road," said Captain. "If not, we'll clear the road for the next train."

Tolls paid; the Bridgewater caravan moved on. The toll road was not smooth or level but was relatively clear, and the train made good time until arriving at Laurel Hill.

*****

CAPTAIN BRIDGEWATER STARED down the steep hill—nearly a cliff—and addressed his group leaders. "Laurel Hill is the worse part of the Barlow Toll Road—perhaps the worst part of the entire Oregon Trail. Even the name is wrong—those plants are rhododendrons, not laurels. This is almost bad enough to make me not take the toll road, but we can get down it if we are careful." Captain Bridgewater reminded the emigrants of Frank Allen's death on Windlass Hill.

At its top, Laurel Hill had a mass of rhododendrons, but the sides were bare and steep. The hill dropped 2000 feet in five paths called chutes, each about a mile long. Each chute was three to five feet deep, and the slope was 60% in some places. Large rocks were scattered along each chute. Sharp-edged rocky rubble made the chutes even more dangerous.

"Abigail," instructed Captain. "You and Mike unhitch our oxen and lead them down that trail." He pointed to a narrow switchback path. "Wait at the bottom of the hill for the wagon, hitch up the team, and drive to camp. Then come back up the hill to help others with their oxen. We'll be doing this all day."

As at Windlass Hill, the emigrants tied ropes to the wagons, wound the ropes around trees and slowly played out the rope.

The Enchanted Journal

Every tree showed rope burns from previous users. They tied a tree to the wagon and dragged it as an anchor. All four wheels were locked. Even with all this resistance, the wagon would slide down the chute. One by one, they slid every wagon down Laurel Hill.

Captain staggered into camp, exhausted, and plopped down on a stump.

Alice gave him a long hug, a bowl of stew, and a cup of coffee. "I love you, Thomas Bridgewater. I could hardly breathe while watching you on that mountain."

"We've completed the worse parts of the trail, Alice. We are nearly there and it's a good thing because I am exhausted." Captain poured a dram of whiskey into his coffee. "I hope you understand."

Alice held out her coffee cup. "I do."

*****

THE SANDY RIVER was indeed sandy—nearly quicksand, but crossed by a bridge—another toll bridge.

"You don't have to use my bridge," said the toll taker. "But I recommend it."

Most of the emigrants were out of money and provisions. They needed to get to Oregon City soon instead of spending the day fighting to cross the Sandy River. Angus loaned money and bought items from others as necessary to proceed on the bridge.

Captain found a suitable site, and the emigrants stopped for their last night on the trail. Alice and Abigail unpacked the wagon for supper and sleeping while Captain and Mike pitched the tents.

Alice grunted as she lifted the cast-iron Dutch oven from the wagon. "I'll be glad to not live out of a wagon. This may be our last night on the trail, but we'll be living out of the wagon and sleeping in a tent for at least a few more nights. Thomas promised a house as soon as possible."

"We made it, Mama! Two thousand miles in five months. Papa was right—it was a grand adventure; he would be so proud."

"I still miss Michael so much, Abigail. It's the strangest feeling—missing Michael, loving Thomas, carrying Thomas's baby.

Missing Tennessee, but excited to be in Oregon and about to begin a new life."

"What if we had stayed in Tennessee? Would Papa still be alive?"

"I wonder about that myself. Maybe it was just Michael's time to go—that's what some people believe. Michael might have died in Tennessee and we'd be trying to scratch out a living on that small farm. I—or you—might get married just to survive. Who knows? All I really know is that I'm glad to be in Oregon and married to Thomas."

"Me too, Mama. Captain is not Papa, but I love him."

Captain's horn squawked from the center of the wagon corral.

"I love him, too, but isn't that horn awful?"

*****

"I'M NOT MUCH AT SPEECHIFYING," began Captain Bridgewater as he faced the emigrants gathered around him.

"You've been giving us speeches for two thousand miles!" yelled someone. The crowd guffawed.

Captain held both hands high. "We made it!" he shouted. "I've done the Oregon Trail other times, but this is the one I'll remember the most." He took Alice's hand and kissed her. Everyone applauded.

"And now," said Captain solemnly, "let us pause a moment in memory of those who did not finish the journey."

Abigail only half heard Captain's words. *We made it, Papa!*

"This time tomorrow, we'll be on the outskirts of Oregon City. I know you are eager to find a place to settle. Some have already left our train to make their claims. Be patient and make good choices. By the way, follow your own schedule tomorrow," Captain chuckled.

"Finally, before we begin the celebration, let me say how much I enjoyed getting to know you. Together, we've accomplished something special that will bind us in lasting friendship."

Someone began a "Hip Hip Hooray" chant and everyone joined in.

The Enchanted Journal

Ralph Richardson took up his fiddle and people began dancing. Emigrants from a nearby train trickled over to the Bridgewater train.

Abigail found her mother and Captain in the crowd around the dancers. *Mama is the prettiest lady here and here I am, standing by her wearing my trail clothes. What is wrong with me?*

"Well, you've made it to Oregon, Abigail," congratulated Captain. "What's next for you?"

"I'm not sure. I guess it's back to being a farm girl or maybe finding a job in town."

"You seem troubled," noted her mother. "You should be happy. What's wrong?"

"Captain," blurted Abigail, "may I live with you and Mama? I can work on the farm and help with your new baby."

"Oh, Abigail," said Captain in a raspy voice. "Of course you'll live with us. Is that what's been bothering you these past few days? I can't imagine life without you. I love you, Abigail."

Alice wiped a tear from her eye and hugged Abigail. "Someday, Abigail, you may choose to leave us and be on your own, but we will never cast you out."

"May I have the honor of this dance?" asked Captain. He winked at Alice and took Abigail's hand to the dance area. After a brief waltz, Captain returned Abigail to the sidelines and extended his hand to Alice for a dance.

Breathless from dancing and her dark eyes sparkling, Maggie joined Abigail on the sidelines. "Oh, this is so much fun! Have you been dancing?"

"A little."

"I wonder what Oregon boys are like?"

"Maggie, boys are the same the whole world over."

"I suppose so, but we'll find out soon. I'm excited."

Henry Wells drew near and shyly asked Abigail to dance. She smiled her *Yes*. Henry had grown taller and heavier on the trail despite the hardships, but he was still smaller than Abigail. They entered the dance area and began a brisk two-step.

As they returned to the sidelines, Abigail spotted three new boys standing around a bubbling Maggie.

Abigail asked, "What will you do now that we are here, Henry?"

"My plan has not changed. I'll help mama and papa on the farm and try to get a job in the local newspaper."

"It must be wonderful to have an ambition and a plan."

"What about you, Abigail?"

"I'm still searching."

"Abigail, I like you very much."

"I understand, Henry, and I'm pleased and honored to have you as a friend. We went through many hardships on the trail." *I hope I'm saying this the best way. Henry is just not the man I need.*

Henry was silent. They joined Maggie and her new admirers, but Henry left after a brief introduction.

"Would you like to dance?" asked one of the taller boys.

"Thank you," Abigail said politely.

"Where are you from?" asked Abigail's dance partner.

"Originally from Tennessee, but now I'm an Oregonian."

*****

THE NEXT MORNING, Thomas Bridgewater woke habitually early but did not blow his horn. He gazed fondly at Alice, still asleep in their tent, ambled to the banked campfire, and rekindled it. Thomas filled the coffeepot with water and placed it on the trivet. He heard a rustle as Abigail emerged from her tent. She sauntered to the fire and gave Thomas a welcoming smile.

"Good morning, Abigail. Feeling better?"

"Yes, sir. And good morning to you, Captain. I realized last night that I'm an Oregonian now and I'm going to make the most of it—whatever that means."

"That's the spirit."

"Thank you, Captain, for all you've done for Mama, for me, for all of us. We'd never have reached Oregon without you and your help."

"Meeting your family was my pleasure and privilege."

"Do I smell coffee?" Alice joined them at the fire. She smiled at Thomas and bussed his cheek.

The Enchanted Journal

"Nancy and I will make breakfast," said Abigail as Nancy and Angus entered their camp.

"No rush." Captain sipped his coffee. "Let's relax and enjoy our trail coffee for the last time."

"I'll be glad to drink real coffee again," said Alice.

"I will sell real coffee in my store," added Angus.

*****

"LOOK, THERE'S A FARMHOUSE! A real farmhouse!"

And so it was. A neat wood framed farmhouse with front and back porches and glass windows loomed in the distance. A large but plain building was nearby. Plowed fields with early fall crops revealed black fertile earth. A grassy field and creek beckoned their animals.

Phillip Foster maintained a campground and store for emigrants five miles outside of Oregon City. He had a long barn with tables and benches to feed people. His wife prepared beef, potatoes, beans, turnip greens and fresh bread and coffee for everyone. Somehow, people always paid for a home-cooked meal eaten at a table.

A store! Abigail was thrilled. Not just a resupply house along the trail or in the desert, but an actual store. The first she had seen since Independence. She admired the goods while Angus babbled away about this store and the one he planned to build and stock.

"See, one side is for dry goods. Women will select cloth, ribbon, thread, fans, and shawls. Men will choose their hats, shoes, and suspenders." He chortled. "Of course, we all know that it's really the women who buy them.

"Near the front, I'll put candy, toys, tobacco, cough drops, and patent medicines like Beecham's Pills.

"On the top shelves, I'll have crockery, tableware, bowls, pitchers, drinking glasses, lamps, and jugs.

"Groceries will be over here. Angus pointed. "Oh, it will be a grand store. Maybe I'll become postmaster. Collecting mail is a wonderful way to draw customers into a store."

Nancy smiled at Angus. "You can do it, Angus. And I'll be right here to help you."

"Having you in the store will draw even more customers."

Everyone seems to have a plan except me, thought Abigail. *What about me? What will I do?* She smiled at the thought of Angus and Nancy changing their roles and becoming her employer.

The Enchanted Journal

Part 5

Oregon City

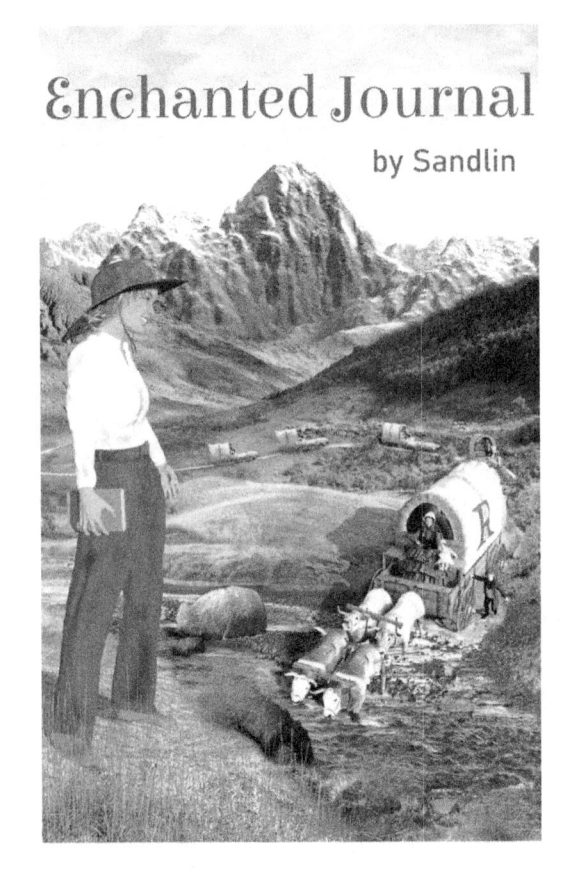

The Enchanted Journal

Chapter 30: September 22 - Oregon City

The Hudson's Bay Company founded Oregon City in 1829 to take advantage of Willamette Falls to power a lumber mill. Pioneers filed their land claims in Oregon City. The population was 1200 people in 1859. The Bridgewater train contributed 88 more.

1843

We are in Oregon City! At Last! We have completed our journey and arrived at our destination. For now, we are encamped at Philip Foster's farm outside the city.

The land leading into Oregon City is everything we hoped for. The soil is black as the night. The flatlands are green and lush. There is much water and tree-covered hills. Papa is beside himself with excitement.

Some people separated from the train early in search of land they could claim, but we continued all the way into the city. Papa wants to talk to the Land Agent before searching for a claim.

Oregon City is the provisional government of Oregon and our center of activity. It is more like a village than a city, but this is the most people we have seen in one place since Independence.

Oregon City is between the Willamette River on the west and the Cascade Foothills on the east. It has about 150 buildings, including shops and stores with goods from Boston! There are two sawmills and two grist mills.

My William plans to work in one of the sawmills, but first, he must help his father get settled. William says he will claim land when he turns 18 (next year!) and will save his earnings from working in the sawmill until then. William proposed marriage to me and I said YES! Together we can claim 640 acres. What a wonderful life we will have!

I sometimes forget that Milli's adventure was years ago. If Milli is in Oregon City, I will find her and return her enchanted journal.

We're here, Papa. Oregon is beautiful, just as you read and told us. But now, what do I do? No more trail for me. I suppose I'll become a farm wife in Oregon instead of Tennessee, but I don't even have a sweetheart.

Chapter 31: Finding Milli

THE DAY AFTER SETTING UP their camp outside Oregon City, Captain urged, "Let's get to the Land Office as soon as we can."

"Abigail," said Alice. "Come with us and be sure to wear a dress—not those raggedy trail trousers. And wear a bonnet, or nothing, instead of that old trail hat. Your hair is long now and beautiful and you should show it off. Brush it well. I'll help you with your corset."

"Mama!"

"Thomas knows you wear a corset, Abigail. We're going to town. Dress like it."

Abigail fussed but followed her mother's instructions. She hoped to find Milli Madison and make a good impression. Abigail climbed awkwardly into the wagon somewhat hindered by her best calico dress. They left Mike and Sue with friends.

"Whoa!" cried Captain as he pulled back on the reins in front of a small wood framed building in Oregon City. The sign over the closed door read *Land Office*. Captain helped Alice and Abigail from the wagon. He knocked on the door.

"Come."

"We're looking for land," explained Captain.

"Well, you've come to the right place," said the agent. "And you look old enough to file a claim. What do you intend to do with your land? Farm? Prospect? Timber?"

"Farm," answered Captain, "and I want to purchase land that already has a house and some improvements. We've been on the trail for many months and are eager to sleep inside a house on a bed."

"I have just the land and house you need. Besides being the land agent, I also act as a broker. A family recently moved out and I represent them."

"Why'd they move out? Land not good?"

"The land is fine, the house is well made, and even has some furnishings. The Wilcoxes simply were not farmers and have returned to the east."

"Oh, I hope the house has a stove!" exclaimed Alice.

"I want a bed," added Abigail.

"This house has both," replied the agent. "Let me tell you how to get there. It's easy to find." He pointed down the road, made a few notes on paper, and handed it to Captain

"Excuse me, Mr. Agent," interrupted Abigail. "Do you know a Milli Madison? Her married name might be Anderson."

"Indeed, I do. Mrs. Anderson is a fine, upstanding woman and lives just outside the city. She and her husband, William, were among the first emigrants to settle here. They received 640 acres of prime land. Do you know her yourself?"

"No sir. I found something of hers along the trail and want to return it to her."

"Well, you're lucky. As it happens, you'll pass in front of her house on your way to inspect the Wilcox house and land. Mr. and Mrs. Anderson would be excellent neighbors."

"Thank you, sir. We'll go check it out now."

"This is exciting," gushed Abigail. "I don't know whether I'm more excited about the house and land or meeting Milli—guess I better call her Mrs. Anderson. She is about seventeen years older than me. I'll bet she is nice and will make a good friend for you, Mama. She must have a family as well."

"How did you know her married name?" asked Alice.

"She wrote about meeting William Anderson on the trail. His family was part of her train. She wrote more and more often about him and I could tell that they were becoming sweethearts."

"Are you jealous that you did not find a sweetheart on the trail? Or did you? That handsome David Murray was interested in you. He was ready to leave his father's train and join ours."

"Mama! I'm not even sixteen." Abigail blushed.

"Well, young Henry Wells certainly likes you."

"Henry is nice and I'm glad to have him as a friend, but he is too small and immature."

"Henry is a good boy," said Captain. "He was a great help on the trail. He'll grow and the trail experience matured him."

"Size and maturity come with the years, Abigail."

"Henry is not for me, Mama."

They continued down the dirt road, speculating on the house and land ahead. The farms and houses along the way appeared prosperous.

*****

ABIGAIL STUDIED THE NOTE from the Land Agent. "Oh, look! I bet that's the Anderson house." She pointed to a large, neat wood-framed, white-washed house. It had a large covered front porch; a smaller back porch was barely visible. Seated on the front porch, a woman and a young girl shelled peas. The woman smiled pleasantly at them.

Captain turned off the main road and onto a narrow driveway leading to the house.

"Howdy, ma'am!" Captain greeted the woman.

"Hello. Anything I can do to help you?"

"I hope so, ma'am. The Land Agent in Oregon City told us about the Wilcox house and land for sale. We want to see it. Are we on the right route?"

"Yes, indeed, you are on the right road."

"How far?"

"About two miles. But before you go, please come inside for coffee. In fact, please stay for lunch. You must be hungry and we have plenty to eat. My husband will return from the fields soon."

The Enchanted Journal

"Thank you, Mrs. Anderson," replied Alice. "Please excuse us if we ask too many questions. We're just coming in off the trail and don't know the people or the area."

"I'll be happy to answer your questions if you'll tell me about traveling the trail these days."

They entered the house and Mrs. Anderson placed a coffee cup in front of each person. "Real coffee. Not trail coffee. Oh, how I dreaded that stuff, but it was all we had."

"Milli," began Abigail, "excuse me, I mean Mrs. Anderson."

"Quite all right, my dear," answered Mrs. Anderson. "Most people call me Milli. Some still call me Milli Madison, my maiden name."

"I-I know. Mrs. Anderson, I have something special for you. I found your journal on the trail." She handed the worn leather journal to Milli.

Astounded, Mrs. Anderson was speechless for a moment, then tears flowed. She stepped to Abigail, and hugged her. "I thought I'd never see this again. Oh my!" She wiped the tears from her eyes and thumbed excitedly through the journal.

"Mrs. Anderson," began Abigail again.

"My dear, of all people, you may call me Milli."

Abigail smiled. "Milli, I have a question. When I first found your journal, only five pages contained writing. Your journal gave good advice about crossing a creek. But the next day, I noticed a new page had been added. Not every day, but often a new page would appear. How was that possible? I call your diary the Enchanted Journal. I tried to use your diary as my own, but my writing would disappear the next day and be replaced by yours."

Milli laughed. "I don't know. I was extremely upset about losing my journal. Every night I would review the events of the day and think about what I would write if I could. I'm pleased my journal was helpful and I'm especially pleased you found it and returned it. I'm even more pleased to meet you."

"It was indeed helpful, Mrs. Anderson," said Captain. "To my eyes, your journal read like a wagon master's notes, but Abigail saw it as a personal diary. The appearance of new pages was more than a bit spooky and we could not explain them. I didn't tell others about the journal. Too much superstition."

"I compared our version of the trail to your journey," said Abigail. "Much was the same but there had been significant changes. You had a much more difficult trail than we did."

"What was your favorite part of my dairy?"

"The lye soap kiss," replied Abigail. "I laughed and applauded you."

Mrs. Anderson blushed. "So my thoughts really did get into my diary. Amazing, but I have no explanation for the new pages. Perhaps this is part of God's plan and guidance for us."

Mrs. Anderson turned to her daughter. "Patsy, go to the woodshed and tell Will to clean up and come in for dinner and to meet company. Insist that he clean up." She smiled at Abigail.

Abigail's eyes followed Patsy out the back door and into the backyard where she skipped up to a tall, strapping young man. He was slim but had broad shoulders. His shirt was spread neatly over a stack of split wood. Lean muscles rippled as Will swung the axe and split a log. Patsy pointed to the house and said something. Abigail's eyes locked on Will. *Thank you, Mama, for insisting that I wear a dress and brush my hair.*

Alice had a partial view through the door. "What are you staring at, Abigail?"

Abigail murmured, "Admiring God's handiwork."

Alice's coffee went up her nose as she snickered, and Milli swelled with pride.

Will lifted his head from Patsy, glanced toward the house, and stuck the axe in the chopping stump. He dipped his cup into the nearby pail and took a long drink of water. After dumping the pail over his head, Will dried off hurriedly with a tattered towel and pulled his shirt on. He combed shoulder length tawny hair with his fingers before following Patsy to the house.

Mrs. Anderson explained to Alice and Abigail, "I must apologize for my son. He knows better than to remove his shirt if we have company, but we were not expecting anyone."

Abigail blushed more brightly. She had seen boys and men without their shirts and she was accustomed to men chopping wood. She chopped wood herself, but somehow, this was different. *What is going on with me?*

Will entered the house and came to an abrupt stop at the sight of Abigail. He threw a warning glare at Patsy. Patsy giggled.

"Will, let me introduce you to the Bridgewaters. They are on their way to examine the Wilcox house and property. They may be our new neighbors."

Will turned politely to Alice and said, "Pleased to meet you, ma'am." He stepped to Captain and shook his hand firmly. "Sir."

Mrs. Anderson smiled and said, "This is Abigail, Will."

"My pleasure to meet you, Miss Abigail." Will's face was flushed but he did not look away and his eyes were bright.

Abigail remembered how William Anderson always called Milli *Miss Milli. What does he call her now?*

"And I, you, Will." Abigail gave him her best smile. Was Will blushing? He was far too handsome to be shy.

Will stood there silently, his eyes locked on Abigail.

Mrs. Anderson came to Will's rescue. "Will, get us a bucket of water for the dishes." He obediently picked up the bucket and sauntered to the well.

Abigail's eyes followed Will to the well. His father joined him and they returned to the house. Will locked eyes with Abigail as soon as he entered. He fumbled the bucket of water onto the counter.

"Howdy and welcome. I'm William Anderson. I see you've met my family."

"William, this is Captain and Mrs. Bridgewater and their daughter Abigail."

Captain held out his hand to William. "Call me Thomas, please. No more wagon trains for me."

"And call me Alice," said Mrs. Bridgewater. "I should explain our family. I am indeed Mrs. Bridgewater, but Abigail's surname is Roberts. My husband, Michael, died on the trail from cholera." She dabbed at her eyes. "We all might have died without the support of Captain Bridgewater. Thomas and I married on the trail."

"William and I met on the trail but did not marry until after we arrived in Oregon City."

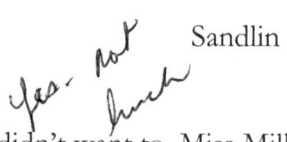

"Not that I didn't want to, Miss Milli," William chuckled. "What do you have for dinner?"

"Chicken and dumplings, beans, corn, and cornbread. Fortunately, I made a large dinner. Will always eats as though he is starving. I'll cook again for supper."

The heavy wooden table easily accommodated three extra people and there were stools for everyone. Will seated himself across from Abigail.

"Mama, Will is sitting in my place," complained Patsy.

"Hush, Patsy. There is room for everyone."

William asked the blessing and gave thanks for new friends. Bowls were passed around and conversation soon shifted to tales of the trail.

"William, Abigail found my journal from the trail and has returned it."

"I had just met you, Miss Milli, but I remember how upset you were to lose your journal after just a few days of traveling."

"The strangest thing, the journal is now filled in with my thoughts from the trail. Abigail says it is enchanted."

"I want to read that journal," ventured Will. "I always hear of your adventures and I'm jealous. I want an adventure. Maybe I'll go east on the trail."

"You won't be reading my journal," laughed Milli. "Only Abigail and I get to read and discuss it."

After dinner, Mrs. Anderson said, "Will, show Abigail our new puppies. Patsy, you go with them." She smiled at Alice.

Will said, "Patsy, you don't need to come. You've seen the puppies."

"Oh, yes, she does," responded Milli with a laugh.

Alice nodded her head at Abigail. "Go see the puppies, Abigail. I'll help Milli with the dishes, while the menfolk talk about the Wilcox farm and farming."

Will opened the door for Abigail and they walked toward the barn with Patsy skipping behind them.

*****

AS MILLI AND ALICE WASHED DISHES, Alice said, "Your son is extraordinarily handsome."

"Thank you. More importantly, Will is a Christian gentleman. Smart and strong too. We are extremely proud of him. I don't know if Oregon City can hold him. He wants more education than he can get here. Plus, he wants an adventure—you heard him."

"Oh, he will find his adventure, I'm sure."

"Your daughter is beautiful and sweet. I'll bet she broke hearts all along the trail."

"None of the boys in our train interested her. Actually, she has never paid much attention to boys." Alice giggled. "Well, until today!"

Milli joined Alice's tittering. "Oh, to be young! Will has no idea of how to act or what to say. He is bumfuzzled such as I've never seen him."

"I wonder what they are talking about," said Alice.

"Puppies!"

Their laughter increased until they were gasping for breath and could no longer wash dishes.

*****

ON THE WAY TO THE BARN, Will desperately tried to think of something to say but all he came up with was, *She sure is pretty.*

Abigail ventured, "You certainly have a nice place here. I hope we can find something as nice."

"The Wilcox place is nice," Will assured her. "You'll like it." *And close by as well.*

"I hope so. Plus, Mama needs a good friend nearby and I feel I already know your mother from her journal. She must be a wonderful mother. I'm so glad to have found her."

"Mama was excited to get her journal back," Will said. "I-I'm glad you found her too."

They reached the barn and Will pointed inside. "So you like puppies?" *What a stupid thing to say. C'mon, you can do better than that.*

275

"I haven't seen cute puppies in a long time," answered Abigail. "That is, except for puppies in the Indian villages. Indians eat their puppies so I couldn't allow myself to think they were cute."

"Mama told me about that. Seems inhuman."

"I didn't eat any puppies on the trail but a few times I was so hungry I could have."

Will led Abigail to a bed of straw where six puppies lay with their mother. "Patsy, go get them some water."

"Mama told me to stay with Abigail," Patsy giggled.

"OK, I'll get the water." Will grabbed a bucket and sauntered to the well swinging the bucket over his head. *She sure is pretty.*

Abigail knelt by the puppies but watched Will instead.

*****

"WILL LIKES YOU," giggled Patsy. "I can tell."

"Why do you say that?"

"Because he doesn't act this goofy around other girls."

"Oh? Does Will know many girls?"

"Yes, especially from church. All the girls like Will. Why, I don't know, but they do."

"Does Will have a sweetheart?"

"No, but many girls wish they were his sweetheart. Do you have a sweetheart?"

"No, do you?"

"Of course not," replied Patsy. "I'm only eleven."

"Your brother seems to be a fine young man."

"But do you like him?"

"We've just met. Time will tell."

"Then why are you blushing?"

"I haven't been around young men in a long time," Abigail alibied.

"Hush, here he comes. Play with the puppies."

*****

WILL RETURNED WITH THE WATER and poured some into a nearby bowl. He waved his hand around the barn. "The Wilcox barn is like this one. I helped build it," he bragged.

"So you are a carpenter?" asked Abigail.

"I'm learning. I enjoy working with wood. What do you like to do?"

"My mind is still trapped on the trail. Mostly I walked and walked in the dust—it's boring. Some days, I drove the wagon or rode the mule. I loaded and unloaded the wagon every day. I got firewood and water. I cooked meals and cleaned up. Day after day. The trail is lots of suffering and hard work."

"But what did you do for fun?"

"Many nights, we'd sit around the campfire and listen to people tell tall tales. I've heard some good ones."

"Mama said their train had musicians and singing."

"Yes, some nights we had music and even dancing. Can you dance?"

"A little. You'll have to teach me to dance better."

"I'll try if you like." Abigail's eyelashes fluttered and she blushed. *I can't believe I did that.*

Patsy giggled. Will glared at her.

"Was there hunting along the trail? I like hunting."

"Lots of hunting. We had a hundred people to feed. I enjoy hunting too."

Will blurted, "You can shoot a gun?"

"Yes, I can shoot a shotgun, plains rifle and revolver. My papa taught me. I like to shoot."

"What did you hunt?"

"Mostly deer, but I did kill a buffalo."

"I'm impressed. I've never even seen buffalo."

"Captain says they are disappearing."

"All the more reason for having my own adventure," said Will.

"What will you do?"

"I don't know, but I feel the need to get away from here for a while." Will kneeled beside Abigail and they were silent for a moment.

"I hope you find your grand adventure, Will". *Will feels the same way Papa did. He will leave this place.* "My next adventure lies here in Oregon." She came to her feet.

Will picked up a spotted puppy, took a step nearer Abigail and handed her the puppy. "Here's a puppy for you, Miss Abigail. Not as pretty as you are but it's cute."

Patsy giggled.

*****

ABIGAIL AND WILL returned to the house with Abigail carrying the spotted puppy. "Look, Mama, how cute. Will says I can have him. Can I, please?"

"Those puppies are still too young to leave their mother," Mrs. Anderson answered. "Let's wait a couple of weeks. You can visit your puppy, Abigail." She smiled at Will.

William and Captain returned to the house talking about farming in Oregon and the Wilcox property.

"Alice," said Captain. "The Wilcox property sounds better all the time. Let's go take a closer look."

"Papa, I can show them the way and around the farm," ventured Will while smiling at Abigail. "I sometimes worked for Mr. Wilcox. I know the place well. I even have a key to the house."

"It's the next house straight down the road," explained William. "You can't miss it."

Milli glanced at William and he understood. "But if Thomas has room, I suppose you can go with them."

"Be glad to benefit from Will's experience and opinion," said Captain.

The group strolled to the Bridgewater prairie schooner. Captain stepped beside Alice and helped her get in. Will hurried to Abigail's side. From her seat, Alice looked down at her tomboyish daughter in disbelief. Several times every day for months, Abigail had climbed into that wagon entirely on her own. Now she needed assistance!

The Enchanted Journal

Will placed his large hands around Abigail's trim waist with his palms on her hips and gently helped her into the wagon. Wide-eyed, she beamed down at him. "Thank you, Will."

Will was bright red but grinning from ear to ear.

Milli nudged William with her elbow and dabbed at her eye with her other hand.

Captain and Will climbed in and they drove off.

*****

"Poor girl. Six months on the trail and she still needs help to get into a wagon." Milli giggled as she watched them leave. "Do you realize they are the same age we were when we met?"

"Are you sure? Thought we were older."

"Yes, I'm sure. Fifteen and seventeen."

"They are so young."

"Yes, they are. I'm pleased you let Will go to the Wilcox place."

"Figured I might as well. The boy would have been useless the rest of the day."

"Is that what your father told you the day we met?"

"Oh, Pa worked me hard that day. Then that night, he said, 'Boy, what was wrong with you today?' You'd better pay attention to what you're doing or you'll get hurt."

"What did you say to him?"

"Oh, I just said, 'Yes, sir.' But I caught his meaning."

"I'm glad Abigail and Will met. I like her very much already. Maybe my journal really is enchanted."

*****

AS THE WAGON BOUNCED along the road towards the Wilcox place, Will took advantage of every bounce to move fractionally closer to Abigail. She did not move away and their knees were nearly touching by the time they reached the Wilcox gate. Will was eager to help Abigail out of the wagon and already looking forward to helping her get in again. Plus, perhaps she would get out again at his house!

They stopped in front of the Wilcox house and Will leaped out. He grasped Abigail's hand to help her, expecting it to be soft; instead, it was calloused. *Of course her hand is calloused. She's been working hard on the trail every day.*

Holding Will's hand, Abigail stood and stepped onto the sideboard. Will placed his hands around her waist as she stepped to the ground near him. He hesitated a moment before releasing her.

Abigail smiled up at Will towering above her. "Thank you, Will. You're quite the gentleman."

"My pleasure, Miss Abigail."

Similar to the Anderson house, the Wilcox house was wood framed and whitewashed with front and rear porches.

"This is a lot like our house," explained Will. "My dad and I helped build it."

"Windows with glass!" exclaimed Abigail. "I love the windows."

"The house looks good from the outside," said Captain. "Let's see the inside."

Will led the way with Abigail at his side; Alice and Captain followed, unnoticed. Alice shook her head and laughed silently.

Will unlocked and opened the door for Abigail. He abruptly remembered Mr. and Mrs. Bridgewater and turned to them. "Welcome to the Wilcox house!"

Alice entered the house and immediately found the kitchen. "A cook stove!" Alice was excited. "I'm so tired of cooking over an outdoor fire."

"There are two bedrooms and a loft," added Will. "I sleep in the loft at our house."

"The Wilcoxes left a lot of furniture," observed Captain.

"I'm glad," replied Alice. "We have almost none."

"Show me the barn and land, Will," requested Captain. "Let Alice and Abigail finish their inspection."

Will glanced at Abigail and reluctantly followed Captain out the back door.

*****

The Enchanted Journal

ALICE TURNED TO ABIGAIL, who watched Will leave.

"So, what do you think, Abigail?"

"Will said that I am pretty."

Alice snorted. "You are far more than pretty, Abigail. You've just been too busy to notice. Many boys and young men out here will be attracted to you. Be careful what you do to encourage them."

Abigail still stared out the back door. "Yes, ma'am. Will is quite handsome, isn't he?"

"Yes, he is. But enough about Will. What do you think of this house?"

"I like it. I suppose Sue and I will share a bedroom and Mike will sleep in the loft."

"First, let's see what Thomas says about buying it."

"Mama, can I have a new dress? For church. Will says the circuit-riding preacher comes this Sunday. We should be sure to attend. We can meet people."

Alice chuckled. "We have a lot to do between now and Sunday, Abigail, but I'll try. Maybe someone in town can fit you for a new dress by Sunday."

Thomas and Will returned to the house and Will casually strolled to Abigail. She smiled up at him. *He is so tall!*

"Alice," said Thomas. "This looks fine to me. If you are happy with the house, we can buy it and move in. What do you think?"

"We will be happy here."

"Let's get Will back to his house and then return to the Land Office."

"I'm glad you'll be our neighbor," Will said. "I can help you move in and work for you sometimes." He smiled at Abigail.

They returned to the wagon and Thomas helped Alice on board. Abigail turned expectantly to Will, who was more than pleased to assist her. Will climbed in and sat close enough to Abigail that one good bounce would have them touching.

*****

MILLI ANDERSON HEARD THE BRIDGEWATER WAGON coming and met them in the front yard. "Just in time," she called out. "I took an apple pie out of the oven a moment ago. Come in and tell me what you think of the Wilcox place."

"Thank you," answered Captain. "We can stay a short time. We are going to buy the Wilcox place and must get to the Land Office."

"I can help them get to the Land Office, Mama," offered Will.

Milli laughed. "Will, they know where the Land Office is. You need to stay here and help your father. He's in the fields now."

Milli watched proudly as her gentleman son helped Abigail from the wagon, then realized that his hands lingered on her hips for an extra moment as she gazed up at him. "Will!"

"Ma'am?" Startled, Will turned red but his hands did not move.

"Will?"

"Yes, ma'am." Will slowly detached his hands from Abigail's waist and hips.

"Let's go inside for pie." Milli glanced at Alice, who shrugged helplessly as Abigail lit up.

Pie eaten and coffee drunk, Captain said they must be on their way to the Land Office.

"When will you move in?" Will asked. "I can help you unload your wagon and move into your new house." He glanced at his mother. "It's the neighborly thing to do," he explained.

"Thank you, Will. I hope to move in tomorrow. But we loaded and unloaded that wagon every day for months. We don't even have as many supplies or equipment anymore. We can manage."

Alice gave Thomas a quick glance.

"Of course," Thomas recovered. "Extra help is always welcome, provided your mother approves."

"Will, you may help them move in," replied Milli. "But you must first do your chores before walking to the Wilcox place." She tittered, "Oops, I mean the Bridgewater place."

"We'll load our wagon at our camp," said Captain. "And check to see if Will is ready when we drive past your house. If not, he can join us later."

"I'll fix your dinner tomorrow," said Milli. "That should save you some time. I'll bring it to you at noon."

The Enchanted Journal

Will and Abigail were smiling at each other oblivious to the others in the room.

Milli thought, *He will get up in the middle of the night to do his chores.*

The Bridgewater family walked to their wagon, followed by Milli and Will.

Abigail stopped at the wagon and turned expectantly to Will. Will glanced anxiously at his mother and blushed, but put his hands around Abigail's waist, hesitated a moment, and helped her into the wagon.

"Thank you, Will." Abigail blossomed. "You're such a gentleman."

"My pleasure, Miss Abigail. I hope to see you tomorrow and in church Sunday."

*****

ABIGAIL WATCHED as the Anderson farm and Will faded into the distance. *What a fine day! What an exciting day! Yes, Patsy, I do like your brother.*

"Abigail," said Captain with a grin. "I do believe young Will Anderson has taken a shine to you."

"Why Thomas," teased Alice. "What makes you think so?"

"Well, I, uh, I…"

"Thomas, I want to treat Abigail to a new dress for church. There is a dress shop near the Land Office. Abigail and I will go there while you deal with the Land Agent."

Oregon, thought Abigail, *is about to become interesting…*

References

Buck, Rinker. *The Oregon Trail: A New American Journey*, Simon & Schuster, Kindle Edition.

Hupp, Theresa. *Lead Me Home: Hardship and Hope on the Oregon Trail)*, Rickover Publishing. Kindle Edition.

Marcy, Randolph B.. *The Prairie Traveler: A Handbook for Overland Expeditions*, Skyhorse. Kindle Edition

The Enchanted Journal

About Sandlin

SANDLIN IS THE PEN NAME for Gordon Sandlin Buck, Jr., a retired mechanical engineer with many technical publications. He also has self-published genealogy and photography books. Gordon lives in southern Louisiana, where his hobbies include photography, genealogy, and woodworking. This is his third proper novel, and he hopes to continue professional writing in the future.

Other books by Sandlin:

The Viking Princess: College Romance in 1970, https://www.amazon.com/dp/B09MYSS2T1. Copyright 2021, Gordon S. Buck.

Timepath: Nature Abhors a Paradox, https://www.amazon.com/dp/B09LGV94RL. Copyright 2021, Gordon S. Buck.

Made in the USA
Columbia, SC
09 June 2022